FAMILY MONEY

Nina Bawden

Virago

VIRAGO

Published by Virago Press 1992
Reprinted 1992 (three times), 1993, 1997, 2006
First published in Great Britain by Victor Gollancz Limited 1991

A CIP catalogue record for this book is available
from the British Library.

ISBN-13: 978-1-84408-318-3
ISBN-10: 1-84408-318-7

Typeset in Goudy by M Rules
Printed and bound in Great Britain by
Clays Ltd, St Ives plc

Virago Press
An imprint of
Little, Brown Book Group
Brettenham House
Lancaster Place
London WC2E 7EN

A member of the Hachette Livre Group of Companies

www.virago.co.uk

To George Hardinge

The first man who, having enclosed a piece of ground, bethought himself of saying *This is mine*, and found people simple enough to believe him, was the real founder of civil society.

Rousseau

God has placed men in families.

George Cadbury

1

Towards the end of the party, they began to talk about house prices again. Harry Pye, who found the topic tedious, wondered if he should trot out the story about his friend in Greece. This friend, a senior civil servant, had always spent his six weeks annual holiday in the medieval town of Monemvasia, renting a fairly derelict but still beautiful house that belonged to an elderly woman; a local crone, garbed in black. Harry's friend had once or twice offered to buy it. Not bluntly, just a few tactful feelers. He knew that most Greeks thought it dishonourable to sell family property. An old spinster like this would leave her house to a pack of brothers and sisters, nephews and nieces. Or to the church. But one summer she said, 'I will give you my house when I die. All I want is ten pounds a week for the rest of my life.'

Seventy-five was what she admitted to but she looked at least ten years older; bent, almost toothless. It seemed a good bargain and he took her out to dinner to clinch it before they went before the notary public. She ate a huge meal. Drank like a navvy. Walked up the steep, rocky path home at a pace he was hard put to match. Exhausted, breathless from panting behind her, he reckoned that on this evening's showing she would last out her century, well into her nineties, anyway, eating up his salary and, for God's sake, his *pension*. So he withdrew his offer. She died three weeks later.

'A friend of mine,' Harry began, but his heart wasn't in it. He thought it a comic tale but feared that his audience might find it tragic. And Felix and Ella, his host and hostess, were too firmly established centre stage and in full cry. Their house, in which they were giving this buffet supper, was 'worth' four hundred and twenty-five thousand pounds. At least, that was what a neighbour had sold for last month. Felix and Ella had decided to cash in themselves and move out of London. They had found a converted oast house in Kent, not too far from a main line railway station – although commuting was hideously expensive, rates were much lower outside the city, and the capital gain was enormous. 'Liquid housing' Felix called it. Unfortunately it was not liquid yet. They had a buyer for their London house, a family man who was 'trading up', moving to fashionable Clapham from a dull outer suburb, but he could not come up with the money until the young couple who wanted to buy his neat semi-detached had sold their cottage in the Lake District. They had had an offer from an elderly man whose children and grandchildren lived in the district and who was genuinely anxious to move, but he had to get rid of his bungalow in Birmingham before he could afford to do so and this was turning out to be unexpectedly difficult. After the property chain had been set in motion, surveys and searches made and contracts drawn up, plans had been disclosed by the local authority for a new industrial complex to be built (with EEC money) on derelict land adjacent to the bungalow estate. The old man's buyer, another widower, leaving a rented flat to sink his life savings in his own place with a nice bit of garden,

2

promptly pulled out, and no one had yet turned up to replace him.

'Only thing I can see is to buy the bloody bungalow,' Felix Carberry said. He gave his long, hooting laugh. Hoo, hoo. 'Hell of a lot cheaper than a bridging loan, even if not much of an investment. Though we might even make a decent profit when the complex is finished. Factory workers have got to live somewhere, and property owning democracy is the name of the game nowadays.'

'No more dreary council housing estates,' said Poppy Pye, who had been born and brought up on one. Her tone was flat. But her brown eyes were shining.

'Thank God,' Felix said, following this piety with his loud, mirthful hoot so that Poppy's soft snort of amusement was only caught and understood by her husband. She looked at him brightly and he winked to show he had taken her point and approved it. Of course it was crass of Felix to appear to condone the present Government's doctrinaire housing policy that virtually stopped all local authority building. But he hoped Poppy wouldn't go on all the same. Harry admired his wife because she spoke out and knew that he disappointed her because he didn't speak out often enough. It wasn't that he didn't agree with her. Just that as an unemployed, married woman she was in a privileged position. She didn't have to watch her step with anyone. Felix wasn't *her* boss!

'You're absolutely right, Poppy,' Felix said. 'Once council tenants are encouraged to buy the houses they live in, they start taking pride in them. May not be able to alter the architecture but a smartened up breeding box is better for the spirits than a shabby one. And if you own your house, you've got job mobility. You can sell up and move wherever you want to.'

3

'As long as you can afford to buy in the first place,' Poppy said sweetly.

'True,' Felix said. 'But because a social change doesn't benefit everyone, that doesn't mean that it's bad. You wouldn't give up an immunisation programme – against AIDS, for example – just because a few people were allergic to the injections.'

Someone said, 'Oh, not AIDS *again*.'

Another snort from Poppy. This time Felix heard her.

Harry said quickly, 'That's not a very convincing analogy, Felix. Still, I see what you're getting at. But what I want to know is, are you *really* going to buy the old man's bungalow? Seems a bit drastic.'

Felix looked at him, smiling. He wasn't a fool, Harry thought. He knew I was just cutting in to stop Poppy blowing her top. And, as if to bear this out, Felix said, with a brief glance in Poppy's direction, 'I see it as a bit of a duty as a matter of fact. The way I look at it, if I buy the bungalow, four households, that is, three couples with children and one old man, say a dozen people altogether, will be able to live where they want to live. I may make a bit out of it in the end but it doesn't seem to me a totally selfish action.'

'Oh my God!' Ella Carberry screeched suddenly. 'If I hear any more about that bloody bungalow I'll go *ape*. Really Felix!' She rolled her eyes at her guests and held out her hands, palm upwards. 'I ask you, a bungalow in *Birmingham*!' she cried, inviting them all to share this absurdity. 'Rates, insurance, drains – all on top of the purchase price – and we haven't got a spare penny! It doesn't bear thinking of. Not with interest rates going up and up!'

'My Mama could lend us the money,' Felix said.

'She hasn't got any! Not unless she sells her flat. I know she

4

keeps *talking* about it, how she wants somewhere smaller, but even if she called in an agent *tomorrow* – which is pretty unlikely, given your mother – and got an offer by the end of the *week*, she'll still be caught the same way as we are.'

'I think not,' Felix said.

He looked at his wife thoughtfully, for long enough to convey to his watching guests that he despised her for getting drunk. Then he said with stagey surprise – feigned, and meant to look feigned – 'Didn't I tell you, love? No, maybe I didn't. She's had an offer from the Arab gentleman who lives upstairs. He wants to buy her flat for his sister, or his aunt, or his mother. Or perhaps to put servants in. So there'll be no problem with money.'

'Oh,' Ella said, 'oh, I see. That does make a difference. Still, she'll have to find somewhere to *go*. She's got to live somewhere.'

'Yes. Well.'

Ella said suspiciously, 'What d'you mean?'

'There will be plenty of room in the place in Kent,' Felix said with clear satisfaction. 'More than we need, even when the kids are home in the holidays. You did say, the one problem with the oast house is the ground floor. It's a bit dark. My mother won't mind. She's going blind anyway.'

Ella said, 'When my mother was in that Home, you always told everyone what a good place it was, her own room, her own things about her. Much more true independence for her than living with us.'

'Bill and Bryony were still at home then. That was different.'

'Should have made it easier. Two extra pairs of hands. And, if you remember, they were fond of *my* mother.'

'Okay,' Felix said. 'Okay, you win, darling.' He looked ruefully around him. Seeing empty glasses, he busied himself with the bottles, red wine in one hand, mock champagne in the other.

Harry wondered if he and Ella had any private life. Poppy said the only thing they didn't do in public was copulate and they probably didn't do that in private either. They probably didn't even talk when they were alone together. They quarrelled, made up, and told each other essential information only in front of other people. It didn't mean that they had an unhappy marriage, Poppy said, just that this was the way they had chosen to make their marriage work. She had seemed pleased and somehow consoled by this assessment but Harry had thought that if she were right it was one of the saddest things he had ever heard.

Now that the Carberry's cabaret turn was over, the room was buzzing again. Harry felt no desire to move from the wall against which he was leaning. He had had his last drink half an hour ago because he was driving and he had given up smoking. Without a cigarette or a glass of wine he felt disinclined to join any of the small groups that were forming and re-forming both indoors and out – drifting out of the open french windows into the summer garden. Drink or tobacco, preferably both, were necessary to make conversation tolerable at this sort of stand up and shout party. Not that he disliked anyone here. He didn't know anyone well enough for that. Except Felix and Ella. Felix was his Department Head at the BBC and Harry's knowledge of Felix in that capacity sometimes made him sorry for Ella.

He was sorry for her now, standing alone in the middle of the busy room, smiling secretly at the lees in her wine glass. Embarrassed because Felix had put her down? Or simply too much to drink? Both, probably. He moved towards her at the same time as Felix. She held out her glass to her husband without raising her eyes to his face, and he filled it to the brim. Not a kindly act, Harry thought. Nor was the accompanying remark. Felix said – and Harry had the feeling he would not have spoken if he had not had an audience – 'I suppose I could always give up my job and look after her.'

Ella said, 'You have no intention of doing that, so why say it?'

Felix laughed, lifted an eyebrow at Harry, and went on to refill – rather more skimpily, Harry noticed – other glasses. Tears sprang to Ella's eyes. Harry said, 'Does he really want his mother to come and live with you?'

She shrugged her shoulders, sniffed and smiled. Harry offered his handkerchief. She staggered a little as she took it and wine slopped from her brimming glass, over her dress, over the front of Harry's shirt. She said, 'What Felix *wants* is for me to look selfish. Though it's true she's finding it hard to manage. Rattling around in that huge old apartment. It's ridiculous, really, she has a minute income and yet there she sits, on a pile of bricks worth about half a million. And leasehold, not freehold. The longer she hangs on, the less it's worth. There's no other money and Felix sees his only inheritance dribbling away. Not for himself, he says, he doesn't mind for *himself*, he thinks of the children. Bill's getting married next year, Felix doesn't want to see him landed with a hideous mortgage. And Bry will need somewhere to live when she's through medical school.'

Harry said, 'In Victorian times, a widow would leave the messuage to her sons and retreat to the dower house. I suppose a granny flat would be the modern equivalent.'

Ella frowned. Harry doubted that she had understood him. He looked for Poppy, caught her eye, and was glad to see her signalling departure. He said, 'Sorry, Ella, I'm afraid we must be

7

going. Marvellous evening.' He beamed delight and kissed her on each sweating cheek.

Ella took them to the door. Under the light, her face was flushed and haggard, Poppy's tired and pale. She had no coat and Harry saw her shiver. He tucked her under his warm shoulder and wheeled her round to wave a last goodbye to Ella. But she had turned away to answer the ringing telephone.

Fanny Pye, Harry's mother, had been to the cinema, to the early evening performance of A *Fish Called Wanda*, and then to the cheaper of the two local Italian restaurants. She ate alone, as she had gone to the cinema alone, but she had a cheerful social time. The waiters, all from the same extended family, had been there for years and although their customers came from a more shifting population there were always, on the nights Fanny went to the Roma, enough regulars in the long, narrow room to smile at and say good-evening to. Brief exchanges, casual company – nowadays this was what she felt she needed as well as what she wanted. She and Daniel had always had what people called a 'host' of friends, and in her bad dreams that was how she saw them: a vast, white-robed army, pressing close upon her, menacingly singing. In the first months after Daniel's death it had appeared impossible to escape their claustrophobic kindness; the 'quiet' dinners, the theatres, the invitations to join them in their country cottages. She had found it shaming to admit, even to herself, that she had begun to dread these invitations. It seemed churlish. Surprising, too: she had never thought of herself as a solitary person.

Not that she felt solitary now. Lingering over her pasta and her wine, wondering whether to have a Strega with her coffee, she was content to sit and watch the other diners and mull over her enjoyment of A *Fish Called Wanda* without having to explain it or defend it. Daniel had always wanted to dissect a film or play the minute they had seen it; sometimes he would start to mutter and wriggle in his seat well before the end, eager to get to what was for him the best part of the evening. But Fanny liked to let her feelings settle before she talked about them, keep quiet until she had thoroughly taken in what she had heard and seen. 'Poor Daniel,' she said, silently. 'I did try to tell you.'

The trouble was, she knew what he would say about this film. She shook her head and cleared her throat as if she could physically stop him speaking in her mind and smiled at the nearest waiter who had been waiting for some such sign from her. He removed her empty plate, swept up the crumbs, poured the last of the wine into her glass, placed a coffee cup and a full dish of her favourite macaroons in front of her. Achilles, the oldest member of the family present, brought her a Strega, unasked, and told her the good news that his only son – with whose triumphant scholastic progress Fanny had long been familiar – had won an Exhibition to King's College, Cambridge. Fanny toasted his success with her Strega.

The attentions she received were observed elsewhere in the restaurant. The Roma was not generally noted for the speed of its service. Several less favoured people sighed, snapped fingers in the air, exchanged wrathful or amused glances with their companions. But only one couple turned openly nasty. Their table was close to Fanny's and she had heard them complaining earlier about the spaghetti alla matriciana. There was too much bacon. Or not enough bacon. Now it was the bill. They had been waiting too long for the bill.

Achilles excused himself to Fanny and went to the rescue.

9

He apologised, smiling. The restaurant was busy, they were short staffed tonight, perhaps their waiter, his nephew who was looking after their table, had not realised they were in a hurry. If they could spare the time, he would like to offer them a *digestif*. On the house, naturally.

The offended customer groaned, as if making amends was a snub in his book. His complexion, already high-coloured, flushed several shades darker. An expensive, spoilt boy, Fanny judged him. All people under forty seemed young to her now, but this man really was young. Too young to be making this kind of scene with dignity or conviction. Certainly too young to know how to end it.

A combination of arrogance and insecurity was making him bluster. The bill was presented and he threw a credit card on the table. Achilles explained that the Roma did not accept cards. Only cash, or a cheque. The angry boy looked as if he might explode. For God's sake, everyone took cards 'in this day and age'! His girl – or his wife? – intervened. She had a cheque book. She picked up the bill. The man snatched it from her and brooded. Sweat shone on his smooth, rosy forehead. He slapped the bill down on the table in front of the girl. His long, blunt, very white fingers were trembling. So was his voice.

'You have charged me for service!' he shouted. 'What service, for God's sake? What incredible *cheek*!'

This last word, and the indignant squeak with which he produced it, stripped him of manhood entirely. Achilles stood absolutely still, eyes lowered discreetly, as if unwilling to witness a schoolboy's humiliation. He did not look up until the young man had stormed from the restaurant, crashing the door open and leaving it swinging behind him. The girl, who had written the cheque, held it out to Achilles. He took it with a little bow, and a soft, soothing murmur of condolence and apology. The girl said, 'Oh shit.' She had a dead white face and a great mop of crinkled red hair. The upper part of her body was clothed conventionally enough in a white lace blouse and black waistcoat, but when she stood up to follow her partner she was seen to be wearing nothing between her waist and her ankle boots except a pair of gold and black tights fitting so closely that they appeared to be painted on her thin legs and plump buttocks.

Achilles watched her go with a grave expression that inhibited comment from other diners. When the door closed behind her, he shrugged his shoulders, spread his hands and smiled ruefully – a deliberately 'Italian' gesture to return his small kingdom to normal. There was a ripple of laughter. He stopped at Fanny's table. 'Sorry about that, Mrs Pye.'

'I hope the cheque doesn't bounce.'

Achilles lifted his shoulders again but less definitively. Although his parents were Italian immigrants he had been born in London. And he knew that Fanny knew it. He said, 'No point in asking for a cheque guarantee and making further unpleasantness. I like my guests to enjoy their meals in peace.'

'And mostly they do,' Fanny said. 'I suspect that young man's temper will get him in trouble before he's much older.'

She paid her bill, adding an extra two and a half per cent to the twelve and a half per cent as she always did. (Daniel had always said that fifteen per cent was reasonable.) One of the nephews fetched her light summer coat and opened the door for her.

Outside, in the pedestrian precinct, no one was about. A misty rain fell, polishing the paving stones and sweetening the air. Fanny, who liked rain, turned up her collar and lifted her face to sniff it and taste it. (Daniel would have had an umbrella. He would have opened it above her, protectively, and hurried her home. He would not have wanted to linger as Fanny did now.)

The antique shops in the Precinct, protected by bars and wire mesh against burglary, were full of what Daniel had called 'other people's unwanted possessions'. Which was why Fanny enjoyed window gazing. She had no impulse to buy; years of living abroad, a diplomat's wife, had taught her to travel light. But she liked to look. To look and to wonder. Who had abandoned these objects, died, or grown tired of them?

The rocking horse was still in the shop on the corner. His newly painted coat gleamed in the light of the street lamp; his wild, white eye seemed to roll in its shadow. Fanny and her sister had had a similar horse; when their mother died, Delia had requisitioned it for her children. She was the older and so had first claim, Fanny acknowledged. Nevertheless, taking custody of Dobbin, *snatching* him before Fanny, flying from Ankara, had even landed in London, had seemed a trifle highhanded. Fanny still felt a burn of resentment, not just because she had loved the old horse – riding him for hours, spellbound, enchanted – but because Delia had known that he would be the only thing she would ask for. Not that Delia would have admitted this to herself, of course; her mind had always been carefully organised to keep that kind of inconvenient awareness at bay.

The horse in the window had a price tag. Fanny peered closer; too lazy to take out her spectacles, she screwed up her eyes to get it in focus. 'Five hundred and ninety-five pounds,' she murmured aloud. 'Can you *believe* it, Dan?'

Lonely suddenly, she turned from the window and marched sturdily through the rest of the Precinct towards the road at the end; not a main road, but a wide one that was always lined with parked cars and busy at night, especially around the time the pubs closed. They must be closing now, Fanny thought, hearing car doors slam, voices shouting. She had not thought it was quite so late.

Nor was it. Lights shone in most of the terraced houses that lined both sides of the street and the roadway was still packed with stationary cars. The noise was coming from a group of three or four people yelling at each other around a car that was slewed across the road. Fanny hesitated. She had walked after dark in cities more dangerous than London and knew all the tricks: keep to a brisk, determined stride, stay inconspicuous, avoid other people's quarrels. But two sets of motorists – she could see a second car now, nuzzling the side of the first one – were unlikely to bother with a third party. And this was the quickest way home. Why should she even consider turning back and going an extra quarter mile along the High Street? She was not going to fall into the foolish trap, the prison that kept so many single women indoors. Give way once, give in for ever!

It wasn't until she was almost upon them that she recognised the repulsive young man from the Roma. It was his car, she guessed, that had rammed the other; the three men surrounding him were more likely to have come out of the old Vauxhall than the white BMW. And, indeed, the girl was getting out of the passenger seat of the BMW now, long, twinkly legs waving like insect tentacles as she reached for the ground. One of the men shouted 'fucking yuppies', and she gave a frightened scream at the same time as her companion seemed to choke – a retching gurgle as he was slammed face down on the bonnet of his car.

The girl began to run. She ran past Fanny, her white face a

chalk mask, her mouth a black slash, her eyes black holes. She tottered on high heels up the street, an agitated, spidery silhouette against the brighter lights of the main road.

Fanny stood still, holding on to an iron railing. Looking down, she could see directly into a basement room lit by a television. It was showing some sort of video – women wrestling in mud, Fanny thought, straining to see as if the nature of the programme was of some weird importance. There were people watching it. Of course, she should call for help! The noises the man was making sounded so desperate. But her mouth had dried. And there was no adult there, in the basement; all the watchers were children. Perhaps they might fetch someone. But the man had stopped making those noises now.

He was on the ground. His head was down beside the car. Or under the car. Out of Fanny's sight, anyway. One of the three men was bending over him, another looking up the street after the staggering girl. He gave a kind of *whoop* – a hunting cry – and started after her. The third man shouted, 'For Christ's sake leave the tart go, we've got to get the fucking car away.'

He flung himself at the side of the Vauxhall, trying to rock it free; the other car's bumper must have jammed under its side. '*Christ,*' he said, '*Jake.* For Christ's sake.'

Fanny couldn't hear what 'Jake' said. He was kneeling beside the man on the ground. Then he stood up, scrabbling at the body, hauling it free of the car, rolling it over. Fanny saw the dark blood round the mouth. Jake said, 'The bugger's all right. Only foxing.'

He dragged the man's legs apart and touched his crotch with his foot. 'I'll wake him up,' he said, and laughed. Then he danced back on his toes.

14

'*No*,' Fanny said.

Her voice was a croak but he heard it. He checked himself, rocking on his heels, and looked at her. Fanny clutched the railing. She said, 'Don't do that. Stop this. You must stop it. At once.'

He said, astonished, 'What the fuck's it got to do with you? He did it! He started it. He bashed up the car! Then he came at me like a fucking madman!'

'I daresay,' Fanny said. She thought – ridiculous to be frightened. This was London. Not Istanbul. Or Washington. They were all young. And not drunk. Or not obviously drunk. She said, 'Even if it's his fault, that's not the point now.'

She wasn't sure that he heard her. The other man was making such a noise, heaving at the Vauxhall. She moved closer, still shaky, but gathering confidence. Then she looked down. And felt sick. She said 'We have to get him to hospital.'

Jake said, 'Oh, God!' and looked beyond her. It was the only warning she had. She felt the first blow, a thump at the base of her spine, throwing her forward, but not the second. I'm *going to break my nose* was her last, conscious thought.

Isabel said, 'Yes, Aunt Delia . . . Yes, really sure . . . She came round briefly but she was confused . . . And she's asleep now . . .

'No, Aunt Delia, no need to come. They're doing all that they can . . . Yes, of course they're taking it seriously. They'll be taking more X-rays. Though the doctor said he's pretty sure there's no fracture . . .

'I told you, Aunt Delia. She wasn't making sense. She didn't know where she was now, let alone where she'd been. Or how she got involved. I don't suppose she was exactly roaming the streets looking for trouble, do you? The woman who rang the police said she wasn't **there w**hen she went off to phone. Just her husband and these other men . . .

'No, he's not conscious yet. He and his wife, they'd been to that Italian restaurant. The one Daddy liked. I suppose Mummy might have been eating there too, I wondered about that, and I rang, but they'd closed . . .

'Yes. Yes, Harry's coming, Aunt Delia. He was at a party. The children told me where and I got him and Poppy just as they were leaving . . .

'Why me? Well, she had a birthday card for me stamped and addressed in her handbag. My birthday's the day after tomorrow. I expect she thought she'd put it in the box on the way home so it would catch the first post in the morning . . .

'No. No, I'm not crying, Aunt Delia. Honestly. Look, I must go. I don't want her to come round and find me not there. And I must watch out for Harry . . .

'Yes, I'll ring at once if anything . . . Yes, I'll tell them you'll be in first thing in the morning.'

For a full minute after she had replaced the receiver, Isabel stood very straight, eyes closed, breathing deeply, wishing she could organise herself to get to a weekly yoga class and learn how to relax her body efficiently. Though it was stupid to let Aunt Delia wind her up! She always made everyone feel that they were not handling things as well as she would do if she were there. It was simply Aunt Delia's *natural habit* and it was only because she, Isabel, had always thought of herself as incompetent that it worried her.

Having sorted this out, Isabel felt a lot better. She opened her eyes and shook back her hair and lifted her chin – bracing herself for the return to the stuffy small room off the main ward where her mother lay.

Fanny had been put in the side ward because of the police-woman sitting beside her bed. It might upset the other patients the staff nurse had explained. It was different in the men's ward. So many male emergencies in this inner city area were the result of criminal action that the men's overnight ward was practically a branch of the local police station.

Isabel thought that her mother would be amused to hear this comment on the part of London she lived in. It was precisely what she and Max had been telling her for ages. Well, for the last eighteen months, anyway, ever since Daddy died. Now she was alone, she would be better off in a good block of flats with proper security arrangements. Somewhere near one of the parks and a decent supermarket where she could buy fruit and vegetables properly prepared and wrapped instead of wormy rubbish from the local street market.

Though her mother claimed that she preferred buying from the stalls. 'I like my apples different sizes and mud on my potatoes. It reminds me that things actually grow on trees and in the earth.' Isabel thought this affected and had felt impelled to say so. Her mother had never lived in the country and in the years of Daniel's working life abroad had always had a cook. Isabel had never seen her wash earth off a potato in her life! 'Well, no, perhaps not, dear,' Fanny had peaceably agreed. 'Perhaps it's buying things from people rather than pushing a trolley round the shelves. I like to have someone to talk to.'

'You could come and stay with us more often if you're short of conversation,' Isabel had said.

She argued with her mother in her mind as she walked back to the ward – it was ridiculous for Fanny to be lonely, she was always welcome, surely she wasn't waiting for an *invitation* – and then reproached herself. The diplomatic life, all that formal entertaining, had inhibited her mother; she had forgotten how to live a free and easy social life. Oh, the poor darling, Isabel mourned, how careless I have been! Her eyes filled with sorrow and remorse – impulsive tears that she blinked angrily away, ashamed because they came so easily. An instant emotional response was cheap, no use to anyone. It was as if she were boasting of her tender heart!

A nurse came clattering past, wheeling a kind of gallows looped about with rubber tubes and swinging bottles. Isabel gasped and ran, but this sinister apparatus had not been intended for her mother. The nurse banged through the doors into the main ward and, in the side room, Fanny lay as Isabel had left her, on her back, slightly raised on pillows, arms outside the sheet that was folded tight across her chest.

Her large, competent hands looked strange to Isabel, or at least unfamiliar; she realised that she had never seen them so unoccupied and still. Maybe she had never seen them wash potatoes but she had seen them busy with a hundred other things. She stretched out one of her own much smaller hands – with stumpy fingers, bitten nails – to touch the nearest of her mother's, and recoiled. 'She's cold,' she said, and the policewoman, a dark girl with a plump, sweet face, reached from her chair at the far side of the bed and picked up Fanny's wrist.

She held it silently. Then smiled. 'Just cold, that's all,' she said – relieved, Isabel supposed, that she had not been watching by a corpse. 'Perhaps we can get another blanket.' She got up and looked through the glass into the empty corridor. 'You'd think a nurse would come. If only to see . . .' The policewoman stopped, and blushed.

'To see she's still alive? I suppose they've done all they can to stop her dying, and they've got better things to do than hang around just to see she's comfortable! I'll see if I can tuck her up a bit.'

Isabel managed to say all this quite calmly. It was only when she was bent across the bed, freeing the sheet from the mattress to cover Fanny's arms, that she realised what she had said. It had not occurred to her before that her mother might have died. Oh, she didn't think she was immortal! But in spite of her father's sudden death, the prospect of Fanny following him had always seemed remote. Daniel, after all, had always fussed about his health and after he left the diplomatic service he had enlarged upon this interest, taking it up as some men take up golf when they retire, until it had become what practically amounted to a new career. By the time of his heart attack (which gave no warning symptoms) he had directed his family's attention so firmly grave-ward for so long that only his doctor was surprised by it.

In contrast, Fanny's sturdy health, and, even more, her total lack of interest in disease, had reassured her children. A strong, tall, supple woman, who had never to their knowledge spent a day in bed, she had seemed indestructible, particularly to Isabel who was younger than Harry by four years. Now, bending over her mother, adjusting her limp and acquiescent body, Isabel saw this was no longer true.

It wasn't the bruised and bloodied face. Isabel believed what she had been told, that except for a cracked tooth, all that damage was superficial, not as bad as it looked. What shocked Isabel was the discovery that her mother was no longer middle-aged, but *old*. It was almost as if there had been a great leap in time since the last time they had met – time for the flesh to loosen and sag and for the skin to pucker and wrinkle. Last week – it was last week, wasn't it? – Fanny had looked twenty years younger. Of course, she had been talking and smiling, urging Isabel to go and see some film or other that she had just seen and was mad about, not lying mugged and unconscious. 'She looks so vulnerable,' Isabel said and felt the shameful tears well up again.

The policewoman looked at her questioningly, half rising from her chair. Isabel shook her head, and blew her nose, and smiled. She said, 'I saw her last week and she was so cheerful, on about some marvellous film or other that she thought I ought to see. But I didn't go to see it. I didn't even write the title down and now I've forgotten what it was.'

'Does your mother live alone?'

'Since my father died a year ago. Eighteen months, actually.' Isabel wondered if a rebuke had been intended. Or if the girl were gathering information for her notebook. Neglected parent. Uncaring daughter. She said, 'But we see her quite often, my brother and I. And she has *hosts* of friends.'

'That's nice,' the young policewoman said. 'Some of these poor old things, they're scared to go out, and they're stuck indoors, and no one comes one week to another.'

'Oh, Mummy's not like that. She's never been scared to go out alone,' Isabel said. It struck her that this was a foolish boast in the circumstances. She said, in a bright voice, 'Perhaps she should have been.'

The policewoman smiled solemnly. 'It's no life, being afraid.'

Isabel returned the smile. She couldn't think what next to say. Or, rather, she could think of a number of things but none that seemed appropriate. Facetiousness – to cover up her panic – would be misunderstood. And to 'stand up' for her mother as she felt inclined to do, to explain somehow that she was not just another 'poor old thing', but a strong and independent personality of some standing in society could not be done without sounding snobbish. 'My father was in the diplomatic service, my mother was an ambassador's wife.' As if she should have special treatment. How demeaning!

She murmured, 'I'm sure Mummy would agree with you,' and sighed.

A nurse came in with a trolley. She folded back the covers to take Fanny's pulse, holding her wrist delicately with cold, red-tipped fingers, eyes on the watch that was pinned to the bib of her apron. Her scrubbed face was stern. Then she took Fanny's blood pressure. Isabel, who hated having this done to her, forced herself to watch, sympathetically suffering the unpleasant constriction in her own biceps. She cleared her throat nervously. 'Is she all right?'

The nurse replaced Fanny's pale arm beneath the covers. She said, 'Has she come round at all?' And, without waiting for an answer, 'Sister's in her office now if you'd like to pop along. Your brother's here. I'd like to tidy Mrs Pye before he sees her.'

Isabel fled into the corridor. Whatever process was meant by tidying, she didn't want to witness it. Seeing Harry, walking towards her, she began to sob with relief. She ran into his arms.

He hugged her. He said, 'I'm sorry you've had to cope alone. Poor Izzy. Never mind. Here now.'

'She looks so awful,' Isabel wailed. 'All bruised and swollen and her mouth all bloody where she fell. She's broken some teeth, one, anyway. Oh, it's so *horrible*, Harry. I wish I knew what had happened . . .'

'She'll be able to tell us, I hope,' Harry said. 'It looks as if the man isn't likely to. So the Sister told me.'

'You mean he might *die*?'

'She didn't say that, you know what hospitals are. She said *critical*. Apparently his wife told the police that they – her husband, that is – hit the other car, and then set about the driver. There were a couple of other men there. But she didn't see Mother.'

'Perhaps she came along and tried to help. That would be like her. Busybodying!'

Harry frowned at this flippancy. This was not a moment to laugh at their mother, not even affectionately.

'God knows,' he said. 'No point in speculating.' He put his hand on her shoulder. 'Come on. Let's go and see her.'

Isabel saw the muscle twitching in his cheek. When they were children he had been terrified of the dentist, of injections, of the sight of blood. She said, 'It really isn't as bad as it looks, Harry darling. Honestly.'

He made a small, explosive sound of irritation and she knew she should not have spoken. Bad enough to be squeamish without a younger sister rubbing it in! 'Sorry,' she said, penitently, 'I just didn't want you to be too upset.'

What disgusted him was the idea that any man could do this to someone weaker than himself. Harry had never hit a woman or a child – nor, indeed, someone of his own sex since he had grown out of the rough and tumble of his junior school. But he could now, he thought, looking at his mother and clenching his big hands. He could take the brute apart!

Isabel whispered, 'No one hit her in the face, they think that happened when she fell.'

'Whisper, whisper, mutter, mutter,' Fanny said.

She spoke in a soft, grumbling voice, without opening her eyes, and then seemed to slip back into sleep, her swollen lips parted. But she was trying to surface. 'Mouth dry,' she managed to say. She sounded peevish.

The policewoman sat alert in her chair. Isabel said, 'She's not really awake.' She dampened a tissue in the water jug by the bed and moistened her mother's lips. Harry bent over her.

'We're here, darling,' he said. 'Izzy and I. You're all right, quite safe now. How are you feeling?'

'Don't talk if you don't want to, Mummy,' Isabel said. 'We're here, beside you, for just as long as you want us.'

Her voice wobbled with emotion. An odd look flickered across Fanny's purple cheek. A ripple of amusement? She breathed something. 'Con . . . con . . .' – working up the air like a bellows. 'Contradictory instructions,' she said. She sounded croaky but normal, which made her next remark surprising. 'What happened to Dobbin, what did Delia do with him in the end? I suppose I could ask my solicitor.'

She remembered saying something before she woke up but couldn't remember what it had been. She saw Isabel and Harry looking puzzled. Or worried. Harry was going grey at the temples but his hair was still thick and had kept a lot of its colour, a rich, shiny brown like polished mahogany. He looked pale – it made her angry to see him so pale. He worked hard, but that pallor came from too many late nights! Indeed, he might just have come from a rowdy party; the knot of his tie twisted sideways and what looked like wine down the front of his shirt. Unless it was blood. She said, 'Have you been in a fight, Harry? You ought to know better at your age.'

'That's fine coming from you,' Isabel said. 'You're the one who's been in a fight by the look of it. What have you been up to?'

That silly teasing tone was just nervousness, Fanny knew. She was irritated by it all the same. Her daughter wasn't a child any longer. Nor even an awkward girl. Fanny couldn't remember exactly how old she was, but she was old enough to have children. Three children, Fanny thought, even though she couldn't remember their names just at the moment. And her daughter was certainly old enough to stop dressing like an adolescent. She looked like a tramp in that man's ancient dinner jacket. And why all the dusty black, anyway? Such a pity, when she could look so beautiful. She had her grandmother's features: the straight, pretty nose joining her forehead at that classical angle and the long, dark-lashed, grey eyes.

Isabel didn't have her grandmother's temperament, though. Fanny's mother had never been restless or anxious. Fanny saw her, in a flash of clarity, sitting on a swing, a long rope of crystal beads round her neck, feet in pointed, strap shoes.

But that was a photograph of a young woman, smiling. Fanny had never known her as young as that. She said, 'How old is Mama now?'

Her children looked at each other. She knew she had said something foolish. When she tried to think what it could be, there seemed to be holes in her head. Empty spaces.

Harry took her hand. He said, in a deep, solemn voice, 'Darling. I'm sorry. She's dead.'

Fanny felt a rush of black, formless anger. Not directed at anyone. It was like a wind swelling inside her. She beat it down and said, 'Yes, yes of course I knew that. I was just thinking of her in that picture.' There was something missing in this explanation. She said crossly, 'On the swing.'

Isabel said, 'I know the one, Mummy. It's in your study, on the ground floor. What used to be Daddy's study, but you took

24

it over when he died.' She blushed and Fanny understood – instantly, without any effort – that Isabel had dragged in this mention of Daniel to remind her that he was dead too. She went on in what was, Fanny thought, a clumsy attempt to conceal this obvious piece of subterfuge, 'The picture is on the wall behind the door.'

Fanny nodded. Now that she had remembered her mother was dead she had lost interest. There were more important things to worry about. She wasn't at home. She was in a small room. Shiny yellow paint and a high ceiling. Institutional. Beyond a window in the wall on her left was a brightly lit corridor. The bed she lay on was narrow and hard. She said, carefully, anxious not to make a fool of herself again, 'Am I in hospital? I didn't know I'd been ill.'

She tried to smile but it hurt her.

Harry said, 'You've had a fall, darling. Or someone knocked you down. We're not altogether sure what happened yet, but whatever it was has jolted you up a bit. You mustn't be too upset if things seem muddled for a while. Just rest, and relax, and everything will fall back into place very soon.'

He spoke very clearly and distinctly as if he were talking to a deaf person. Or a foreigner. Fanny said, 'Don't patronise me, Harry.'

He grinned. He said, 'Sorry, Mother.' But he looked relieved. He turned and seemed to be answering someone behind him. 'Perhaps, if you want to speak to her, it might be . . .'

That was all Fanny heard. A nurse appeared and squeezed along the side of the bed next to the window. 'Just your blood pressure, Mrs Pye. It's nice to see you awake. Are you comfortable?'

In fact, she was suddenly very tired. She closed her eyes while

25

the nurse fiddled with gadgets, liking the sensation of young, cool fingertips on her bare arms, the feeling of being taken over, looked after. When the nurse had finished, she opened her eyes and saw that Harry and Isabel had retreated to the end of the bed and a young woman in uniform had taken their place.

Surely she hadn't been out in the car? It was kept in a garage at the end of the terrace and she rarely used it in London. She said, 'Have I had an accident?' She thought, with horror – *have I killed someone?*

'We don't know,' the girl said. And then, quickly, as if she had guessed what Fanny was fearing, 'You were in the street, we think walking home. You fell. Or something hit you. Can you remember?'

'Something happened,' Fanny said. She knew this 'something' was there, but it was a shapeless shadow lurking at the very edge of her vision. She couldn't approach it, or bring it closer; it seemed to move, bob about, like a liver spot before the eyes. Once, tantalisingly, she almost had it. She said, 'Was anyone else hurt? Was it a car accident?'

'There were vehicles involved,' the policewoman said. 'But no, not that kind of accident. There seems to have been a fight. A man was seriously injured.'

Fanny waited for the shadow to take shape and declare itself. There was no point in pursuing it. There were a few tricks she knew how to play but memory had its own logic; a code which was hard to break sometimes.

She said, 'It's like a word on the tip of the tongue. A matter of waiting.' She saw how young the girl was. She smiled with her bruised mouth. 'Can you understand that?'

The girl smiled back. 'If it's like that, it'll come. It's important that we know everything you can tell us. So someone will be here all the time. You just have to lift your hand. Or ring the bell.'

Fanny wondered why she had gone into the police force. A friend of Daniel's, a Chief Constable, had once told her that the best policemen were those who had stumbled into the profession by chance. Because they couldn't think of anything else to do.

Her head was aching. She was glad to lie quietly, knowing that Harry and Isabel were beside her. Whatever had happened, she was clearly ill enough not to feel she should worry about their being here at the hospital instead of in their own homes. Where were those homes? Isabel had children. She was married to that dark, Jewish-looking man with the somehow rather incongruous naval beard. Mark. Yes, Mark. He was an architect. He drank when he was depressed. That wasn't a pleasant description and there must be more to him than that, but it must serve for the moment. At least she had a skeletal idea of her son-in-law. Flesh would grow later. That must have been a nasty bump on her head to have knocked so much out of it. And, now she thought about it, her shoulders ached, and her back, and her neck. Her throat was sore, too. Mustn't moan until the children had left, though. It would weigh Isabel down particularly; she always seemed loaded with burdens. Putting a good face on things, a lesson Fanny had learned early, was not one she had managed to pass on to her daughter! Perhaps Isabel did have a lot to bear. Children, drunken husband – no, not Mark, *Max* was his name, it came to her suddenly. Who did Harry live with? Not with her, she was sure. Did he live with Delia? There had been a time when he had been at boarding school and spent the occasional holiday with Delia, but that time was gone now. He was here now, beside her bed, in this

27

small room, this small, brightly lit capsule, spinning through the dark. What lay outside it? For Isabel, the drunken architect, the shadowy children. But for Harry?

She had almost slipped into sleep again. She heard herself snore, and jerked awake. They were still here, looking at her with concerned expressions. Had she dropped off with her mouth open?

She said, embarrassed, 'Are you married, Harry?' She attempted a laugh. 'I seem to have forgotten.'

He concealed his shock quickly, but not before it had answered her.

Isabel said, 'Oh, Mummy! Harry's been married for years! How could you . . . I mean, you're so fond of Poppy!'

She sounded scandalised. And hurt on Poppy's behalf. Presumably Harry must be hurt too, though his kind smile would not admit it. Fanny said, 'Oh, I'm sorry, how silly. Poppy, of course!'

The name meant nothing to her.

Harry said, 'You see? You haven't lost your memory, darling, just mislaid a few bits here and there. Poppy sent her love, she went home to see to the girls, we don't like leaving them alone after midnight, not too late, anyway, but she'll come in tomorrow. Lunch time, probably. I'll try and look in before I go to work in the morning and if there's anything you need I can ring Poppy. Or Isabel.'

'I'll be here in the afternoon,' Isabel said. 'And Aunt Delia said she'd come in the morning. She would have come tonight but I told her there was no need. I'll tell her to come a bit later than Harry. You won't want too many visitors.'

'Although if you want us, we can come any time,' Harry said.

Fanny felt weary. If she knew where the hospital was, or where any of them lived in relation to it, she might be able to make some sensible comment on these energetic arrangements. She could ask where she was, of course. But it would be humiliating if the answer meant nothing to her. Like Harry's wife's name. There had been a Poppy at school. Her primary school, years ago, before Hitler's war. Poppy had one of those false pianos; she pumped the pedals and the music played. Fanny had thought it wonderfully sophisticated but her mother had said it was common. That Poppy would be her age now. Harry's wife must be very much younger. How old were Harry's children? How many? He had said 'the girls'. What sex were Isabel's children? She looked at her children, at Isabel whose grey eyes were washed with tears, at her tall, tired son, and smiled painfully.

'It will be lovely to see you whenever you can come. Just now, I don't know what the time is, but I think I need to sleep. And try and sort things out.'

She thought she had managed that with dignity. Well enough to hide the extent of her ignorance, anyway. There was just one thing she wanted to know – that was more urgent than anything else, for some reason. It was something she could ask without offending anyone. She said, 'What are those pianos that play automatically? I don't think I shall rest until I know.'

'Pianola,' Harry said. 'Leave your mind alone, darling. You'll remember everything in the morning.'

Once she had begun to remember, she discovered a kind of restful freedom in her mild confusion. She lay, floating it seemed, in an uncertain sky; one moment choked and lost in foggy cumulus, the next, sailing through feathery cloud into clear and sparkling weather. It was like the best kind of dreaming that comes between sleeping and waking. Surprising, she thought, that falling down in the street and banging her head should turn out so agreeably. Although it was probably the pills she was being given for pain that were making her feel so idle and easy, not the 'accident'. Whatever the 'accident' was. She knew she had been to the cinema because she thought she could remember buying a ticket. But she couldn't remember what film she had seen. She knew she had eaten at the Roma because they had told her. (The nice police girl had spoken to Achilles and he had sent her a pot of African violets.)

Other memories came. They were a mixed bag; she saw them at one point as a jumble of objects on a white elephant stall at a bring and buy sale. She made no effort to summon them. She lay in her hospital bed and bits of her life drifted through her, leaving a gentle imprint behind them; she felt herself to be soft and absorbent, like blotting paper.

Harry's wife, Poppy. A small, plump girl with a smooth, pale skin and brown eyes. How odd to have forgotten her. Remembering seemed an arbitrary business. Perhaps there was only space to remember one Poppy, and the schoolgirl with the pianola had taken preference. (This time the word *pianola* appeared in her mind without effort.) A daughter-in-law, you would think, was of more immediate interest than a childhood friend. Harry and Poppy had been married some time. She liked Poppy very much indeed. She was an unusual girl for Harry to have married in some ways, though what those ways were, Fanny couldn't quite pin down at the moment. Harry and Poppy had twin girls. Molly and Minerva.

Isabel's children were Adam, George and Jennifer. Isabel's husband was Max, not Mark. And it was Mark who drank, not

Max. Mark was Max's father. Poor Max. How lucky that she hadn't said anything stupid to Isabel. What could she have said? 'Oh, Isabel, is Max sober tonight?' Surely not. Though she had made that idiotic remark to Harry.

She said, to her sister, Delia, 'I seem to be a little vague at the moment. But if you've come to view the corpse you'll be disappointed. I'm to stay here several more days and I must admit I'm enjoying it.'

'It's a disgrace,' Delia said. 'Not you, Fanny. The hospital. Only one lift working, four wards closed, and the flooring in the corridors pot-holed like the streets of some Third World city. Though the comparison is an insult to the Third World. I should have said New York or London.'

'I came in unconscious so I didn't notice,' Fanny said. 'And the staff are lovely. I meant I was enjoying being ill. It feels wonderfully irresponsible.'

'Oh, it's not the fault of the doctors and nurses. It's the Government. This nonsense about turning the National Health Service into a more cost efficient operation is simply an evasion of public duty. If you're going to apply economic arguments to hospitals, the most effective measure would be to reduce the number of sick. Sick old people especially. Why not free fags and free booze dished out to all pensioners? Maybe a few mind blowing drugs too. Carry 'em all off as soon as possible. Wouldn't work on you, Fanny, you're indestructible. What on earth happened? Isabel says that you've lost your memory. I rang Harry, of course, but he said the same. What are you playing at?'

'Don't make me laugh, Delia,' Fanny said. 'It hurts to laugh.'

Delia scowled at her. 'I wasn't conscious of making a joke.

Don't be perverse, Fanny. But I can see it must hurt. You look absolutely ghastly. Your right eye is crimson. A sight to frighten the crows.'

Fanny said, 'There was some sort of fight over a car. It was in that street that runs through the Precinct up to the main road. The houses on either side are built in a crescent so the street bellies out in the middle, wide enough to park a third line of cars. It's the way I would walk home from the Roma, if that's what I was doing. Apparently I had eaten at the Roma. So had the man who was beaten up. His name is Hobbes. Like the philosopher. Andrew Hobbes. His wife was with him. She saw the other men but she was too frightened to look at them properly. Though she was sure the other car was a Vauxhall. She and her husband were driving a BMW. Of course, I don't *know* any of this. All I know is what they have told me.'

Fanny thought – why can't I remember? I was there, must have been, since they say so. I can remember other things, sometimes too many things, all at once, crowding in much too fast. Like flicking through snapshots. Pictures of Delia. Young and pudgy in long white socks. Shouting at me because I couldn't catch the ball she was throwing. Delia important in her new school uniform, hair in two heavy plaits. I cried because my hair wasn't as thick or as long as Delia's . . .

Delia had been so pretty. A lovely strong jaw, smooth as marble. Age had thickened and loosened it; mottled dewlaps swung from it. When had the change taken place? The years descended like a slow moving glacier, crushing, destroying . . .

Fanny said, 'I don't know what I look like. They haven't brought me a mirror so I presume that my appearance is pretty horrendous. I'm sorry if it upsets you to look at me.'

'Don't be a fool.' Delia shook her stiff helmet of hair in an

32

irritable gesture. Fanny could smell her hairspray. Delia had her hair done at Harrods and Harrods hairspray was distinctive; sometimes, at West End cinemas in the afternoons, it pervaded the atmosphere. Particularly now people were not allowed to smoke any longer. Years ago, when Delia had been Chairman of her local borough council she had smoked thin, black cigars.

Delia said, turning on, Fanny noted, her soft, concerned voice, 'I don't want to bully you, duckie. But you really must try to pull yourself together. Make a real effort. Surely you ought to be able to remember who hit you?'

Fanny said, 'It's like asking people who have decided to get divorced if they have thought about it.'

'But you have never been divorced, Fanny!'

'If they have decided, they must have thought, don't you think?'

'Well. Yes, I suppose so.'

'If I could remember, I'd tell you.'

The logic of this exchange seemed impeccable to Fanny. 'That squished you up,' was what the children used to say when they reckoned they had won an argument. Her success made her feel more kindly disposed to her sister. She said, 'If you've been concussed, it's usually what happened just before that gets lost. You can't force it back. So they tell me.'

'Perhaps your mind doesn't want to remember,' Delia said. She paused, frowning, considering the implications of this remark. Then she said, 'I don't mean you would deliberately forget, why should you? It's just, you sound so much like yourself that it's hard to believe . . .'

'You have never been very imaginative, Delia.'

Fanny heard herself saying this with some surprise. She had often addressed her sister rudely in her mind but never out loud. Or not since she had been a frantic small girl driven into uncontrollable fury by a bossy older sister. She thought that she ought to apologise but felt no impulse to do so. Nor any necessity. She was licensed by her condition to say exactly what came into her head without censoring it. She was conscious of a moment's wicked pleasure – and then a warning light flashed in her brain. She said, 'I hope I'm not getting senile dementia.'

'Absolute rubbish, Fanny!' Delia gave a short bark of scornful laughter. 'You've had a bonk on the head, silly girl. That's absolutely all.'

'Senility has to be started off somehow.' Fanny spoke reproachfully but she was reassured as she always had been by Delia's brisk convictions. She thought of a long-ago Delia, turning on her bedroom light, flinging wide the cupboard door to show that there was nothing there but clothes and her school hockey stick. A bracing wind, scolding, blowing the shadows away. 'How do you think a witch would get in, anyway?' Delia the bully was also Delia the comforter.

She said now, 'You need to rest, duckie. I can see you're going to need a bit of looking after for a while. I'll talk to Harry, we'll work something out. You mustn't worry, that's the main thing.'

'I'm not worried,' Fanny said. Although this was true, she knew that her weak and passive tone denied it, and that Delia would assume that she was happy to be taken over. But just then, quite suddenly, she felt too tired to care.

'She mustn't go back to that house alone,' Delia announced to Harry. She was ringing her nephew from the House of Lords. Harry, who was holding an editorial meeting in his room, had left it to pick up the telephone in his secretary's outer office.

He said, 'Aunt Delia, I'm sorry, but I thought it was urgent. I'm caught up at the moment. Can I ring you back?'

'It's urgent enough, Harry. And I'm due to speak in the debate in ten minutes so I won't keep you long. I had a word with the consultant and they're thinking of discharging her tomorrow. Disgracefully sudden as I told him. Now. We both know she'll insist on going home. Fanny has always been mulish and offering her alternatives would be a waste of time. She can get herself to and fro from the bathroom so she won't need nursing. Food is no problem. I can nip into Marks and Spencer and fill her freezer. I'd stay with her only Buffy's lost without me, he really can't manage his artificial leg. He'll get used to it I tell him, but it's early days. I suppose Ivy can come in a few hours extra in the daytime, and there's that nice Partridge woman next door, but that leaves the evenings and the nights and so I think the best thing would be if Becky moved in for a spell. It'll suit her as well as Fanny, she won't have to trail up from Sussex at the crack of dawn.'

Harry thought of his cousin Rebecca, so much younger than he was, years younger than her two bouncing, beautiful sisters. A witch's egg, the runt of Delia's litter, and the only one still at home. Painfully shy, painfully silent – when she did speak she tended to spit. Harry said, 'I didn't know she was working in London.'

Or working at all, come to that. Who would employ her?

He said, 'Have you asked Mother?'

'Fanny's fond of her.' Delia was expert at dodging the issue. 'And I'm sure she'd want Becky to make a success of this job Buffy's got her. Look, Harry, I really must go.'

She sounded suddenly indignant as if Harry had been importuning her.

He laughed as he put down the receiver. His secretary, who was new and young, looked at him anxiously. 'I'm sorry,' she said. 'I did say you were busy but I couldn't persuade her . . . She, well, she *boomed* at me.'

'She does boom,' Harry said. 'And she makes use of the Baroness bit to steamroller people. Tell yourself she's just an old Labour work horse put out to grass in the Lords and be firm with her.'

He crinkled up his eyes at this nice new girl and hoped that she wasn't going to turn out too timid. She was looking so crestfallen at this tiny failure. He said, 'Though as a matter of fact you were quite right to call me this time. My mother got mugged the other night and she's being turfed out of hospital.'

'I know,' she said. 'I saw it on Breakfast Time. They didn't say names, just what had happened and where, and that the police were looking for witnesses, but one of the other girls told me it was your mother. I wanted to say I was sorry. I mean, it's so awful for elderly people. London's so awful now, everyone says so.'

Harry smiled. 'I think the dangers are exaggerated. And it was a young man who was badly hurt, not my old mother.'

'It must have been a terrible shock for her, though,' she said sternly, rebuking him. 'And it was dangerous, wasn't it? It sounded as if the poor man was going to die.'

They had taken Fanny to see him in the intensive care unit. Hearing this from the Sister, Harry was furious. He said, pompously, 'Presumably the police are putting the pressure on, hoping to jog her memory, but if she has a set-back as a result, I shall hold the hospital responsible.'

He was seething. Dragging an old woman out of bed to view

a dying man – who was probably some sort of criminal, anyway, people who got themselves killed in the streets were seldom respectable – would have distressed her enormously. God knows how much damage she had suffered already!

The Sister said, 'It seemed to perk her up a bit, actually.'

He had to admit she looked better. Her face was still puffy, and even more discoloured than yesterday, but she was sitting up, combed and tidy, with a peacock blue shawl round her shoulders. He said, 'That's pretty. Where did you get it? Not exactly NHS issue.'

'Poppy brought it. She thought it might distract attention from the bruises.'

'Do they hurt badly?' He sat on the bed and looked at her in what he hoped was an unmoved and clinical manner.

'Only when I laugh. Poppy made me laugh – she looked so appalled when she saw me. It was so good to see her. She brought me *He Knew He Was Right* as well as the shawl. She said I once told her that Trollope was good for long waits at air-ports and she hoped he might work in hospital too.'

Running on, Harry thought, to compensate for having for-gotten Poppy before. He wanted to tell her not to worry, that Poppy was the last person to be offended. But perhaps that would be rubbing the salt in. He said, 'Do visitors tire you?'

'I like to see people. I was especially pleased to see Max, of course.'

She frowned, as if wondering why she had put that so posi-tively, then dismissed her internal query with a little shake of the head and a sigh. 'There are so many blanks still. I went to see Andrew Hobbes. Or, rather, I was trundled along in a wheelchair. But, well – just nothing.' She leaned back against the hard hospital pillows and her eyes seemed to darken, as if a light had been switched off behind them. She said, 'All those tubes and machines. His poor wife.'

'Was she there? Did you recognise her?'

She moved her head restlessly. 'I don't know. I mean, yes, she was there, and I thought, for a minute, I'd seen her before. But that may have been just because I'd been told she had been in the Roma, because then it went, and she was a stranger. Just a strange girl who'd been crying . . .'

Harry thought she looked frightened. Surely she wasn't fit to leave hospital? She might seem more sparky, but once she was home reaction was bound to set in. Perhaps Delia was right about Becky.

When he told her she laughed – and put her hand to her swollen mouth. She said, 'Delia always passed her toys on to me when she got tired of them.'

'That's a bit hard, isn't it? She may have thought Becky would be company for you. But it's up to you, isn't it?'

Fanny smiled carefully. 'Not if Delia has made up her mind. If I say no, she'll get her own back. She'll put social workers on to me. Meals on wheels, library services, home helps. The whole boiling. Community care is Delia's baby. She'd love to have a guinea pig to demonstrate on. Show how well it all functions without being personally inconvenienced.'

Harry said, 'Delia just doesn't like to think of you being alone. Nor do any of us. Poppy and I would be happy if you came to us, you know that. So would Izzy, only her house is noisier.'

'You're all very kind,' Fanny said. 'But I want to go home.'

Isabel, coming to fetch her the next afternoon, saw her sitting beside her bed, dressed in the clothes she had been wearing when she came in. Fanny looked up and smiled with what seemed to her daughter a pathetic eagerness, like a child who has been waiting too long to be collected from school. Though if Fanny had been a child, Isabel would have put her arms round her and hugged and comforted her. Instead, she was first of all stiff with embarrassment, and then suddenly, blazingly angry – with herself for not bringing clean clothes to the hospital, with the hospital for not telling her to do so, with everything that had conspired to reduce her strong, competent mother to a frail, shrunken old woman huddled in a wheelchair and dressed like a tramp. She said, shaking with rage, 'I should have brought you something decent to wear, I'm so sorry.'

Fanny looked down at herself. 'It's only dirt and a bit of blood, dear. Is it so bad?' She opened the handbag perched on her knees, and started fumbling for her glasses.

'Oh, don't *fuss*, it's all right,' Isabel said. 'Though they might have cleaned your coat up a bit for you.'

'I think the nurses have enough to do without playing lady's maid to me.' Fanny's voice was amused and equable but she looked disappointed. Her eagerness had gone. She said, 'It's my fault, really. They would have helped me after the ward rounds, but I insisted on dressing myself. I didn't want you to have to wait for me.'

Isabel said miserably, 'And I was late, wasn't I? I thought I had masses of time but the traffic was absolutely bloody, Chelsea Bridge was closed, one of those enormous lorries jack-knifed on the roundabout and the tail-back was simply miles . . . There'll be a terrible snarl up if they don't clear it before the rush hour. Each time I drive into London nowadays I swear I'll never do it again. I suppose what we ought to have done was to ask them to send you home in an ambulance.'

'I'm sorry to be such a nuisance,' Fanny said, rather sharply.

She started to struggle up. A nurse came running. 'It's all right, Mrs Pye. We'll take you down in the wheelchair.'

'I can walk perfectly well,' Fanny said.

Above her head, the nurse looked at Isabel. 'The trouble is, there's only one lift working at the moment and we're only allowed to use it for patients in wheelchairs. It has to be kept as free as possible for the operating theatres.' She bent over Fanny and said, much more loudly, 'Do you understand, dear? I don't think we're quite up to three flights of stairs are we?'

Isabel looked at her mother nervously, but Fanny's expression was patient.

Except to thank the nurse in a gentle voice, and with a fixed, polite smile, Fanny didn't speak again until she was in the car and attempting to fasten her seat belt. Isabel leaned across and did it for her. 'Sorry,' Fanny said. 'I don't seem to be very competent.'

'Nonsense,' Isabel said. 'I'm just in a hurry to get you away from that place!'

'I suppose the assumption is that if you are old you are likely to be deaf. Well, deaf certainly. Probably dumb and blind, too.'

'Why is only one lift working? That's a *teaching* hospital, for God's sake.'

'Delia was in that hospital once,' Fanny said. 'Years ago, before the war. I remember my mother taking me to see her in this great long ward, beds lined up either side like white soldiers. It was all very military, rank and ritual and patients never allowed to speak to the doctors or the matron directly only through a staff nurse or a sister. And the nurses wouldn't tell you anything. That drove Delia wild – everyone so superior and treating the patients like criminals, there by their own fault. That's changed now, or mostly changed, you'll always get those who think sick people are idiots. But the place was run down then and it's still run down. Delia will say it's a lack of political will, that the Government wants to tear down the Health Service. I just remembered, lying there, that there never did seem to be enough money.'

Isabel believed that Delia was right. She and Max had once belonged to the Liberal Party; they had voted Green at the last election, but had decided since then that the only way to achieve a society that paid a proper regard to education and housing and roads was to vote Labour. (She and Max and the children had always been so healthy that standards of hospital care had not, up to now, come into their reckoning.) Her mother's loftier attitude to political questions, as if she looked down at the world from on high and saw six sides to every question, had always seemed to her specifically designed to annoy Delia. But Fanny was in no state just now to be faced with this argument.

Isabel said, 'What was wrong with Delia? It's hard to imagine her being ill. Either of you, for that matter.'

'I'm not sure anyone told me. I was only seven – this was about 1938. Delia would have been twelve. I think I thought she had appendicitis, I had a friend who had appendicitis and I suppose I thought that was what you went to hospital for. But no one told me, as far as I can remember. All Delia talked about when she came home was how they all put her down. She said the doctors and the nurses had treated her like a little girl with no money. She said she wished she could have told them she was a Princess. Or at least the daughter of a Lord. Someone must have snubbed her, I suppose. But she was always very conscious we were poor.'

'That sounds odd, coming from her,' Isabel said.

'Oh, Delia was determined to get her own back. Not that we were really poor, you know. My father was never out of work, he was proud of his job on the railways. But Delia would have felt more socially secure if he'd worked in a bank. A white collar job . . .'

Her voice trailed into silence. Isabel glanced sideways and saw her lying back, her eyes closed, her hands loose in her lap. Isabel put out her own hand and touched her mother's gently. Fanny smiled. She said sleepily, 'My friend who had appendicitis was called Poppy, too. Her parents had a house on the new estate. They had a goldfish pond in the middle of a rockery. I liked going there because of the goldfish and the pianola, but my mother thought they were uneducated because there were no books in the house. Delia agreed with her, she was snobbish about that sort of thing like our mother. Even though Poppy's parents had bought this smart new bungalow. And a little car.'

Her voice was slowing again; there were distinct gaps between words. Isabel, turning off the main road near the Angel junction, said cheerfully, 'Don't go to sleep now, darling one. You're very nearly home.'

'Home' was a five-floored terrace house, jobbing-builder's Georgian, built in the 1840s. It had been slum property when Daniel had bought it for his young bride in the Fifties; a base for home leave and a store for belongings unwanted abroad. Now Sickert Terrace had been largely yuppified; bright paint and window-boxes, Volvos and BMWs lining both sides of the narrow street. Behind the houses the small gardens that went down to the Regent's Canal were prettily landscaped, furnished with mock Victorian iron furniture, romantic stone statues of a suitable size, plant pots and amphoras brought home from holiday raids on Provence, Tuscany, Greece.

Daniel had paid fifteen hundred pounds. 'How much do these houses go for now?' Isabel said. She asked the question idly, seeing a For Sale board several doors from her mother's, thinking at the same time, and more importantly – all those stairs! How will she manage them!

'Four hundred and eighty thousand was the last figure,' Fanny said crisply. 'Going on half a million. And when you think my parents bought the home I grew up in for eight-and-six a week. I wasn't going to sleep, Isabel. I was thinking.'

There was a parking space outside the house. Luck, Isabel thought, but Ivy Trench, coming down the steps to the car, smiling her welcome, had not trusted to luck. 'I got Dr Partridge to move his car just twenty minutes ago and I've been keeping a lynx eye ever since.' She opened Fanny's door. 'How are you, dear? You don't look half as bad as I feared, I must say. But you're glad to be back, I expect.'

She helped Fanny out of the car. Fanny tottered and laughed. 'A bit weak on my pins still. Oh, Ivy, thank you for being here, such a relief, you can't imagine.'

Watching the two women embrace – Fanny, old and tall and angular; Ivy, old and short and stout – Isabel tried not to feel disgruntled because her mother had never greeted her like that, with such undisguised affection. She should be grateful that her mother had a staunch and loving friend to call on, and one whose services, since they were paid for, could be accepted without guilt. (How this squared with her left-wing feminist conscience Isabel preferred not to discuss with herself.) Ivy Trench had been living in the street, in a rented ground floor flat, when Fanny and Daniel moved into the terrace and had 'kept an eye' on their house while they were abroad; later, when she had married and moved into a council flat half a mile away, she had continued her caretaking, adding other services like baby-sitting as they were needed, and since Daniel's retirement she had come to tidy and clean three or four times a week.

Isabel hoped that her mother paid her the going rate; Fanny had been absent from England so long that she was probably unaware what that was! Perhaps it hadn't mattered, or not until now: a friendly, *ad hoc* arrangement that had suited them both while Fanny was able to look after herself and Ivy could come and go as she pleased, fitting Fanny in between the demands of an old and immobile husband, was no longer appropriate. Mr Trench had been a fireman who had injured his spine in a fall from a burning building the year before he was due to retire. Always sour natured and disputatious he had become 'impossible', so Fanny had once told Isabel. 'His life's not worth living so he makes damn sure hers isn't either.'

If he really didn't want to live, pity he couldn't die, Isabel thought suddenly, then Ivy could move in and look after Fanny! Blushing with self-reproach, she got out of the car. 'Ivy, I'm so glad you could manage to be here,' she cried. 'I know how difficult it is for you and we all do appreciate it. Of course, we shan't expect you to do more than you *can*. I just wish I lived nearer and could be more useful.'

'Oh, I won't make any trouble of it,' Ivy said. 'I know how busy you are. I've talked it over with my daughter and she says she can help me out with her Dad, sleep at the flat for a night or two. He'll lead her a cat and dog life, I told her, but she said, don't you worry about that Mum, your place is with Fanny.'

Isabel saw Fanny looking at her with an amused smile, and

thought she was comparing her daughter with Ivy's. She said, 'If only my children were a little bit older!'

Neither woman replied to this. All Fanny said was, 'If you are staying, Izzy, perhaps you had better put your car on a meter. This is a residential parking area and while I'm sure the neighbours won't complain, any warden that comes by will be sure to give you a ticket.'

'Mind you, if I catch them they get the rough side of my tongue,' Ivy said. 'Busy as bees in this sort of street, harassing the people who live here. That's an easy job, that is. Those wardens are an idle lot. When do you see them on the main road, going after parked vans? I'd sort them out if I had the chance, I can tell you!'

She drew in her breath with a satisfied hiss. Fanny's colour rose a little. She said, 'Sometimes I think the whole world must be secretly trembling for fear Ivy turns her wrathful gaze on it.'

She looked shyly at Isabel. Her mild sarcasm was meant as a discreet apology in case Isabel should feel dismissed or rejected. Understanding this, Isabel smiled at her mother. Fanny said gratefully, 'Thank you for bringing me home, dear. I'll be fine now. I'll ring you this evening.'

She didn't feel fine. She felt papery. The word came into her head, unsought for, unbidden. While Ivy settled her in the comfortable Victorian chair in the ground floor room – Daniel's study, that was her study now – she puzzled over its origin. If her mind was going to play tricks on her, she must learn how to deal with them. If she could trace the source of each random thought, hold tight to the thread that wound through the labyrinth, then she would be in control again, not at the mercy of her own mind bent on mischief.

'Papery,' she said – aloud, but speaking softly so that Ivy, on her way down to the basement kitchen, would not hear her. The word was flimsy on her dry tongue. Crumpled. Tissue paper. Smooth tissue paper between the folds of silk dresses. Flat. One-dimensional. That made sense intellectually, there was no *depth* to her at this moment, but she felt no answering leap of recognition, no tug on the line. 'Don't force it,' she murmured. 'Don't worry. It isn't important.'

'Talking to yourself?' Ivy said, coming in with the tray.

'Was I?' Fanny said vaguely. 'You've been quick.'

'I had the things ready and the kettle was boiling.'

Ivy put the tray on a stool and sat on the low chair by the long window that looked on the garden and the canal. She poured from the round teapot with the chip in the lid that had belonged to Daniel's Aunt Josie. Fanny and Daniel had cleared out Josie's flat when she died, saving the small amount of good stuff for her son in Australia, and taking the china teapot with the chipped lid for themselves because Josie had always used it when Daniel went to visit her. She had been much older than her sister, who had been Daniel's mother. 'More like a grandmother,' Daniel had said, sitting among the newspaper and packing cases on the floor of the flat in Bayswater where his widowed aunt had lived as long as he could remember. 'She always had time for me.'

As his more youthful mother had not, presumably. It was the nearest Daniel had ever come to a complaint, Fanny had realised. She had never known Daniel's parents, who had died before she met him, killed in the wartime bombing of London. Daniel had shown Fanny two posed, studio photographs, one of his mother in a chiffon dress with flowers at the waist and one of his father, smiling, in Air Force uniform. Daniel had said,

'Now you know almost as much as I do about them.' He had laughed as he spoke and Fanny, who had been very young, had assumed that his laughter was gallant camouflage for an aching heart. It wasn't until they were tidying up his aunt's flat in Bayswater that she knew better.

She said, 'That teapot belonged to Daniel's Aunt Josie. Daniel was fond of her.'

'It's still a good pourer,' Ivy said. 'I'm sorry I couldn't get the blackberry tea you're so fond of. Nearest thing was Cullen's camomile.'

'Anything,' Fanny said. 'I'm so thirsty. Josie was wonderful to Daniel. His father and mother never stayed anywhere long and in the war his father was in the Air Force, stationed all over the place. While he was growing up, this aunt was the only real home Daniel had. Josie's own son was in Australia, he was an agricultural engineer. He didn't even come home for her funeral.'

'That's the first time you've mentioned Daniel's family to me,' Ivy said. 'What set you on them, all of a sudden?'

'Seeing what I can remember,' Fanny said. 'There's so much that I can't. Nothing about what happened after I walked into the cinema. I feel such a fool.'

'You saw that film about a fish. A fish in the title, anyway. You said you were going last time I came.'

'A *Fish Called Wanda*. The girl told me, reminded me. The young woman sergeant. Detective sergeant her rank is, though it's hard to believe. She looked about thirteen.'

'Oh, they all do.'

Fanny smiled. 'I'm so glad you're here, Ivy.'

'Because I make predictable remarks?' Ivy smiled back, without malice.

47

'Because I don't have to watch my tongue. It's running away with me at the moment. I upset Isabel.'

'You've always done that. She's a loving girl, though.'

Fanny sighed. Ivy said, 'Drink your tea. Then we'll clean you up a bit and get you to bed.'

'There's only one of you, Ivy. Why say *we*?'

'Just a manner of speaking,' Ivy said. 'I suppose it's a way of making children or sick people feel they're being cared for and looked after. I thought you'd like to get a bit tidy for visitors. Harry's coming. And he arranged for Dr Partridge to look in after his surgery. He's ever so worried about you. Harry, I mean.'

'I forgot he was married,' Fanny said. 'I forgot my mother was dead. Bits of me slipping away. It frightens me, Ivy. And that young man is dying. No one knows how it happened. I may have been the only witness, it seems. And I can't remember. I'm a dotty old woman.'

'We're all getting that way,' Ivy said. 'It's the stairs always remind me. Harry wondered if we should get that old sofa bed out of the basement and put it up for you here, in the study. You'd have to make do with the ground floor cloakroom but at least you'd be on the level.'

'The only reason you don't like climbing stairs is because you have got too fat.' Fanny spoke on a spout of irritation that took her by surprise; it eased, rather than shamed her. Like opening a pressure cooker valve and letting off steam, she thought. She said, 'Sorry, Ivy. But you do puff a bit.'

'Old women go one way or the other,' Ivy said calmly. 'You're getting scrawny. Not that you weren't always thin. Though it suited you up to a point. My husband used to say, a bit more on the bust and you'd be a real beauty. Of course, that was when he was still up to it. Capable. He liked a woman to have something

48

on her he could get hold of. But fat or skinny, stairs can be the death of you when you're getting on. They can be a death trap. That's just what Harry said to me on the telephone, his exact words. The stairs in that house are a death trap. That's why he was thinking of you sleeping on the ground floor. If you are in your own bed and you need the toilet in the night you have to go down a floor.'

'Being concussed hasn't affected my bladder,' Fanny said, rather stiffly. Though it was absurd to be put out because her son had been discussing this natural function with Ivy. In fact, she had never needed to empty her bladder more than twice every twenty-four hours, once in the morning, once at night. When the children were young and they all went together on long, family walks, she had always been left sitting on a rock, or a gate, while the others disappeared into woods, behind hedges. A long time ago, of course. Harry had forgotten. He had just lumped her into a sack labelled *old women*. Old women had weak bladders. They fell down the stairs and broke brittle bones. They lost their memory. Well, she had lost her memory, hadn't she?

But she was more than put out. She felt humiliated; hurt in a pained, petulant, childish way that was in itself another cause for shame. Not because her son seemed to think she had suddenly become an incontinent invalid but because Ivy had apparently agreed with him. It was as if being knocked on the head and taken unconscious to hospital meant an automatic relegation to the ranks of the simple minded as well as the feeble bodied. She had endured it in hospital. She would not endure it from Ivy! To think that she had been relieved to find Ivy waiting! To think she had trusted her!

She looked at Ivy, at her square, pleasant, fleshy face with thick, dark brows drawn together above puzzled eyes. The eyes were tea-coloured, the brows flecked with grey, like her strong, wiry hair. Fanny thought, spitefully, that Ivy ought to pluck those eyebrows. And the bristles on her chin. She said, 'What other arrangements have you and Harry made for me behind my back? I think I'm entitled to know.'

'Come on, dear, don't take it like that,' Ivy said. 'There's no behind-your-back nonsense. Harry and I just had a long chat about the best thing to do. He and Isabel had been bothered for ages about the house being too much for you, and it just came up naturally. I wouldn't have been the first to mention it, I mean it's none of my business. But when he brought it up, well then, I said what I thought. An awkward old kitchen and five flights of stairs and none of us getting younger. I know what I'd do if I were you. What I'd have done years ago if I'd had your chances.'

'A nice little bungalow at the seaside?' Fanny was shocked to hear herself sounding contemptuous, as if this innocent ambition was something to be sneered at. Even if it had been, she should never have made a remark like that, in that tone, to anyone, let alone Ivy, who wasn't – as she had just pointed out – as lucky as she was! Ivy, who lived in a wretched flat in a run-down council block where the lifts were usually out of order and the stone stairs stank of urine; Ivy who had never once, in all the years she had known her, complained – or even remarked on till now – the capricious assignment of 'chances' that made such a difference between them. Oh, she should be ashamed!

Ivy said, 'I've never fancied a bungalow, to be honest. Nor the sea. But I wouldn't say no to a little house near my daughter in Bow. Somewhere I could go upstairs to bed and get a night's sleep without having to listen to the old devil grinding his teeth. That's all I was meaning. I daresay Izzy would be glad to have you a bit nearer her. Though, as I said to Harry, he'd have a job shifting you. You get to our age, I said, it grows harder to change, and your mother's had enough of that in her life, she wants to stay put now.'

'Thank you for sticking up for me, Ivy,' Fanny said meekly.

She didn't feel meek. She felt outraged and fearful. Half an hour later, upstairs in her own double bed, propped up on two sets of pillows (Daniel's anti-allergic Dacron, hers a mixture of goose and duck down) she realised that she was even fearful of Ivy. It was as if she had suddenly been thrust back in time into an artificial and terrifying childhood in which all adults were enemies in league with each other, talking over her head and sealing her fate without ever consulting her.

Old people, of course, were helpless as children. Though she wasn't so old. It was paranoid to imagine that she could hear them whispering among themselves. She thought – whisper, whisper, mutter, mutter, and plucked at the sheet with her fingers.

She forced herself to lie still and listen. Nothing now, except the sounds she was accustomed to hear from her bedroom: traffic rumbling steadily on the City Road several streets away, birds calling in the gardens and in the trees that lined the towpath on the other side of the canal, a dog barking, the chug of one of the narrow boats charging its engine. Familiar sounds. Calming sounds.

Daniel had not been calmed by the noise of the boats. He had claimed that the fumes from the engines brought on his asthma. There were no official moorings on the short stretch of canal at the back of the terrace, but it was an attractive place to stop, the tall, pretty houses on one side, towpath on the other, and there were usually between twelve and twenty boats more or less permanently parked there. It was the illegality of these moorings that had upset Daniel just as much as the damage to his health. He had written angry letters, to the local Council, to the British Waterways Board. Some of them had been answered but only in cautious buck-passing terms which translated into the straight message that neither the Board nor the Council were willing to take any action. Neither had the staff or the money to police the canal, neither wanted the unwelcome publicity that would surely follow any attempt to 'harass' the boaters. Rightly so, Fanny had argued. People had to live somewhere. If they couldn't afford to buy houses in London and were moved on like vagrants or gypsies when they found a cheaper alternative, there would be no one to do the low paid jobs that kept the rest of the population comfortable. Was Daniel willing to be a hospital porter? Or go round with a dust cart?

Remembering this disagreement with Daniel, Fanny found herself smiling. Her point about hospital porters and dustmen had been deliberately disingenuous. Apart from a few independent spirits who, with the assistance of the occasional social security payment, had opted out altogether and really had nowhere else to live, the inhabitants of the narrow boats were a very mixed bag. Some were students or lecturers at one of the city's polytechnics, others were weekenders with flats or houses elsewhere; not a dustman or hospital porter among them. The truth was Fanny liked the boats, and not only because the better ones were agreeable to look at. The idea that a more chaotic and exciting life than her own was going on at the bottom of her garden had always intrigued her. She didn't even mind a noisy, late party; to Daniel's astonishment she could fall asleep when shouting and laughter and music provoked the rest of the terrace into a loud slamming of windows and (after midnight) telephone calls to the police.

'Showing off,' Daniel said, in her mind. 'Parading your superiority to the infuriated bourgeoisie of Sickert Terrace. A working-class girl stuffed full of inverted snobbery!'

The telephone rang. It was out of her reach, still on Daniel's side of the bed. He had always kept the telephone by him in case there should be an upsetting message, a death or an accident in the family, or an obscene caller, as he always slept nearest to the door to protect her against an intruder. Fanny tried to shift herself in the bed but pain made her slow and Ivy had already picked up the receiver. When Fanny lifted the extension, Ivy was already talking to Harry. Fanny heard her say, '. . . not too bad, really, a bit rambly, but I couldn't keep her downstairs, well, you know how stubborn she is.'

Harry laughed. Fanny replaced the receiver as gently as she could manage. She would never listen in to a private conversation. Even when the private conversation was between a pair of conspirators.

She lay back, her heart pounding. She had been right to suspect them of plotting against her. *Whisper, whisper . . .* The soft susurration of treacherous voices seemed to surround her, seeping up through the bed springs, the mattress, the pillows.

Rambling, poor old thing, stubborn. Of course, you have to make allowances, she's had a nasty shock, but she's always liked her own way, you can't deny there's a selfish streak in her, what has she ever done for anyone? Leaned on other people all her life! Oh, she looked after Daniel, but what woman wouldn't? Look how he looked after her! What kind of life would she have had without him? Bit of luck for her, wasn't it, being sent up from the Foreign Office typing pool when Daniel needed a temporary secretary, she wouldn't have got on like her sister Delia, neither the drive nor the brains not the interest – what does she care about other people? Look how she treats Ivy Trench for example! Oh, she pays her for what she does, before Ivy got fat she used to pass on her pretty clothes to her, but would she drop everything and move in and look after Ivy if she were to fall ill?

Fanny said, fiercely, aloud, 'Shut up, you moaning, self-pitying trollop. Playing at being mad!'

She wished she could be certain it was only play. The voices were hers, of course. It was only a trick of her mind that had seemed to give them independent existence. She must cling on to that, to a sane way of thinking. People often became suspicious when they were ill. It was helplessness that brought it about. She had seen it happen to her mother when she grew deaf. She had complained that everyone muttered! She began to imagine they were talking against her. Of course it was her mother's voice she had been remembering; *mutter mutter, whisper whisper*. Although now, in her own case, it was natural they should all be concerned. That didn't mean they had suddenly turned into enemies. Not her dear, loving children. Not Ivy, her friend!

All the same, she sensed danger. There was always a point when the roles of parent and child were reversed; when the children took over. She must make it clear to them that in spite of her silly forgetfulness she had not reached that point yet. She was still in control of her own life; what she must do was to make decisions about her own future before they started to do it for her; take firm hold of the reins, stay one jump ahead. As soon as she felt a little less tired she would buckle down to it.

54

When Ivy came up half an hour later, Fanny was sleeping peacefully.

Harry said, 'Do you think it's really what she wants to do? I mean, *really*? It seems so sudden. She's had this tremendous upset and she's not over it yet. After all, she still can't remember. Ivy says that bloody policewoman was round again yesterday.'

'Why bloody? She's a nice girl.' Isabel frowned at her brother reproachfully. 'You're always saying that the police ought to do more to catch criminals. Look at the fuss you made when your car got nicked! There's this poor devil lying in hospital. All this policewoman does is pop in occasionally. She doesn't bully Mummy, or anything,'

'I don't think Fanny minds too much, Harry,' Poppy said. 'Honestly, love. Maybe she felt a bit of an idiot in the beginning, but now she knows it's quite usual not to remember what happened just before or just after an accident. It's – oh, what do they call it? – post traumatic stress disorder, or something. It could be hysterical amnesia, that's what Delia likes to think anyway, she said to me that Fanny had been so shocked that her mind had suppressed what had happened. But I don't think so, Fanny isn't so shockable! And, actually, I think she's finding it all a bit of a challenge. Gives her something to think about. Looking for the lost key . . .'

'Maybe it's just as well if she doesn't find it,' Max said. 'Think for a minute. Suppose she was able to tell the police something that led to an arrest? Or they trace the other car and pick up the owner, perhaps that's more likely, and Fanny recognises him? If she saw it all happen, saw them beating up Andrew Hobbes as she was walking home from the Roma. Mrs Hobbes didn't see her before she ran off, so Fanny wasn't involved to begin with.

But suppose she did have a chance to see what the men looked like, enough to identify at least one of them . . .'

'So?' Harry said, smiling.

Max was a passionate reader of old-fashioned detective stories. Commuting from Surrey to his office in Clerkenwell where he ran an inter-city courier service, he read at least one a day. This innocent obsession amused Harry. Max, who was aware of Harry's amusement and saw it as condescension, pushed his heavy glasses up on his nose with a hairy forefinger and said, 'So, if it came to her being a prosecution witness, she would have one hell of a time in court. The defence would tear her to pieces. But we understood that you could not, at first, recall these events at all, Mrs Pye! You had lost all memory of them, had you not? And then, to the jury, it is a little dangerous, is it not, to convict on the evidence of a witness who was unconscious in hospital for so many hours after this accident and who, even when she recovered, could not remember. And so on.'

Max flushed slightly. He had been rehearsing this trial in his mind, appearing, as he usually did, first for the prosecution, then for the defence. At school he had wanted to study law but his father's drinking habits had led to frequent periods of unemployment and there were two younger brothers to provide for as well as his mother. Max had left school and ridden a motor bike for one of the delivery services that were starting up at that time, taken an evening class in accountancy, and put aside his ambition. He had told no one about it, not even Isabel, whom he loved, but he was sometimes afraid that Harry had guessed it.

He was unnecessarily sensitive. Although Harry saw the flush he had no idea what had caused it. All the same, he felt vaguely guilty as he often did in Max's company. As if Max were silently accusing him of feeling superior. He said, 'You've made my point for me, Max. A jury wouldn't like to convict on the basis of evidence given by someone in Fanny's mental condition. So is it sensible for us to treat her as if she were in a fit state to make important decisions about her own future?'

This was a family conclave, summoned by Harry but taking place at Max and Isabel's large, battered house in Surrey suburbia. It had once been a vicarage, then an expensive, private kindergarten; after that enterprise failed it had stood, empty and decaying with woodworm and damp, until Max and Isabel bought and repaired and converted it, installing Max's mother in the biggest room on the first floor and making over the loft (screening the hot water tank and putting in dormer windows) for Max's brothers who were now at northern universities in the term time.

They had had an early family supper. Max's mother and George, the younger boy, had gone to their rooms; George to sleep, Max's mother, who had a bad back, to watch television from the comfort of her bed. The two older children, Adam and Jennifer were playing croquet on the sparse grass of the long lawn. Beyond the light of the house it was almost too dark to play; bats darted above them, between the tall trees either side.

Max was smoking his pipe to deter the midges. Harry, who had his father's allergic disposition, sneezed from time to time, and shifted his bottom uneasily. Max and Isabel's garden furniture was a mixed bag, bought from boot sales and rummage sales and scavenged from skips. Sitting in their garden was always a lottery, and this evening Harry had drawn the short straw: an old wicker chair with wounding spikes in the seat.

Isabel said, 'I thought we'd all agreed ages ago that it was daft for Mummy to stay on in that awkward house after Daddy died. Now she's decided to agree with us. So what's wrong?'

Poppy laughed. Isabel winked at her. Conniving against him, Harry thought. He said, 'You know perfectly well.'

He wished he still smoked. He could have taken out a pack, fiddled for his lighter, found it was out of fuel, asked Max for his matches. Allowing time for someone else to break in, come to his rescue.

He said, 'It just seems precipitate. She hasn't thought where she wants to go, what kind of house or flat. Nor how much money she'll need. It makes a difference if she wants to stay in London or not.'

Poppy said, 'She'll have enough money, surely. Unless she wants to buy some ridiculous luxury apartment with a jacuzzi. Or a stately home in the country. Neither would be Fanny's style.'

'She won't know what she wants till she's looked. I would hate to see her land up somewhere unsuitable, some awful place with tiny rooms that wouldn't take her furniture, for example, just because she hadn't left herself enough leeway. And we don't know what kind of lasting damage has been done to her health by this episode. That's the main thing that worries me. It may turn out that she needs some kind of long-term nursing care.' Harry shook his head, miming a ponderous sadness. 'Even if she recovers completely from this awful trauma there's no reason to suppose she'll stay fit for the rest of her life. And the house is her only capital. Her pension would never pay the full fees of a really good nursing home and although we could chip in, it would be a strain she would hate to think she was imposing on us.'

'If she was senile she wouldn't know,' Poppy said.

'Oh Poppy, how can you?' Isabel said, flinching.

Harry said at last, reluctantly, 'No one knows what might happen next year or the year after. And a hundred thousand pounds or whatever might make all the difference.'

'It would make all the difference to Ivy now, wouldn't it,' Poppy said. 'If she had a house of her own with enough room to get away from her husband occasionally.'

Harry sighed patiently. 'I know that, of course. And of course, in principle, I think it's marvellous that Fanny has thought of it. Socially and morally her instincts are impeccable.' He laughed in what he hoped was an easy way but it seemed to grate on Poppy who looked at him coldly. He cleared his throat. 'Seriously, though. I think we've established that she isn't thinking quite as clearly as she usually does at the moment. We don't want to let her rush into something she might regret later. And we must remember, if she does sell the house, it will be the first major decision she's made in her life, on her own, without Father.'

'You make her sound horribly feeble,' Isabel said. 'A kind of wilting, witless lily. I think she and Daddy made decisions together. What you really mean is, if Mummy has money she doesn't want, you'd rather she didn't waste it on Ivy.'

'That's unfair, Izzy,' Max said.

'True, though. Isn't it, Poppy?'

Poppy looked at Harry's reddened face and said, 'A thing can be true and unfair. I happen to think it would be a fine thing for Fanny to buy something for Ivy. And she hasn't been vague about it. She's looked through the local papers and telephoned agents. She says you ought to be able to buy a decent small house in Bow, which is where Ivy wants to be, for around a hundred thousand. But it's unfair to suggest Harry wants the money for himself quite in that crude way.'

'I didn't mean he wanted it for himself,' Isabel said – flushing up, Poppy noticed, in the same angry fashion as her brother, mottled patches on cheek and throat marking the resemblance between them. 'What he thinks, though, is that it's family money locked up in the house, all Daddy left, in a way, and so it's not up to Mummy to decide on her own what should be done with it. Or not altogether. I don't agree with him as it happens, after all we have houses of our own to live in and Ivy hasn't, but I know what he means, all the same. It's a sentimental indulgence to hand out a large sum of money to strangers – not Ivy, I don't mean Ivy's a stranger, but if Ivy dies, it will all go to her horrible husband, or to her daughter, and I can't think Mummy could really want that. Nor do I think Daddy would have agreed to hand over a chunk of his life's savings – which is what it is really – if it meant cutting out his own grandchildren in favour of Ivy's.'

She looked reproachfully at Poppy, moisture glistening in her grey eyes. Max said, 'You'll have to make up your mind, Izzy darling. Ivy, or Jennifer and Adam and George.' He smiled at her with love. He loved her most of the time but he loved her especially when she got into this kind of intellectual muddle. Her father had thought she was stupid and Fanny wasn't much more perceptive. *His* sweet Isabel turned to him now, eyes still bright, but with laughter suddenly.

She said, 'I can't, can I? Here and now, of course Ivy. But in ten years, who could tell? Suppose George wanted to go to medical school, something like that, and we couldn't afford it? Suppose you had some crippling disease. Or Jennifer had a drunken husband and five children. I can't think of a suitable disaster for Adam just at the moment.'

'I think we all get the point,' Max said. 'I don't think, in fact, you can take the future into consideration in this sort of thing. If Fanny wants to help her friend then she ought to do so whatever happens afterwards.' He saw Harry's expression and amended hastily, 'Of course it's none of my business, not my family's money.'

'Don't be absurd, Max,' Harry said. He had been thinking with some resentment that it would have been tactful of both Poppy and Max to have been a little less free with their advice but as soon as Max put this thought into words he was ashamed of it. He said, 'Has anyone spoken to Delia? One would be interested to know what she thought. If she knows, that is. If Fanny has spoken to her.'

'Delia will egg her on, I'd have thought,' Poppy said.

Harry thought – easy enough for Aunt Delia to be generous when she had nothing to lose. But it seemed coarse to even think that, let alone say it. At this moment a sudden puff of wind made him sneeze violently; the sneeze made him jerk in his unsatisfactory chair and a sharp piece of loose basketwork jabbed him wickedly. 'Oh God,' he moaned. 'If any money comes to you, Izzy, from any source whatsoever, buy some decent garden chairs, will you?'

In spite of the sneezing and the pain in his right buttock he was glad of the diversion. He had suggested the four of them met in all innocence. Fanny's declaration of intent had simply seemed something that they should talk about. He realised now that he had been hoping their discussion would solve everything, that in some miraculous way what he saw as a problem would suddenly cease to exist. Instead he was more uncertain now than he had been before. He knew Poppy was angry with him. He was shocked that he and Izzy who had known Ivy all their lives were so much less concerned about her comfort and happiness than Poppy and Max. And he was irritated with Fanny.

He said, 'I suppose Izzy has put her finger on it. What our mother is planning to dispose of so lightly is really family money. When our father bought the house he put it in her name but it was the little bit that he inherited from his mother and father that paid for it.'

This bald, pernickety statement offended him. It sounded venal and mean whereas what he was feeling was a whole complex of warmer and richer emotions connected with his father, his children. He said, 'My father was very careful with money. I don't mean he was stingy. But he was obsessional about paying bills on time, that sort of thing. And at the same time he was always anxious that we, that Izzy and I, and Fanny, of course, should feel as secure and be as secure as he could make us. I don't know how he would feel about what Mother means to do and I wonder if she has even thought about that side of it.'

Poppy said, 'Once, when I was canvassing for the Labour Party, I met a woman whose husband had just died. She said she had always voted Labour but she wouldn't this time because her husband had been Conservative. So she thought she should vote Conservative herself now, out of respect for his memory. It's what he would have wanted, she said.'

Max smiled. Isabel was looking tearful again. Harry said, 'I doubt whether my mother has quite that degree of familial piety.'

Fanny was in her tiny garden, in a reclining canvas chair that filled up most of the minute patch of grass. Harry sat on the ground beside her. Fanny was sipping a glass of sherry that

Harry had brought her; Harry, who had felt that he needed a stronger drink, held a whisky in his hand.

Fanny was saying, 'I thought it would be a wrench to begin with. So much of our lives spent in houses that didn't belong to us. This was the only house that was home. But since I realised about Ivy, what it could mean to her, that's all changed. What is a house, after all? Four walls and a roof. And a fortune, it seems. So ridiculous.'

She was looking better, Harry was pleased to see. The bruises were fainter, little more than a purplish blush here and there. And even if her memory was still uncertain, she seemed to have learned to cover up when she couldn't remember.

He said, 'There'll be a lot of clearing up to do, won't there? So you shouldn't rush into it, darling.'

'Rebecca will help me. She's willing to do anything one asks. In fact, I'm surprised Delia passed her on to me, I'd have thought she'd have found her too useful.'

'Maybe she actually wanted to help you,' Harry said. Mostly he enjoyed his mother's tart remarks about Delia but sometimes he found them undignified.

Fanny smiled. 'Well. I can only say that I'm grateful. Rebecca doesn't talk much, though more than she did to begin with, but she listens, and she runs up and down the stairs to save Ivy's legs.'

Harry said abruptly – at least it seemed abrupt to him – 'Does Ivy know?'

'About my selling the house? Yes, of course. Not about what I'm going to do with the money.'

'Ah,' Harry said.

'What d'you mean? Ah.'

'Oh. Nothing. Not much, anyway.' Harry stood up and

63

stretched his back, rubbing his thighs. 'Sorry,' he said. 'Not very comfortable. Too old to squat on the grass.'

'I don't want her to know till it's done,' Fanny said. 'Not just because things can go wrong but because she'd think up good reasons to stop me if she had too much notice. Probably say I was out of my mind. You think I am, don't you?'

'Of course not,' Harry said heartily.

Fanny looked up at him. He was so much like Daniel – the thick hair, and the heavy chin, and the full, pouting mouth – and not just to look at. There was the same unwillingness to admit to what he was really thinking or feeling, especially if it seemed in any way inconvenient or embarrassing. Daniel had always found it easier if he was on the move; best of all if they were out walking together. She said, 'Help me up, Harry. I've been in the same place too long, I need exercise.'

They walked along the towpath at the other side of the canal. A British Waterways working barge came through the tunnel at one end of the cut and set the moored narrow boats rocking.

'Father never managed to get rid of them, did he?' Harry said.

Fanny had stopped beside one of the boats. In the double bunk below the dirty but uncurtained window two people were very pleasantly occupied. Fanny seemed disposed to linger; when Harry took her arm to move her on, she gave a small sigh. 'If only I were younger,' she said.

Harry laughed, and coughed.

'I meant living on the canal,' she said quickly. 'I suppose now I would worry about the damp. Or someone would worry for me. It's all right, Harry, I won't do anything totally foolish.'

'Have you any ideas?'

'A nice little cottage in the country with a thatched roof. That's what old ladies like me are expected to want, isn't it?'

She sounded suddenly snappish. Harry determined to be calm and cheerful. He said, 'I'd think you'd probably enjoy living near enough to London to come up for the day and go to the cinema.'

Somewhere in Surrey, not too far from Isabel and Max; a small, well-arranged house on two floors with a small garden, perhaps near a common. Fanny had always liked walking, hadn't she? He saw her striding across the heather. She might enjoy a dog as a companion. He said, 'You've never had a dog, have you, Mother?'

She didn't answer. Well, there was no need to answer. Harry knew there had never been a dog. He had begged for one when he was twelve or so but of course it was impossible for a diplomat's family, always on the move. Unfair to the animal, all those months in quarantine kennels whenever they came back to England. The expense of the kennels had to be considered too, as Daniel had explained to Harry, taking him for a long evening march as he usually did when he intended a serious man-to-man conversation. They had gone for miles along the Appian Way, Harry remembered; Daniel had just been posted to Rome and Harry had flown out for the Christmas holidays. It was cold on the Appian Way and he had been sulky. If he had been going to get the dog in the end, it would have been worth this boring trudge in the darkening and icy air; as he quite clearly wasn't, he would rather have stayed at home with Isabel and watched the marvellous advertisements on Italian television. 'It's not that we can't afford it,' his father had said. 'Just that we want to spend the money on other things.' Harry couldn't remember now if he had asked what those other things were and been told. He was sure that it would have been made painstakingly clear that the expenses that took priority over a dog's quarantine bills were either absolutely necessary like food and shoes, or of a very worthy nature like language lessons in the holidays so that he should get full advantage from the fact that his father's job gave his children the privilege of being at home in so many different countries.

He wondered if he should ask his mother if she had known how much he would have preferred a dog to Italian lessons four mornings a week but decided that she had probably forgotten. Or would pretend to have forgotten. It seemed to him that since her 'accident' – as he preferred to think of it – she had begun to withdraw into old ladyhood; treating her age as a kind of useful disguise to be assumed when she didn't want to be bothered.

She said, pausing with her hands on the white railing between the towpath and the canal, looking down into the oil-streaked water between two of the boats where an accumulation of plastic rubbish bobbed up and down gently, 'You don't resent my doing this for Ivy, do you? I can see that some children might. But I thought, since neither of you is exactly homeless, or poor . . .'

She turned to look at him with embarrassed apology. He heard himself saying, 'Do you have to ask, darling?'

She put her hand on his arm. 'I'm sorry,' she said. 'I just felt that I should. In case there should be something you'd all hidden from me, some crisis, some terrible debt.'

'No, no of course not.' He put his arm across her shoulders and patted consolingly. 'Of course I can't speak for Izzy, or not absolutely. That is, there's nothing she's told me, but one can't help realising that those two have a few financial problems. Max's mother, his brothers . . .'

'They are Max's business, dear. Ivy is mine. All my grown-up life she has made a lot of things possible for me. Looked after the house, taken care of you children when Daniel and I were in London, picked you up at stations, taken you to airports to fly to us for the holidays. We lived on her back, Harry. All those years. It isn't a sentimental impulse on my part. It's something I owe her.'

He nodded gravely. He said, 'I understand, darling.' It was hopeless to try and explain to her that it wasn't so simple. Or he was too cowardly. Weak. He couldn't bear to look mean in her eyes so he had said none of the sensible things he had come to say. On the other hand, since she had decided to keep her intention a secret from Ivy, there was some breathing space; some comfort to take back to his sister. It might not be totally false to hint that his presence had had something to do with persuading this concession from her. After all, it might seem a reasonable compromise: it would have been foolish, probably counter-productive, to have appeared absolutely disapproving of what could be assessed, on the whole, as a very proper decision. His mother had always seemed gentle to him, willing to listen to other people, not like her sister, blaring her foghorn opinions. But gentle people could be quite resolute, and old women, particularly, were sometimes contrary.

Fanny said, 'I haven't discussed this with Delia. So please don't mention it, Harry.' She wrinkled her nose in a smirk that made her look like a wicked child suddenly. But she looked weary, too. The smudges under her eyes had turned darker.

'All right,' Harry said. 'I'll warn Izzy. I think we'll turn back now. Far enough for today.'

She leaned on him heavily. He reproached himself for not noticing sooner that she was tiring. He said, 'Take it easy, no hurry.' And then, to divert her, 'It seems our young lovers have finished.'

They were sitting in the open stern of the narrow boat, each holding an open can of Coke; a plump girl in tight jeans with frizzed hair and a round, sweet face, smooth as a baby's. The boy was thinner, more lined around the eyes, but seemed scarcely older. Seventeen, Fanny judged, but recognised that she could be wrong by a number of years. People stayed young for much longer nowadays. It was partly the jeans, the uniform that stamped them in her eyes as children. But there was something more, too. 'Freedom,' she said. 'They are freer than we were.'

'Oh, I don't know,' Harry objected, piqued that his mother appeared to be lumping him with herself, locking them both into the same grey prison of an extended middle age. Did she really think that his generation had been as frustrated as hers must have been? He wasn't so much older than that man in the boat! Well, no more than ten years or so. Twelve, maybe. He said, with a laugh, 'Honestly Mother, when I was growing up they had actually invented the Pill.'

She shook her head. It was not what she had meant. But she was feeling so exhausted now; no breath left to explain. Sex came into it but only as part of a much larger whole. She made an effort. She said hoarsely, 'When I was young, I seemed to waste so much time trying to be what other people wanted. It seems different now.'

Harry said, 'Do you know that young man and the girl?'

They had reached the wooden steps that led from the tow-path up to the street. Fanny paused, clutching Harry with one hand, the wooden rail with the other. 'I'm not sure. I mean I know most of the boat people to look at and a couple to speak to. I didn't recognise those two for certain but of course the boats come and go.'

'They seemed to know you. Or he did. He gave you a bit of an odd look.'

More than just odd. Piercing, that was the word. Piercing and hostile. And yet, as he had looked up to begin with, when he had first noticed Fanny, there had been another element, too.

'A bit wary, I thought,' Harry said.

'They all knew it was Daniel behind the complaints to the Waterways Board and the Council. So they might know who I was. Maybe they thought I was out on the war path. Trying to catch them chucking their rubbish into the water.'

'Or prying into their private life?' Harry grinned at her affectionately as he helped her up the last steps. 'Come on now, my lovely, almost home.'

The relief in her face at that moment, and then again, a bit later, when they were indoors and she had collapsed into a chair, stirred his conscience uneasily. He said, 'If this really is the only house that was home to you, perhaps you ought to think a bit harder before you leave it. Honestly, darling. There are all sorts of things we could do to make it more comfortable for you. We could get someone else in to help Ivy. Someone younger. And if you've really found Becky useful, perhaps, when she goes, you could bear to put up with a housekeeper. Or some such arrangement.'

There must be plenty of women, younger than Fanny, better able to nip up and down those steep stairs. A widow in her forties, perhaps. Someone who would be glad of a home in London with a lively-minded if ageing lady. Even a dependent child would not be out of the question – as long as it was at boarding school in the term time it might indeed be an additional interest for his mother. He had a pleasant momentary vision of dropping in after work, on his way home, and sitting in front of a log fire watching her play chess with an eleven-year-old boy while a pretty woman of around his own age poured drinks for them all.

He said, 'Do you ever light a fire? Not here in the study, but upstairs in the drawing room. In that charming early Victorian grate.'

'We are in a clean air area,' Fanny said. 'And lugging up coal or wood a couple of flights from the basement is hardly a suitable job for the ailing valetudinarian you seem to think I shall shortly become.'

'No,' he said. 'No, I suppose not. Sorry, Mother.' He bent to kiss her and said, 'You don't play chess either, do you?'

She smiled, not making the connection for once, but assuming that there was one and it would come to her later. It struck her that she never had these non-sequential conversations with Isabel. An almost painfully strong feeling of gratitude and love towards her son rose within her. She said – a little stiffly, trying to control the constriction that emotion produced in her throat – 'I know you want what's best for me, darling. But I would rather leave this house under my own steam, in my own time. I don't want a housekeeper. When your father retired we thought that one of the nicest things about living here was being private, getting up when we liked in the morning, being able to boil an egg in our own kitchen. We'd had enough of servants in our working life. I know Isabel would say that is a frightfully privileged remark, and I am such a coward, I don't suppose I would make it in front of her.'

'You don't mind Becky?'

'Rebecca is the nearest anyone could get to being invisible. Though she has been a little more evident lately. I think she isn't as cowed by me as she is by her mother. But this job is a nightmare for her. Dogsbody in the publicity department of a smart publisher, can you imagine it, Harry? How Delia and Buffy could have thought it suitable for her defeats me. Not the work, she's not incompetent, it's the other girls. They terrify her. She goes off every morning looking like a frightened *rabbit*. And so thin! Those tiny legs, it seems a miracle of engineering that she can actually stand on them.'

Harry was not interested in his cousin. But he was glad to see his mother grow animated in her defence. 'Well, then,' he said, grinning. 'Two birds with one stone.'

'No,' Fanny said. 'At the moment I need her, maybe she needs me just a little. For a while, anyway. But she should become independent. And I have learned to be solitary.'

Harry looked at her. Not much wrong now, he thought. Not up top. Unless the slight physical weakness she was showing was functional. He said, 'Is that policewoman still bothering you?'

'She isn't bothering me, dear. But no, nothing's come back. Not even a flick or a whisper.'

Shapes and sounds. A soft voice behind her, a dimly seen cloud, or balloon, on the edge of her vision. Signs that something was there, just out of her reach; if she held still it might slowly develop like a photographic negative in an acid tank. Other memories had returned in this way, though some remained ill-defined, flimsy. So how could she be sure, how could she trust them?

'I should think it's too late now,' she said, faintly ashamed to realise that this thought relieved her. She gathered it up, and, filing it away with other, related thoughts, she summed them up to settle them all. 'Old women shouldn't live alone in London,' she said.

*

What a disingenuous old thing she is. Who does she think she is fooling? Oh, yes, her poor son! She knew what he wanted to say and she knew he was too nice-mannered to say it. Not a matter of manners, exactly, but that will do for an overall term embracing the civilised values; a decent delicacy, a wish to be magnanimous, or at least to appear so which probably comes to the same thing in the end. In practical if not spiritual terms anyway. Oh, poor Harry – chained as firmly as anyone ever was to what is expected, to what looks right, to what other people would like him to be. What a frightful hypocrisy, going on to him about freedom!

'That's not fair,' Fanny said aloud. She indulged the malicious voices that sometimes plagued her, but only up to a point. It was useful to know what they might be saying about her so that she could be prepared, arm herself against them. And she had not meant that Harry was 'free', in the way of the girl and boy on the boat. Or as his own children were free. Not free from family pressures, but from hang-ups about sex and money. That was the Welfare State, Daniel would have said, not altogether approvingly – although he had always voted against any Government that appeared to want to dismantle it, he had deplored some of its manifestations. Those 'idle layabouts', the boat people, among them . . .

Fanny was standing at the bathroom window looking down at the canal. It was soft, late summer twilight. Lights were coming on in the houses, framing a variety of lit stages within which people moved unselfconsciously; the dark not yet intrusive enough to make them draw curtains. Some of the canal boats were lit too, their yellow lights reflected in the slowly wrinkling water. There was no light in Fanny's bathroom. She stood slightly to one side of the window, a position in which she was fairly sure she could not be observed from the towpath. Although there was no one there at the moment.

The telephone rang on the floor above, in her bedroom. She pulled down the bathroom blind, felt her way to the door, and switched on the light. She climbed the stairs, muttering, 'All right, I'm coming,' hurrying to get there before Rebecca, who hated the telephone, should feel it her duty to answer it.

Poppy said, 'Are you all right?'

There was a controlled urgency in her voice that warned Fanny that there was likely to be more to this question than the maddening over-solicitude the children had been showing her lately. She said, quickly, 'Is anything wrong?'

Poppy said, 'Oh, Fanny, don't worry. It's just that we wondered . . .'

It was so unusual for Poppy to hesitate that Fanny had a sudden attack of acute maternal anxiety. 'Is Harry not home yet?'

'No. But he's all right, Fanny. It's just that he went to the hospital. Andrew Hobbes died. We were afraid the police might come round and upset you. Harry rang me a couple of minutes ago. He thought it would be better if you heard it from us. He's on his way home now. But we can drive over to you as soon as he gets home, if you like.'

'Thank you, dear. There's no need.'

'Are you sure?'

'Absolutely.'

Poppy said, 'I suppose it isn't so much of a shock. I mean, in a practical way he was dead already. They simply decided to switch off the life-support systems.'

Fanny wondered if his wife had been with him. What a strange moment. Would they have consulted her? Or his parents? She had watched Daniel die. In such terrible pain she would have given her own life to stop it. But if someone had asked her, had said, 'Shall we make an end now?', what would she have answered?

She said, 'That poor girl. Such a long time.'

Poppy said, 'Harry says it's his mother who hasn't been able to come to terms with it. Wailing and carrying on. That's why Harry's not home yet. The father was worried about driving home with his wife raving, and although the girl was all right, she wasn't much help. Harry managed to persuade someone to let them leave the car at the hospital and found them a taxi.'

'That was kind of Harry,' Fanny said.

'Well, he is kind.'

Poppy gave a short laugh. It sounded almost angry. Fanny thought – does she think I don't appreciate Harry?

She said, 'I'll let you know if the police come round. I suppose they will, although I wouldn't expect them to call until tomorrow. I think they've given me up for a dotty old woman.'

'They'll be looking for a murderer now,' Poppy said. 'It might make them more persistent. That was why Harry was particularly anxious about you.'

There was still a suggestion of reproof in her voice. Fanny said, 'I know dear, I'm sorry to be such a nuisance. But it wouldn't be a murder charge, surely? From what I understood to have happened, it could only be manslaughter.'

'That's bad enough,' Poppy said sharply.

'I thought it might worry Harry less. A kind of accident, not deliberate. Tell him I'm not worried anyway, there's a good girl. Tell him he's got quite enough to do without fussing over his mother!'

She used the word 'fussing' deliberately, almost adding, 'Harry was always a boy to make a rod for his back,' only refraining because she was sorry that Poppy should feel she had to defend Harry to her. And putting the telephone down she felt a little sorry for herself, too. She had always found Poppy so easy to get along with. Perhaps they were all worn out with the trouble she'd caused them. She must try not to burden them any more than she had to in future. There was no reason to after all. There was only one small thing that concerned her that she would have liked to mention to Harry – or to Poppy, to pass on to him – but the way Poppy obviously felt at the moment, she had better keep quiet about it. She ought to mention it to Rebecca but she shrank from the necessary explanation. It would be awkward to explain what she assumed might be one cause of this unpleasant phenomenon. If it went on she would have to do something but when she last looked there had been no sign of him. Perhaps she was overwrought. Imagining things.

She switched off the bedroom light and went down the stairs to the bathroom. She turned off the landing light before she opened the bathroom door so that she would not be visible from outside, crossed to the window and drew up the blind.

The moon was almost full and very clear, throwing its flat silver light over the water, and the boats, and the trees beyond the towpath and the houses beyond the trees, turning shadows blacker and the boy's uplifted face paler, a bleached coin gleaming out of the darkness. He was standing perfectly still in the stern of his boat, hands thrust in his pockets, shoulders hunched forward. His stance was patient and uncomfortably permanent. There was no doubt about it. As he had been doing off and on, all the evening, he was watching the house.

2

The fire started in the Partridges' house. Sickert Terrace was handsome but flimsy. Although they used the pattern book, speculative small builders in the mid-nineteenth century tended to cut a few corners. If a front door slammed at one end of the terrace, windows rattled along the whole row. And the gap at the top of the Partridges' fourth floor window frame was large enough for a small bird to enter and nest in.

Archie Olds, painter and handyman, sang from his favourite opera as he blasted away with his blow lamp. *Now my philandering days are over.* He did not notice the gap, or the now empty nest, and there was no wind to alert him to danger. In the Partridges' garden, smoke from a bonfire rose in a vertical column, and although their Tree of Heaven was already bare, other trees in the gardens of the tall houses and on the towpath on the other side of the canal remained dressed over all, not a yellow leaf stirring.

Archie was pleased with his day's work. Now the old paint was burned off he could start priming and undercoating tomorrow. The wood of one window frame was rough at the bottom; a perfectionist might decide to replace it but Archie tried to keep his bills down and a bit of filler would serve almost as well if he remembered to bring it tomorrow. He laid the heavy ladder on its side behind the parapet of the first floor balcony, safely out of sight of the towpath, so that no casual burglar should seize the opportunity. This part of London was considered a high risk area by insurance companies and Archie was very conscious of his clients' security. He was always careful to leave windows fastened and locked; he approved of burglar alarms and chains on front doors.

Climbing into the drawing room, he bolted the sash window behind him and removed his shoes before padding across the carpet and down the creaky stair. Reaching the ground floor, he poked his head round the half-open door of Dora Partridge's study. 'I'm off now,' he said. 'Hope the weather holds for us.' Communing with her word processor, Dora nodded absently. 'All right today but it's getting a bit late for an outside job,' Archie said.

He waited patiently, and she looked up, fingers still poised over the keyboard. Her eyes focused on Archie. She dropped her hands and swivelled her chair round to face him. She said, 'Sorry, Archie.'

'That's all right,' he said kindly. 'I'm the same when I'm working. All I said was, you get to this time of the year, there's always a chance of wind or rain settling in.'

Dora gave him the appropriate answer. 'Keep our fingers crossed. We've been lucky so far.'

'Right,' Archie said. He found Dora hard going socially. He smiled his open, engaging smile that in other houses brought him more appreciation and flattery. 'You get on, then,' he said. 'Nothing to worry about upstairs. I've locked up, left everything shipshape.'

'Thank you, Archie,' she murmured. After the front door

banged behind him, she waited a minute, hands loose in her lap, in case he should have forgotten something, or decide to pop back for a last, friendly chat. When it seemed safe she pushed her glasses up on the bridge of her nose with her forefinger and returned to the chapter on literacy among working people in the 1890s, the penultimate chapter of her book, *After Mayhew*, that she was hoping to finish by the end of November.

She heard the wind half an hour later but it only distracted her briefly. A soft rustling and pattering made her glance sideways to see the narrow leaves streaming from the ornamental cherry that shaded her window in the spring and the summer. They had hung for so long on the tree that next year's fat buds were already appearing. How pretty, she thought, watching this shower of gold, and went back to work smiling.

The house martins had come back to the terrace several years running, building nest upon nest, each new one pushing the old straw and grass and mud pellets deeper into the gap between the wooden frame and the bricks and the mortar, trapping dust and other dry rubbish, flakes of paint, blown scraps of paper, all packed so tight by now that if the air had stayed still, the fire would have smouldered a while and then slowly died, starved of oxygen. As it was, the wind played with it gently to start with, teasing it, coaxing it with small, flirty puffs, sudden rushes. Tiny flames flickered and spurted yellow spears before blackening and petering out; then, as the wind strengthened and thumped in the chimney a spark flowered at the tip of a dead, brittle stalk and flew to a pitch pine joist that rested on the inner wall and jutted into the cavity between the Partridge house and its neighbour.

The muck trapped in the cavity wall was desiccated stuff, builder's rubble, not much to feed on. The little fire trickled backwards and forwards along the joist as if searching for something. There was enough air to keep it alive in the cavity while it waited for the next gust of wind to carry it across to the opposing joist of the next house. Meanwhile it lay quiet, a somnolent fire, more smoke than flame.

In the Partridge house, the smoke detector halfway up the stairwell started whistling. Tom Partridge's mother, who had just come in from the garden and was changing her clothes in the guest bedroom on the top floor, thought it was the door bell and called down to her daughter-in-law from the landing. 'Oh, that bloody thing!' Dora Partridge said, emerging from her own bedroom on the floor below, wearing a shower cap and bathrobe and carrying a stool with her. 'Always going off at the wrong moment. As if it knows when you're busy! I expect it just needs a new battery.'

Alice Partridge, peering over the landing rail, said she was sure she smelled smoke herself. Oh you would, Dora thought, sniffing crossly. Just because Tom and I are going out for the evening and leaving you alone with the kids.

Dora Partridge had been a social worker before her marriage, and although she was now more absorbed in her literary ambitions, she still reckoned she knew about motivation. All the same, she had to admit that there was more in the air at this moment than an old woman's jealousy. She gave the loud cheerful laugh with which she had always concealed irritation with her elderly clients. 'I know what it is, Mother darling! That wretched bonfire! You've been burning leaves, haven't you? Marvellous of you, it's a job needed doing, but if there's the least bit of wind we get it all over the house. I expect that's what set the thing off!'

And she hopped on the stool and disarmed it.

*

Next door, Fanny was on her knees, surrounded by packing cases, box files, cardboard boxes, sorting out Daniel's papers. Who would have thought anyone could leave so much clobber behind him? Oh, it was all in meticulous order: all bills paid before the due date and suitably stapled together, each major category separated by a bulldog clip. What astonished Fanny was the quantity: every bill back to 1978, a solid ten years of receipts, kept, she had begun to feel, against some mythical auditor who might suddenly appear in a thunder clap, threatening debt collectors, court proceedings, humiliation. For a law-abiding man, Daniel had been absurdly afraid of the law. Though perhaps there was no incongruity there. She should have asked him, Fanny thought. She said aloud, 'Too late now.'

Rebecca, also on her knees, looked at her questioningly.

'Nothing,' Fanny said. 'Talking to myself. First sign of madness. This lot's for the black sack. Old bills. Things not worth keeping. No, not that purple file, dear. I think those are the insurances. I ought to go through them. They can't all be necessary.'

Daniel had been a compulsive insurer with an eye for a bargain. He could never resist an economical offer even if the cover was for an unlikely contingency. Although the Pyes had never owned a domestic animal he had always ticked the box on the household insurance form that paid compensation to guests who might be bitten by a visiting dog on his premises. And, for the children's sake, since accidental death in late middle age was comparatively cheap, he had insured his own life and Fanny's several times over, with the RAC, the AA, and with all his credit card companies. Remembering him *gloating* over these policies, totting up the thousands of pounds the children would get should both of them be killed in a car crash,

Fanny smiled to herself, very tenderly. Daniel's fear that his family could be left homeless or hungry was painfully real, not in the least comic.

The purple insurance file went in the bottom drawer of the bureau. Old bills in the black plastic sack. Also yellowing batches of newsprint filed in brown envelopes marked *Crosswords*; *Useful News Items*; *Theatre Reviews of Plays Seen*; *Obituaries of Friends and Acquaintances*. Fanny disposed of these memorabilia without a pang; Daniel's passion to collect and categorise had seemed footling when he was alive, and now simply bored her.

Letters were another matter. Most of these were put aside to be dealt with later – next week, next month, next year. When she felt stronger. She had already burned a bundle of her own letters, written to Daniel before they were married, when he was Second Secretary (Information) in Moscow and she was still working in London. On a slip of paper tucked inside the elastic band that held them together he had written, in his decisive and upright handwriting, *Typical Fanny!* Criticism? Or loving amusement? Fanny had no wish to speculate, still less to read what she had said and confront her nineteen-year-old self. It struck her that to attach such an ambiguous comment to a young girl's letters was 'Typical Daniel', and although she had not examined this thought or tried to explain to herself what she meant by it, she had found herself flooded by such pain that it had seemed she could not, physically, bear it. This pain – that made her sway backwards and forwards, clenched hands tight against her mouth, groaning loudly had taken her by surprise. The first months after Daniel died she had got through the immediately necessary paperwork, tidied up his things, his clothes, his books, given his collection of walking sticks to

Oxfam, divided his cuff links and watches between his son and his son-in-law, gone through all the photographs of their young married life, children, friends, holidays – and remained most of the time calm and dry eyed.

She had realised that it was likely to be the small, silly things that took her unawares, and had taken care to be alone with the more private letters and photographs and, above all, alone with Daniel's diaries. These, to a stranger's eye, would seem to be mostly meticulous accounts of the weather but Fanny could not pick one up without remembering Daniel standing in front of an open window – in Rome, in Ankara, in Athens, in London – at night, in pyjamas, saying, 'What do you think, Fan? Seven out of ten or eight out of ten for today? Lovely afternoon and not bad this evening but there was that patch of threatened rain before lunch.'

Impossible to explain, even had she wanted to, why this reminder of a boyish obsession should produce such an agony of grief. It wasn't guilt or remorse: she had been amused by Daniel's nightly ritual, never irritated. But whatever the cause of her tears she preferred not to have to try to explain them.

Especially not to Rebecca. The resentment against the girl that she had felt to begin with – or, rather, the resentment she had felt against Delia for dumping her daughter like an unwanted kitten – had gone. It was clear that she needed more help, at least for a while, than she could reasonably expect Ivy to give her, and she suspected that if she didn't put up with Rebecca she might have to endure something worse. It had been Delia's suggestion that she might ask Dora Partridge next door to look in occasionally that had finally settled the matter. And in fact she was finding her niece's timid presence more acceptable than she had expected; having Rebecca in the house was the next best thing to being alone, rather like having a discreet and well-trained pet animal. But she was not the sort of girl you could *talk* to, Fanny thought, or only in the way you would talk to a five-year-old child.

She said, as she tied up the neck of a full plastic bag, 'I'm so grateful that you're here, Becky. So much rubbish turns up when you start clearing a house, and it can't be delegated. No one can really decide what to throw away except the person the rubbish belongs to. And you've been so patient with me.'

Rebecca blushed, darkly and painfully.

Fanny said cheerfully, 'What one could do with every now and again is a really big bonfire. Some of that stuff we've lugged up to the attic could have been dumped without anyone missing it. We should have been *firm* with Harry and Isabel and told them to come and sort out what they wanted when it suited us!'

Rebecca said huskily, 'Perhaps they thought there might be something precious you might not notice. Grown-ups don't always know. Mummy threw away my stick insects one time I wasn't there. She said she thought they were dead. I don't mind helping you, Auntie Fanny.'

Rebecca was twenty-six, a bit old to be talking about 'grown-ups' Fanny thought. But she looked so like a child with those skinny limbs, and a tiny neck, like a flower stalk, supporting a head that seemed much too large for her. Not unlike a stick insect herself in fact. Did stick insects have large, pale, prominent eyes?

Fanny said, 'Delia was always disposing of other people's possessions in my recollection.'

Rebecca laughed in a high-pitched, excited way and put her hand over her mouth. 'Oh,' she said. '*Auntie Fanny.*'

Fanny felt mildly ashamed. Really, *she* should be more

'grown-up' herself. It was contemptibly childish to be scoring off Delia in this silly way. Particularly now, when she should be feeling sorry for her sister. Having a leg amputated could hardly have improved Buffy's always uncertain temper. And for Delia to have a child like Rebecca would be a humiliation as well as a sadness.

She said, 'I'm sure I've done the same thing to your cousins from time to time, too. More often than Delia; we were always moving about after all. Never mind. Thanks to you we have saved a lot of cardboard boxes up in the attic for them to look through.'

Rebecca was looking woebegone. The top-heavy head, weighed down by the heavy plait of coarse brown hair pinned around it, drooped further sideways than seemed physically possible without breaking the fragile neck. *Oh*, Fanny thought, remembering Harry's constant cry, aged fifteen, when he was exasperated by Isabel, *Don't be pathetic*.

She said, 'The Fosters want to move in a month. I can't put them off any longer because of the baby, they want to get settled in before it's born, obviously. And we've exchanged contracts now, anyway. But that gives you enough time to look around, doesn't it? Have you asked the other girls at work? People are always moving in and out of flats, aren't they?'

Who in their right mind would have Becky, though?

Fanny said with forced brightness, 'I'm sure we'll think of something between us. I'll ask about, and I'm sure your mother will. At least, you could always go home. I know it's a bit of a bore trailing up to London from Sussex, but Delia does it without complaining and she's a lot older than you!'

Fanny didn't look at Rebecca. She felt she had been brisker than she should have been but a doleful expression would be more than she could bear at the moment. She said, 'I'll take these two boxes up to the attic, and if you'll put the rest of the books into that packing case, we shall be done. Then if you like, I'll take you out for supper. We'll go to the Roma.'

'I'll take the packing cases up to the attic, Aunt Fanny,' Rebecca said.

Most of the householders in Sickert Terrace had converted their attics, raising the roof beam and extending the top floor to provide extra bedrooms for children, or a studio flat 'with a fine view of St Paul's', that could be let to defray the mortgage. When Fanny and Daniel had bought their house it had been in fair condition, rewired and painted throughout except for one of the small attic rooms that was occupied by an elderly Irishman, a sitting tenant whose death the owners had been hoping would come in time for them to sell the freehold with vacant possession. Luckily for the Pyes they grew bored with waiting and were forced to sell at a price that still gave them what was at that time a thumping profit for a house in a run-down inner city area, but which was one Daniel could just afford. His parents, killed by a flying bomb in 1943, had left their son nothing except the overdraft on their joint account; the three thousand pounds Daniel received on their deaths came from an insurance his maternal grandfather had taken out on his daughter's life for his grandson's benefit, a policy so tortuously and expensively drawn up to prevent his daughter or her husband getting hold of the money, that the amount Daniel received was very little more than the original sum his grandfather had invested. By the time he had paid for the house and the legal costs of the sale he was left with three hundred pounds in his savings account; enough to furnish sketchily, not enough for much renovation. When the Irishman died, they refitted the bathroom he had used on the floor below and moved their bedroom to the other room on the top floor because it looked on to the canal and the trees, where birds sang in the mornings, and used the Irishman's room for storage. They cleaned it out, put a coat of white paint on the walls and the ceiling and replaced a rotten window but left the old gas fire with its slot meter and broken elements. Daniel had said it was a nostalgic reminder of the first flat he and Fanny had rented in London.

That had been in 1953. The gas fire went back further still, as did the pre-war gas piping under the floor boards.

The room was quite tightly sealed: a fall of mortar and soot had long ago blocked the chimney and the wood of the small window frame had swollen during the heavy September rains. Although most of the attic's contents were highly flammable – photographs not good enough to be stuck into albums, water-colours painted by Fanny's mother's two maiden aunts, long unread books, time-spotted papers, broken cane chairs, a wicker hamper full of Christmas decorations, the cardboard boxes full of more recent and miscellaneous discards waiting for Harry and Isabel to go through them – the fire, starved of oxygen, was still only smouldering slowly. The temperature was very high by now, high enough to blacken the timber, curl the cardboard, melt the solder in the old joints of the gas pipes, ignite the gas, but the supply of air was too meagre for the gas to burn.

Until Rebecca opened the door of the attic.

She felt the heat. She smelled the gas. She managed to close the door before the flashover. Even so, the impression of a sheet of flame seemed to be stamped on her retina, momentarily blinding her. And the explosion that blew out the attic window kicked her halfway down the first flight of stairs. She scrambled to her feet, slipping on the contents of the cardboard box that were showering around her, and screamed for her Aunt Fanny.

Next door, Alice Partridge was playing Scrabble with her granddaughters, Letitia and Amy. Although Alice was aware that they would have preferred to watch television she thought they needed more mental stimulation and since they were good-natured girls they were prepared to indulge her. But when they heard what sounded like a bomb, or like gunfire, they ignored their grandmother's orders to stay where they were, and raced to the street door in time to see a wonderful dragon's lick of yellow flame snaking halfway across the street from the Pyes' attic next door. Letitia ran out, wild with excitement. Amy, two years older and more responsible, picked up the telephone in the hall and dialled 999. Alice, joining her, proud to hear her granddaughter requesting the fire service and giving her name and address in such measured and confident tones, took coats from the hall cupboard and went into Dora's study. The word processor was too heavy but there was a folder beside it that contained what looked like small discs, and a pile of manuscript that was (to Alice's eyes) more obviously useful. As she picked up the manuscript it struck her that there must be other things in the house just as important as Dora's fledgling book; things that her son might indeed value more. She worried about this for a moment, both ashamed and amused to recognise that her wish to placate her daughter-in-law should be so dominant, and then picked up the folder that held the discs, just to be sure.

Out in the street, hearing the approaching wail of the sirens, she thought she need not have bothered. Although the fire had been dramatic in its eruption (at first, hearing the bang, Alice's mind had flown to an earthquake) it appeared to be confined to the upper floor of the Pye house and at the end of the street the first fire engine was already making a majestic entry, manœuvring carefully between two lines of parked cars, brass gleaming, young men in helmets and yellow trousers ready to leap to the rescue.

Luckily no one seemed trapped. Alice had already seen Fanny Pye emerge from her house, half carrying, half dragging her frail, childlike niece who was covered in black smuts and wailing. The girl was quiet now, sitting on a chair someone had provided and sipping a glass of water. Fanny stood some distance away from her, far enough to suggest that she had deliberately relinquished responsibility, with her hands thrust deep into the pockets of her long, brown cardigan and her head thrown back, staring up.

Watching her house burn. Alice wondered if she should approach Fanny, and at least offer her one of the warm coats she had brought from the house for her granddaughters, but there was something inhibiting about her stillness and silence. Alice affected to find Fanny formidable, anyway. After Daniel Pye's death, Dora had made several attempts to bring them together – *two old widows, such nice company for each other* was her obvious assumption – and resenting it, but lacking the courage to say so, Alice had chosen to interpret Fanny's polite reserve as coldness and condescension. 'Why should she be interested in me?' she had grumbled to Dora. 'A woman like her, who's led such a busy life, entertaining the high and mighty all over the place! I shouldn't think Sickert Terrace has got much to offer her socially!' Alice had meant this as a sly way of putting Milady Dora down; now she felt she had traduced Fanny unfairly. 'Oh, the poor soul,' she muttered under her breath, and after looking around to check on Letitia and Amy, made her way towards her.

Two more fire engines had followed the first. People hurried to move their parked cars and then stood with other inhabitants of the street, crowded as close to the burning house as the firemen would let them. Smoke and flames tore into the night sky. Sound crackled and splintered and hissed. Sight and sound were familiar from televised disasters; what was new to most of the watchers was smell and temperature. Heat reddened faces; the thick air smelled of scorching. These unpleasant physical sensations apart, the fire had rapidly become a spectacle, a piece of theatre. Although it had been established early on that no one's life was in danger, the Partridge girls and their grandmother safe in the street and the neighbours on the other side of the burning house known to be in America, eyes scanned windows with a certain shameful hope. But as entertainment it was all over too soon. Flames died, the smoke became darker, more choking, more acrid. Blackened firemen began to emerge from Fanny's front door and from the front door of the couple who were innocently holidaying in Vermont. 'They must've broke in round the back,' Alice Partridge heard someone say. 'Stands to reason, they've got to get in somehow, haven't they? Stop it spreading.'

Alice wondered if she should have given someone her key. Or had she left the door open? Turning back to check, she lost sight of Fanny.

It seemed to Fanny that there were faces around her that she had never noticed before. Not because they were newcomers to

the street – these were easily identified by their generally youthful prosperity, their clothes, their motor cars, their clear-voiced,
confident children – nor because they belonged to the shifting
population of boys and girls who lived in the squat in the
derelict house on the corner. The seeming strangers who suddenly caught Fanny's bewildered attention were all old, and
dressed, with an almost theatrical uniformity, in string vests or
ragged pyjamas beneath ancient coats and dressing gowns, bandaged or crippled legs shod in shuffling, felt slippers. It was as if
they were collectively auditioning for the chorus line representing Age and Poverty in a contemporary musical about the
inner city, Fanny thought, as she recognised first one, then
another. She realised that what had thrown her to begin with
was seeing them all together: now, regarding them individually
she could place them, place most of them, anyway, as pensioners who had probably lived all their lives in the street and were
now hanging on, stubbornly, helplessly, in other people's base-
ments and attics; protected tenants like the elderly Irishman
who had clung to life long enough to enable her and Daniel to
buy their house so remarkably cheaply.

And who of course, conversely, Fanny thought wryly, had
prevented the previous owner from selling his property to them
with vacant possession, at the full market value.

She caught the eye of a woman of about her own age who
was looking at her. This woman was bald as an egg and wearing
a quilted nylon dressing gown. Trying to ignore her shiny pink
skull, Fanny smiled shyly and tentatively. She was disgusted
with the way she had instinctively lumped a lot of people
together just because they were old or poor or physically hand-
icapped. To make amends, she smiled rather more fulsomely.
She said, in a bright voice, 'Thank God for the fire service. If

they weren't so quick off the mark the whole street might have gone.'

'Oh, it makes you realise,' the woman said. 'I mean, I remember the Blitz. I thought for a minute it was a bomb going off. It's your house, isn't it? You all right, dear?'

Fanny wondered why she didn't wear a handkerchief or a wig. Perhaps she did normally; perhaps she had been getting ready for bed. 'Well,' she said. 'So-so.'

'Bit shaky, I expect. Safe as houses, people used to say, didn't they? Do you know how it started?'

Fanny shook her head. An explosion in the attic. Something electrical. Faulty wiring. She said, 'I don't know, of course. There was a lot of old rubbish up there, on the top floor. Papers and things. Boxes of photographs, old pictures, all dry as bones I expect . . .'

Her voice seemed to be booming inside her head. The sound of the sea, as if she held a shell to her ears. She hoped she wasn't going to make a fool of herself, be silly and faint. There had been enough of that sort of nonsense, bringing everyone fussing around her, pushing her into old age long before her proper time. She heard herself, speaking hollowly, echoing through a long tunnel, 'Memories, really, old family history, the sort of lumber everyone carries round with them. It was time for a good clear out, anyway. Moving house . . .'

Now, thankfully, she was coming back. The world was in focus again even if she still felt at some distance from it. The bald woman's expression was solicitous but not unduly concerned; presumably she had not noticed anything wrong. Relieved, Fanny said, 'I don't mean, of course, that I'm glad of the *fire*. Doing the job for me. That would be monstrous.' She thought that if Delia or one of the children were to hear this repeated they would decide she was mad. She said, quickly, 'It's lucky my niece wasn't hurt. Though she was badly frightened. I think I should go to her.'

Leaving the bald woman, making her way through the crowd that was diminishing now it was clear the excitement was over, Fanny thought that she should speak to someone, to thank the firemen, discover the extent of the damage and what they considered had caused it. She had forgotten about the old gas fire for the moment and merely had a vague sense of guilt that attached itself to the shambles in the dead lodger's attic room and the memory of Daniel saying at some time or other that they really ought to see to the electrics, have the whole house rewired. How recently had that been? If it had been a long time ago the responsibility for inaction was not hers altogether. Daniel had often spoken of things that ought to be done without any intention of doing them, simply handing them over to someone else, or to Fate. This was not idleness on his part but another kind of economical insurance or superstition, like carrying an umbrella on a calm, sunny day.

She saw the young man from the boat before he saw her. He was standing by one of the fire engines that had mounted the pavement, looking at the broken paving stones and saying something to his girl. She was looking up at him, one hand raised to push back her hair from her face, the other resting lightly on the gently pregnant swell of her belly. Fanny thought – if he looks up, I could smile at him. He can't still hold a grudge because he thought I had spied on him.

But he didn't look up until she had passed him.

The firemen had taken up the stair carpet in the Partridge house, removed a couple of treads, and found the blackened remains of the pitch pine joist in the cavity wall. Investigating, they discovered dried mud pellets, all that was left of the house martin's nest. Alice Partridge, hovering anxiously, confided that she had smelled smoke several hours ago. 'Of course,' she said, emboldened by the knowledge that she was in the clear, 'my daughter-in-law didn't believe me.'

The young fireman she spoke to had heard this sort of story before. He had already pointed out the disarmed smoke alarm to his senior officer, who had learned from one of the boat people that someone had been using a blow lamp on the back of the Partridges' house. The fireman hoped that the decorator, whoever he was, had a proper insurance, and was relieved that it wasn't his business to ask Alice Partridge his name. Instead he spent some time reassuring her. The house was safe now, safe for her granddaughters, and someone would be along first thing tomorrow to check the cavity wall and the window frame and replace the stair carpet. If her daughter-in-law was worried she could ring the station at any hour of the night, though she, Alice, could be quite confident that there was no danger at all. The Partridges had in fact got off very lightly; the only real damage done was to Mrs Pye's house and even that damage was limited to the two upper rooms. A ceiling had come down on the floor below, in a bathroom, but the joists, though badly scorched, seemed to be holding. They would put props in to make it secure of course, make it habitable, even if the upper part of the house might be a bit draughty. 'Oh, the poor things,' Alice cried. 'They must come here, of course.'

Fanny was happy to go to the Partridges for a wash and a drink and a sandwich, but about staying the night she was firm. Rebecca must make up her own mind, though her room on the

93

ground floor, on the street side, was quite sound. But for herself, she would be comfortable enough either in the spare bedroom next to the bathroom, or if it was decided that ceiling might collapse too, on the sofa bed in the basement. There was so much she had to do; telephone calls to be made, both tonight and tomorrow. She would rather get on with it.

'Can I make some calls for you?' Dora offered. She had arrived home while the fire engines were still in the street and was eager to establish her role.

Fanny shook her head, smiling her gratitude.

'Of course I'll come with you, Aunt Fanny,' Rebecca said bravely, struggling up from her chair. 'I wouldn't dream of staying here and leaving you to manage by yourself.'

Dora beamed at her. 'It's a blessing you were here when the fire started, Lord knows what might have happened to your aunt if she'd been on her own.'

Dora looked complacently at Fanny. The right approach to a girl like Rebecca, who was so obviously crushed by her noisy, successful family, was to praise her!

'Actually,' Alice said, 'poor Rebecca was overcome. Fanny had to carry her out of the house.'

'There was an explosion,' Fanny said. 'Becky was carrying stuff up to the attic. She was blown down the stairs.' She added with a piece of half-hearted diplomacy, 'I suppose I was lucky she was there in the sense that it was her and not me. I would have been more likely to break a leg.'

Dora said in a triumphant voice, 'There you are, Mother.'

Alice Partridge raised her eyebrows at Fanny who allowed herself only the tiniest of smiles in reply. She had been caught between these two before and had no wish to take sides. She said, to make a diversion, 'The ironic thing is, Rebecca and I

94

were sorting out stuff for the children to go through, just in case there was something they wanted. Though there was nothing worth fussing over. History, really.'

They looked at her uncomprehendingly. Perhaps she had not made herself clear. But perhaps she was unclear what she meant anyway. Her mind was a mess, she told herself sternly. 'I expect some people might think it foolish but it's always seemed important to me to keep things, old diaries and letters and so on, to pass on to the family so they should know where they come from. And who they are. Now they'll never know, will they?'

A kind of weariness, or nervousness, was making her garrulous, Fanny thought. Unless it was Dora Partridge who had that effect on her. She couldn't be afraid of her, surely? Oh, of course not. It was the spectacle of Dora and Alice together, locked in ritual combat, the stuff of situation comedy, that made her uneasy. Not that it mirrored her relationship with her own children, at least, she hoped that it didn't.

And yet she felt guilty.

Comfortable in her ground floor study, tucked up with a glass of hot whisky toddy in the sofa bed that Tom Partridge had asked one of the firemen to help him carry up from the basement, she telephoned Harry. 'It's all absolutely under control, everyone has been marvellous. The fire service, the neighbours – such a shock for the Partridges. That's where the fire started; the decorator, you know Archie, that nice man we all use in the terrace, was burning off paint with a blow lamp. Not that it makes any difference who is responsible, their insurance, our insurance, what does it matter?'

She lay back against pillows, sipping her toddy, and let Harry run through his expressions of horror, anxiety, and offers to come at once, or if there really was no need for that, first thing in the morning. She thought how much she would like him to be here; here now, at this moment. Talking to her. She could have called him earlier instead of sitting next door having a silly conversation with Dora and Alice. Why hadn't she? Oh – because there was nothing he could have done and a queer inhibition that was probably pride, prevented her asking him to come just because she wanted his company.

She said, 'There's no need. I think I've done everything. I rang the insurance emergency number, the assessors will be coming tomorrow, and a builder to tidy up and make the roof watertight until we find out what needs to be done and how much it will cost and how long . . .'

'At least that's not your problem,' Harry cut in decisively. 'Okay, you'll have to get a builder in to make good, and so forth, but that's the extent of it. I'll ring the solicitors tomorrow and check exactly what the form is, but I'm sure there's no need for you to worry.'

The whisky was warming her. It was the first time she had drunk whisky since Daniel's death and the first time in her life that she had prepared a toddy herself. Squeezing the lemon, mixing the juice with the sugar, pouring the whisky, she had wondered why she had denied herself this simple pleasure so long. She said, 'It doesn't worry me, Harry. We ought to have done up that old attic ages ago. Even if the fire did start with poor Archie's blow lamp, I should think some of the blame must be ours. There was such a lot of stuff there, all the Christmas decorations for one thing. Do you remember those angels we bought in Germany?'

Daniel had been posted to Bonn. They had stood in the

snow looking in the shop window; Isabel asleep in the pram, Harry holding her hand. He had been fair then; a blond child in scarlet leggings and parka, pressing his pink nose against the glass, tugging her hand. '*Mummy, please Mummy, let's buy them for the tree, I'll lend you my pocket money.*'

Fanny said, 'You were right about them. They were beautifully made. They were there, up in the attic.'

The grown up Harry made a curious, huffing noise. Like an impatient walrus, she thought. He sneezed and huffed again, managing to hold on to the second sneeze. There were further squeaky and juicy sounds. He said huskily, 'I must be getting a cold. It's not your business, Mother. Not your house any longer.'

For some reason this simple statement upset her. Something to do with the fire, perhaps? Watching all those years of her life going up in smoke? Daniel had *given* the house to her; thinking of his own wandering childhood, it was the most precious gift he could think of, a roof over her head. (Did Harry really think leaving it was so easy?) She said, irritated suddenly, 'We haven't completed yet.'

'You've exchanged contracts. So they can't get out of it.'

Fanny said, 'Harry! That poor girl is enormously pregnant.'

'Oh, I agree. It's rotten timing for them.'

She said, 'I can't keep them to it.'

There was quite a long silence. Then he blew his nose. She said, 'Harry?'

'Look, Mother. You've had quite enough for one evening. Let's leave it. We'll talk in the morning. Oh, hell, I haven't got too much time tomorrow. I've got a production meeting. *Hell.* Perhaps I can get out of it. I don't know. I'll have a word with Isabel. Or maybe Poppy . . . I mean, you can't just . . .' He stopped. Fanny waited. He said, in a strained voice, 'Darling,

97

don't you think you had better move in with us for a bit? I mean, obviously you've coped marvellously. Been wonderful. But you must be exhausted.'

She said, amused, 'I'm quite all right, Harry. A bit tired now, that's all. As anyone would be. But the house is perfectly habitable below the top floor. I could have slept in the spare bedroom if it wasn't for the smell. That really is unpleasant, though it's not so bad in my study. I couldn't possibly leave the place empty. Or leave Becky here alone, either. Don't *worry*, dear. Or worry anyone else tonight, either. You know what Isabel is. And Delia might worry about Rebecca.'

'Ha ha!' Harry said.

'Well, maybe not,' Fanny said. 'But she'll worry *me*, ringing up.'

'Mmm. I suppose so. Are you really all right? I mean, honestly?'

'She really did sound all right,' he said. This was at least the tenth time he had said this to his sister in about the same number of minutes and he was beginning to feel dog tired at the likelihood of having to go on repeating himself for what was left of the night. But just as he was resigning himself to this gloomy prospect, Isabel gave up bleating for reassurance about their mother's health and safety and her own carelessness in not worrying more as a good daughter should, and said, in a totally different, completely business-like tone, 'I suppose she won't go all mushy and decide she can't sell the house now?'

It astonished him, as it always did, how quickly Isabel could switch between over-heated sentiment and what seemed quite icy appraisal of the situation under discussion. Or the other way round. Although he could usually follow her train of thought and knew it was much the same as the kind of private, internal agonisings he sometimes went in for himself, he also knew that there were quite a few who found it a bit convoluted if not actually tortured. His father for example. 'Scatty' was one of the words he had used when speaking about his daughter – though being a kind man, it was only behind her back, and only to his wife, or to Harry. And Harry had always stood up for her. Most people make huge, erratic leaps in their thinking. Now he thought that the crucial difference between Isabel and apparently less agitated folk, could be that when she argued with herself she usually did so aloud.

He said, 'Bloody nuisance if she does. She sold to the Fosters at the top of the market. There's been quite a fall in house prices since. Interest rates on the up and up, I suppose, no chance of them going down again for a while.'

'I wasn't thinking about the price, Harry!' Isabel sounded shocked. 'I meant, it would be just like her to worry much more about the poor people who're paying it. The Fosters have two small children, haven't they? Well, a three year old, and one coming. I think that's what Mummy said. They'll be terribly upset when they hear.'

'Upset or not, they're committed. Legally. The only way out for them would be if she let them off.'

'But would anyone else buy it if she did?'

'Only as a bargain, I imagine. She'd have to drop the price a fair bit. Unless she decided to wait until the repairs have been done.'

'Oh, Harry! That would be an awful hassle for her, wouldn't it?'

'That's one of the reasons I'm concerned,' Harry said, although he had not thought of it until now. He felt faintly ashamed and cleared his throat before he continued, 'In fact, it has to be the main one. I know she's a tough old bird. It's amazing how completely she's recovered from that unpleasant accident. She was even quite perky when she talked to me just now. Oh, she was a bit wandery once, on about some Christmas decorations, the rest of the time she was absolutely on the ball. Though how she'd cope with builders is another matter.'

Isabel said, 'When we bought this house it was a ghastly mess. The kids were all small, and we had the boys a lot of the time, Max's brothers, and not a spare penny! But it turned out quite jolly, really, and the children adored it. The big boys, especially, all those lovely men doing things and letting them help sometimes, bang in a nail or two, or splash on a bit of paint here and there.'

'I hardly think that Mother is itching to get her hands on a hammer.'

Isabel giggled. 'Oh, don't be so *thick*. I meant the *Fosters* might enjoy it. And they'll have the insurance, that means they'll be able to do it all up just as they want to, a proper roof extension like most of the other houses in the terrace. I should think, once they've got over the shock, they'll be glad of the chance.'

'Let's hope they see it that way,' Harry said. 'Can't rely on it though. I think we may need a concerted effort to stop Mother going mushy on us as you said. And of course we've got to see how bad the damage to the house really is. I can go most easily tomorrow afternoon. Late-ish. Poppy's got the dentist tomorrow. Not just an in and out job, an impacted something or other. What about you? Or Max?'

It occurred to Harry during the ensuing haggle over priorities that there was one small thing nobody seemed to have hoisted in. Or had not mentioned, anyway. If Fanny were to postpone the sale (for what would have to be quite a while when you thought of all that had to be done, comparing estimates, getting planning permission, let alone finding a builder who might be likely to turn up at moderately regular intervals and not leave the place draped in flapping tarpaulins interminably), what were the chances that she might change her mind about buying a house for Ivy? He refused to go into the moral implications of persuading her to give up the idea. He thought he could safely leave that to his sister. Particularly when it was a fair certainty that when it came to the crunch, to the actual disposal of what she thought of as family property, Isabel was likely to be a good deal more beady-eyed than the rest of them.

She said, confirming this, 'I suppose it's not impossible that house prices will go up again? Max and I were talking about it last night. The sort of people who've made a lot of money in the last ten years, ordinary people, not dealers, aren't the sort who are used to putting their spare cash or savings into stocks and shares. There was a really huge slump in the property market years ago, it went down about forty per cent just after the turn of the century. But though that was partly high inter-est rates, as it is now, it was also because there was an enormous increase in cheap public transport! That's not exactly true now, I could tell you.'

'No, indeed,' he agreed quickly, before she could amplify these gleanings from whatever financial article she had been reading recently by telling him how much Max's season ticket cost and how dreadful the conditions were on the crowded trains to Waterloo in the morning. The fact that Harry could drive to work from his more convenient area of south London, and was able to use the BBC executive car park was, in Isabel's view, a typical example of managerial privilege which in a juster society would have been stamped out years ago.

'I expect prices will recover,' he said, allowing himself to yawn with a good noisy squeak to warn her that he was ready for bed and would not be talking much longer. Though as he yawned he was seized by a sudden, brotherly desire to torment her. 'Of course,' he went on in a tone of sweet reason, 'in many ways it would be a good thing if they didn't. I should have thought you'd agree with me that the boom has been a disaster socially. No cheap rented accommodation. Too high a proportion of income going on keeping a roof over your head. Too much talk about how much it all costs and about how much we've all made just by sitting and doing bugger all in our breeding boxes. The encouragement of *greed*, in a word.'

'Oh, shut up,' she said. 'That isn't the point and you know it.'

'If the action's going on, you want a piece of it?'

'Precisely,' she said, with perfect good humour.

'That's my Izzy,' he said affectionately.

'It's not being *selfish*. I've been thinking of Max, if you want to know.'

'What's Max got to do with it?'

'Oh, you know, really, don't you? He deserves some sort of a break. He's been doing this boring job for so long. If money was a little less tight, then he'd have a chance to do something he really liked doing. Like Law. He's not too old to get qualified. If Mummy really wants to chuck money around . . .'

She stopped. Appalled, by her own coarseness, Harry assumed. He was appalled himself. Although he decided, almost immediately, that what she had just said was not entirely unreasonable, he was still appalled by her actually saying it instead of just thinking it.

She said – crossly, as if *he* had spoken aloud, 'Oh, don't be so niminy piminy.' And then, in a much lower tone, hurriedly, 'Don't tell Max what I said, for God's sake?'

Harry assumed that either Max had come into the room, or that she had been seized with shame. He said, cheerfully, 'Of course I won't, idiot. Don't you tell him either. However much Max may feel *himself* that he might have done something else if things had been different, I mean if there had been more money around at the right sort of time, he won't want to know that you think what he actually has done, running his own delivery firm all these years, is a boring old rubbish job and you wish he could have a chance to fulfil himself properly. That really would put him down, don't you think?'

There was silence at the other end of the line. Then Isabel said, 'Yes. Yes, I see,' in an artificially thoughtful way as if the conversation she was engaged in was about some issue that required a certain amount of intellectual attention but that didn't really concern her.

Harry wondered if it was Max in the room with her, or Max's mother, or one of his brothers. Her children were probably in bed by now. He thought that it couldn't be easy, an unwieldy household like that; only four in his own and that seemed sometimes too many. And Izzy very rarely complained, the way some women did, of too much to do, lack of time, lack of money.

He said, 'Sorry, love, I know you were just thinking aloud. I didn't mean to be spiteful, just wanted to stop you rushing in where angels fear to tread before you've asked yourself whether it might be that the angels know something you don't.'

She laughed affectionately at this silly joke, not because it was funny, but because it was the kind of silliness that they had shared when they were children together; it had been one of the ways they signalled making up after a quarrel. She said, 'Goodnight, Harry, sleep well. Wish Poppy luck at the dentist and I'll ring tomorrow when I've been to see Mummy.'

Fanny had had an exhilarating day. Insurance assessors had been and gone; a builder who was one of Tom Partridge's patients, a robust, cheerful Welshman, had fixed things up temporarily, made the roof watertight, boarded the windows and hung a heavy dust sheet at the top of the stairs. Although blackened and charred the attic floors were still safe to walk on. 'Stout stuff, those old pitch pine joists,' the Welsh builder had said. 'Though I wouldn't recommend you to hold a barn dance up there exactly.' He had a lovely lilt to his voice and a friendly, confiding manner. He came from the Gower peninsula, he told Fanny as they sat in her kitchen over a pot of tea; he and his brother had only recently moved their small family firm up to London. 'Bit of a change,' he said. 'Bit of a challenge. More going on for our boys if they don't want to go in for the building. We've got five between us and there's nothing much for them at home now the mining is more or less finished. Just a bit of light industry, and that's for the women.'

Fanny was charmed and reassured. She had heard how difficult it was to find a good builder in London and until now she had not needed one. Archie Olds had been competent enough as a handyman for simple repairs and maintenance and neither she nor Daniel had felt any urge to go in for anything more ambitious in the way of home improvement. This made them a unique phenomenon in Sickert Terrace: in the four years after Daniel's retirement almost every other house had undergone some radical reconstruction. There were always workmen in the street, laden skips, scaffolding, huge vats of simmering tar. Walls were knocked down, or put up, whole rooms refurbished, bathrooms modernised, early Victorian fireplaces either ripped out or replaced, plaster cornices and other 'period features' restored to houses that had thrown them out earlier as old-fashioned and fussy. To the Pyes it seemed that in the years they had been living out of the country, titivating their houses had become a major English pastime, a compulsive new game.

House fever. They had looked on, bewildered. It was the rise in prices, Daniel suggested. And more money around. People who were not accustomed to investing put their spare cash where they could keep their eyes on it: in double glazing, extra bedrooms, garages, conservatories, fashionable fitted kitchens, or at least in a whirlpool bath or a fan-assisted oven. To spend money that way could be counted a virtue: it would add value to the house as an investment. Fanny had thought it was more basic than that. A house was the urban equivalent of the rural small holding: people wanted a stake in the land. Both of them felt, perhaps smugly, that they were immune to this fever, although there had been times, lately, when Fanny had found herself thinking that now Daniel was no longer around to object to it, she might have a television with a large screen installed in her bedroom so that she could watch the late night movies or a video of an old favourite; a Preston Sturges film, or a Hitchcock. And since the attic bedroom was small and the ceiling sloped on one side, she would need to get rid of an obtrusive cupboard to make enough space for a generously designed and convenient shelf.

She had done nothing about it because it had seemed too much trouble to turn out the cupboard, find a good carpenter (and along the way explaining to Archie Olds why she was employing someone more skilful), buy a new smaller bed, new curtains and carpet, redecorate. It would cost a lot, too. Even though she could afford it, Fanny was puritan enough to resist spending an unnecessary amount of money just for her own comfort and pleasure. And once she had decided to sell the house there was no point, anyway.

But now Fate had intervened; the fire, changing everything. Her solicitor, whom she had telephoned first thing in the morning, had – a little to her surprise – agreed with her almost instantly. He would be unhappy himself to force through a sale in this situation. If the buyer was still keen to complete that would be another matter. Or if his client were desperate to sell. Even then he would have to point out that there might be tiresome complications. Structural problems, for example, that might appear later and although in theory the sale was not complete until the money had been passed over, if the buyers were held to the contract against their will they would have a grievance. If it could be proved, for example, that the fire had been caused by some carelessness.

'Let's find out what they want to do first,' Fanny had interrupted, cutting short what threatened to be a lengthy legal lecture, and to speed things up had rung the Fosters herself, at once.

'So that's all sorted out,' she said to Isabel in the late afternoon. 'Of course they were upset but only up to a point. Once they realised the extent of the damage, I think they were vastly relieved – and not only because they would have had to deal with it. After all, they were paying a really huge sum for this house, and presumably got a huge sum for their own. If they decide to let their sale go through they'll have won on the swings *and* the roundabouts! More money to play with. And since it **seems** that they can stay with her mother until after the baby **is born, t**hey have time to look around.'

She beamed her satisfaction at her daughter. 'That was the one thing that was worrying me, that poor, pregnant girl having nowhere to go.'

Isabel was regarding her with an amazed expression. Not quite open-mouthed, Fanny thought, but it was true, jaws did droop when people were startled. Keeping them closed was a conscious act.

Isabel said wonderingly, 'I said to Harry that you'd be putting the Fosters first.'

'Well, it's not quite like that is it, dear? Though surely, anyone would . . .'

'But I didn't *believe* it. Honestly, Ma!'

Isabel laughed rather unpleasantly. Fanny said, 'You usually call me Ma when you are displeased with me.'

'Do I?' Isabel flushed. 'Oh, I'm sorry, how awful! Of course I'm not displeased, what a word to use! It's just, Harry and I thought, well, hoped, I suppose, that you wouldn't rush into anything, at least, not as fast as you seem to have done. I mean there are so many things to be thought of, and your own comfort is one of them. You can't really want to hang on here, in this mess, on your own.'

'Rebecca's here,' Fanny said. 'Not at the moment, she's working. As a matter of fact I was quite impressed with her, going off this morning as if nothing had happened. Then I thought, well, it gives her something to talk about. Like a child going off to school with a nice bit of news. As I remember, you and Harry were always pleased to report a good drama. And it's not such a mess, is it? Mr Jones hung a dust sheet to stop the dirt coming down from the top floor and when Ivy comes tomorrow we'll clean up the rest of the house.'

'Ah!' Isabel said. 'What *about* Ivy?'

Fanny looked at her. Then she got up from her chair and went to the corner cupboard and opened it. She said, 'Would you like a whisky, darling?'

Isabel observed that her mother was already holding a glass in her hand. She must have picked it up from the floor beside her chair. Isabel said, lightly, 'You been at the bottle, Mummy? I thought that sherry was your tipple.'

'A habit I fell into after your father died,' Fanny said. 'People offered it. I imagine it is thought a suitable drink for widows. Odd, really. I have always understood it was bad for the liver.'

She poured two glasses of whisky – reasonably generous, but not remarkably so – and gave one to Isabel. She said, 'If you want ice there is some in the refrigerator. I'd get it for you but I am rather tired.'

This was a lie. Fanny was not at all tired, quite the opposite: she felt astonishingly wide awake. It was simply a coded way of expressing a mild reproach: after all her demonstrations of concern and affection on the telephone this morning, Isabel had delayed her arrival until much too late to do anything useful. Not that she had wanted her to come earlier, Fanny reminded herself dutifully, but Isabel could not have known that.

Isabel leapt to her feet at once. 'Of course, you must be *exhausted*,' she cried. 'As if I would want you to run around after me! I don't want ice, as it happens, but I'll get some for you. Now you just sit down and put your feet up and *relax*. I'm sorry I came bursting in, asking questions about what is really and *absolutely* none of my business.'

'Rubbish,' Fanny murmured. She sat down and allowed

Isabel to pick up her feet and place them on a stool that was slightly too high for her chair. Leaning back to ease the discomfort this caused in her calf muscles she wondered if a supine position made her look older and more helpless than she was. She said, 'Thank you, dear. I don't like ice either. That is, unless the whisky is being served warm as it sometimes used to be at those embassy functions. Do you remember? Even if the refrigerator was big enough we could never persuade any of the servants to keep the whisky properly cold.' She saw her daughter frown and said, feeling laughter rising in her throat and trying to stifle it, 'I'm sorry I used the word *servant*. What would you prefer? Butler, or steward? Darling Izzy, those good people went with the *job*.'

'I know. I'm sorry.' Isabel looked penitent. Then she said, 'What would you call Ivy?'

'A friend. A helper. A part-time housekeeper.'

'There you are! You wouldn't dream of calling her a *maid* or a *servant*.'

'No. I should have called the embassy people the *staff*. Is that more dignified? I can't call Ivy the *staff*. That has to be plural, I think. A member of the staff, you say. But I think of her as my friend. Should I find another name for her because I pay her for some of the things she does for me?'

'Drink your whisky,' Isabel said. Her grey eyes were warm and merry. 'What about your plan to buy Ivy a house? If you don't sell, then that's all off, isn't it?'

So that was what she was looking pleased about, was it? Fanny said, 'I didn't say I wasn't going to sell eventually, Isabel. Just not to the Fosters. Nor immediately to anyone. This builder I seem to have acquired through Tom Partridge seems both nice and competent. I think I would quite enjoy being around while he fixed up the top floor. I told him I'd like to have one big room up there and he's promised to do me some drawings. I wouldn't feel comfortable, dear, if I got rid of the house as it is at the moment. Your father and I were happy here and I think you and Harry were happy here, too. I would like to pass it on in good condition to another family.'

How revoltingly sentimental, she thought. She wouldn't get away with this soft sort of talk if Harry were here. But Isabel, bless her, was nodding respectfully! 'Just don't wear yourself into a frazzle,' she said. 'If the building work gets you down you can always move out. I'm not sure that you ought-n't to anyway, until the smell gets a little less foul. It really is *horrible*!'

'Luckily my sense of smell isn't as acute as it used to be. Fading. Like my memory.'

Isabel looked sidelong at her mother. Fanny understood that this subject had become embarrassing to her. It was, Fanny thought, as if Isabel saw her loss of memory as an unmention-able disease.

She said 'Even if I had cancer, I would hope we could talk about it. People my age do forget. It's just that one of the things I seem to have lost, mislaid anyway, is thought to be important. Though important to whom? I do ask myself that, Isabel.'

Isabel said impatiently, 'You're not serious, are you?'

Fanny swung her aching legs off the stool and sat upright. She finished her whisky and said, 'You know, Izzy, I would quite like another. A small one.'

She held out the glass. Isabel raised her eyebrows – quite effectively, Fanny considered. Expressing doubt as to the wisdom of her mother's drinking habit but politely refraining from commenting.

Fanny waited until the glass was returned to her. It had been somewhat meagrely refreshed. She said, speaking carefully and clearly, 'I'm not sorry that I can't remember. To begin with, I wanted to. Partly because it was my citizen's duty, but chiefly because I wanted to please that pleasant young policewoman. Just lately I've not been so sure. I think, that man died: I might have died too. Whatever happened – some kind of quarrel, some kind of street brawl – it was nothing deliberate. That would be a different thing altogether. But so many dreadful things happen, famine and wars, hideous diseases. If I *had* been killed, would I want them to find out who did it? Put someone in jail, some young man, at the beginning of his life. I really don't know, Isabel. It may be time passing, nothing seeming quite as urgent as it once did.'

She wondered if she meant this. She meant something like it.

Isabel said, 'You're not asking yourself the right questions, are you? Or using the right word. If someone is killed in a fight it is murder. How would you feel if I had been murdered? Or Harry?'

'Nothing could bring you back.'

'If someone killed one of my children, however it happened, I'd want to tear them to pieces.'

'You were always a violent child,' Fanny said, smiling.

Isabel flushed. 'I was being *serious*.'

'And I'm on my third whisky? I admit that may have something to do with it. Not with what I say, but with the fact that I've said it. I expect that when you and Harry were young, in my charge, so to speak, I might have wanted to kill anyone who threatened to harm you. But that apart, the only person I ever wanted to kill when I was young was my sister Delia.'

Although this was perfectly true, Fanny had meant it as a

joke, to take that solemn look from Isabel's face, and it was as a joke she expected her daughter to take it.

But Isabel didn't appear to have heard her. She was staring at her mournfully, dark brows drawn together, eyes puzzled. Her hair was loose on her shoulders but held away from her face by a band of green silk that matched her green woollen jacket and skirt. Green was a colour that Fanny was fond of and it occurred to her suddenly that this may have been why Isabel had decided to wear it.

She wondered if she had upset Isabel recently by complaining about her usual black garb. She said, 'You look beautiful in that colour, Izzy dear. In fact, you look beautiful altogether today.'

Radiant was the word. Her daughter looked *radiant*. No woman acquired that kind of inward glow from pleasing her mother! And Isabel had arrived much later than Harry had suggested she would. Not that it mattered. Isabel had telephoned. But she had been uncharacteristically cagey about why she couldn't come earlier. Her usual style was to give ten explanations when one would have served. Today she had simply said that she had something to do and that she wasn't sure how long it would take.

Fanny hoped that Isabel wasn't too serious about whoever it might be. She said, watching her daughter, 'How's Max?' – and was sorry to see Isabel blush.

She answered, quickly, 'Oh, desperately overworked as he always is. It wouldn't matter so much if he enjoyed it, if it were something really worthwhile. Then he'd feel quite different about it, I think. As it is, he's quite *drained* when he gets home in the evening. No energy to do anything except fall asleep in front of the telly.' She sighed, very deeply. 'Poor Max!'

The pitying sigh confirmed Fanny's fears. When she had fallen in love, she had always been sorry for Daniel. That was how guilt had affected her.

How serious had those love affairs been? It was difficult, looking back, to remember. Daniel had never known, she was sure. Or she had been sure at the time. But to think about it, about the risks she had taken, frightened her now. And she had a different nature from her daughter, more cautious, colder. Isabel would dismiss any argument for discretion as shameful hypocrisy. Isabel would want to be 'honest' with her husband.

Fanny said brightly, 'For heaven's sake don't tell Max.' She gave an artificial little trill of laughter. 'I mean, of course, don't tell him you're sorry for him. That's a depressing thing for anyone to hear. I expect he does get a little tired now and then. But he keeps all his family going which is no mean achievement. That's a source for some pride, I should think. And not only for him. For you, too.'

Isabel sighed again – but with exasperation this time, not sorrow. 'Oh, *Mummy*, don't preach, you're as bad as Harry! I don't see why you should both stick up for Max all the time! What about me?'

She sounded about fourteen years old. Fanny laughed outright, unaffectedly. Isabel scowled, and then smiled. 'I know, that's childish, I'm sorry. I don't know how we got *into* this conversation! We were talking about you, not about me. I was going to ask you . . .' She hesitated; she seemed suddenly embarrassed, Fanny thought, a bit sly. 'There was something you said. About the man who killed Andrew Hobbes. How do you know he was *young*? Did the wife say so? Did the police tell you? Oh, I'm sorry to *ask*. It sounded as if I'm being inquisitorial! I don't mean to be – for heaven's sake, why on earth should you try and hide anything? It was just. Well. It just bothered me for a minute.'

'I don't know,' Fanny said. 'Isabel, I really don't know. If I said he was young, then perhaps I assumed it. A fight over a car – it sounds like a young man.' This made sense. But she felt winded. As if someone had slugged her.

'I'm so sorry, darling,' Isabel said 'I didn't mean to muddle you. It's so difficult always, trying to sort out what you might remember from what people have told you. I suppose we're all just a bit over-anxious about you. About what has happened. I mean, in a way it would be better if you didn't remember because while you don't, you're quite safe.'

'Safe, Isabel?'

'Oh, you know what I mean. I don't mean safe *physically*, I meant, if it came to a trial, you'd presumably have to give evidence, and Max is worried about that, he thinks the defending counsel would pitch into you, give you a simply frightful time in the witness box. But I'm sorry I brought it up. It was stupid to worry you.'

Fanny thought that it was curious how one could love someone dearly and yet find them as irritating as she was finding Isabel at this moment. And yet to protest, to ask Isabel not to give voice to every thought that came into her head, would be hurtful. An alternative would be to have another whisky. As an anaesthetic. But then Isabel would rush to the telephone and tell Harry that she was afraid their mother had a drinking problem.

She wished Isabel would go home. She wished that she didn't feel angry. She wished that she could remember everything and be finished with it.

She said, 'I think the police have decided that although they want to hear what I have to tell them if it should come back to me, I wouldn't be much use as an official witness for all the reasons you mention. It doesn't altogether please me to know that I am considered too loose in my wits to be cross-examined in court but I suppose I ought to be grateful for everyone's kind concern.'

Isabel giggled. 'Don't be huffy! Though I ought to be pleased! It means you're back on form. Quite recovered.'

'I'm not huffy.' Fanny considered this lie. 'I was a little pompous, perhaps,' she amended.

'Is that what you call it?'

Isabel regarded her mother with mock disapproval, one finger placed against her cheek at the exact spot where she had once, as a plump ten year old, had a dimple. The image that rose up before Fanny was so sharp and so clear that she smiled with remembered amusement. 'Oh, get along with you,' she said, with the same affectation of grumpiness that had once dismissed the teasing child, thinking, in the same moment, that if someone had told her at the time that her fat little girl would grow up so lovely she would have found it hard to believe it. Harry had been the handsome one.

Kissing Isabel goodbye in the hall, she murmured, 'I'm sorry.'

Isabel did not appear to have heard her. She ran down the steps to her car which, parked in a resident's space, had acquired a ticket under the windscreen. She waved, miming horror, and laughed.

Sorry? What for? Closing the front door, Fanny wondered. 'Old sins,' she said aloud, and put them aside. There was always so much to regret between parents and children; things done or not done, things said, or not said. But on the whole Harry and Isabel had not turned out too badly.

Daniel would have said something to Isabel about her careless parking habit. He would have worried about it all evening. If she had told him she suspected that their daughter had a lover, he would have been distraught. But she would never have told him.

Putting the whisky back in the corner cupboard, picking up the two dirty glasses and carrying them down to the kitchen, she thought about supper. There was some cold chicken, not much, but enough for Rebecca and she wasn't hungry. Perhaps she was wrong about Isabel. She knew Ivy thought she was hard on her sometimes. It was a shame about Ivy; she had looked forward to telling her about the house money. Although it was fortunate that she hadn't told her already; it was only her own pleasure in giving that must be deferred.

Oh, but she did look forward to seeing Ivy's face! Was that selfish? Oh, probably. But quite unimportant. You could say there was likely to be an element of selfishness, self-satisfaction, anyway, in doing the right thing but that didn't stop it being the right thing to do. And to make sure that a good, hardworking woman like Ivy had a place of her own to live and take pride in must be right, surely? No doubt Delia would find a flaw in this argument, she would think it too simple. Her view would be that individual generosity could not be an answer to social injustice; giving was charity and therefore demeaning to those who received it.

'What absolute nonsense.' While she laid the supper table – the cold chicken, a cucumber salad, wholemeal bread, cheese and apples – Fanny addressed her absent sister in a loud, indignant voice, and suddenly found herself trembling with outrage against her. She sat down on a kitchen chair, her head swimming, twisting her quivering hands together, trying to still them. 'This is ludicrous,' she said, and attempted a laugh. Why on earth was she angry with Delia? She had been angry with Delia often enough, but this kind of shaking fury was something she had not felt for years, not since the time she had gone for her with the bread knife – oh, years ago, when they were both in their teens. What had that been about? Why should she feel like this now?

She made herself breathe slowly and steadily. Something had gone wrong; slipped out of focus. It was as if some sort of temporal control or governor had suddenly failed, leaving her to spin wildly in time, at the mercy of any long ago passion that happened to seize her.

'Ludicrous,' she said again, very firmly, and felt her pulse slowing down. Thank God for that! If Harry were to come as he had said that he would, she must not appear a batty old fool in front of him. Nor even in front of Rebecca. The girl seemed almost completely indifferent to other people – a defence against Delia, perhaps? – but even she might notice it if her aunt should begin to throw knives about. Had she behaved oddly when Isabel was here? She thought not; the only thing that Isabel had picked on was something she had said about the young man at the scene of the accident, though why that had troubled her Fanny couldn't remember just now and it probably wasn't important. But she did remember one thing: she had spoken a little stiffly, or sharply, perhaps, and after that Isabel had pronounced her 'recovered'.

Fanny thought that there was no point in going into the implications of *that* remark at the moment! She stood up, moving slowly and carefully as if she had recently suffered a bruising fall and held on to the edge of the table as she walked around it, acting the part of an old woman. She looked at herself in the looking glass at the side of the kitchen door, next to the telephone, ran her hands up through her hair until it stood on end and wrinkled her nose. She said, 'Why, you old hag!'

The telephone rang in her ear, startling her. Dora Partridge said, 'Fanny, are you okay? I mean be honest. Say if you're not.'

'I think I'm fine.' Fanny hoped she had injected enough doubt into her answer to give her freedom to get better or worse, depending on Dora's proposal. 'It depends,' she added, for extra caution.

'Oh it's nothing strenuous,' Dora said. 'It's just some people from the boats going round with a petition. They want the Waterways Board to establish permanent residential rights, for about a dozen boats, something like that, and they're hoping some of us in the terrace will sign it. I wasn't sure how you felt. I know Daniel was against anything of the sort, but Tom says he thought you felt differently. Anyway, one of them asked if he should call on you, I suppose he was doubtful because of the fire, it was nice of him to ask really, and not just to come knocking. So I said, let me just ring her up first, see if she's well enough. How she feels. That's all. Say no if you want to. It can wait for another day, though not much longer because there's a planning committee meeting, you know everything always has to be done *yesterday* doesn't it? Or if you prefer I'll just pop in on my own and explain it all to you and they can get your signature later.'

'No,' Fanny said. 'No, it's quite all right, Dora. Send whoever it is along now.'

'Are you sure? Truly? I did promise your sister I'd keep a sharp eye on you! But this does seem important to them, and, after all, here we sit in our warm and comfortable houses . . .

What I feel is, we ought to try and think what it might be like to know we could be moved on any time, at the whim of some official. I think all we lucky ones ought to think about that. I know the boaters have been a bit of an irritant sometimes, the smell from the engines, and the mess on the towpath, but I don't think it would hurt you to hear their point of view. If I really thought it would make you too tired, I wouldn't suggest it.'

'I'm sure you wouldn't,' Fanny said. 'You are always considerate, Dora.'

It was over twenty minutes before he came, long enough for Fanny to wonder if he were still trapped in the Partridge house being lectured by Dora. But when he rang at last, and she opened the door, she had the impression that he had been standing there for some time; he had the still, contained look of someone who is used to waiting and watching.

Perhaps he had loitered because he was nervous. His thin face was very pale, almost waxen under the yellow street lighting; his narrowed eyes, shy and furtive. Fanny smiled her widest and most generous smile, to encourage him.

He gave a short gasp, as if he had been holding his breath, and said, 'I'm Jake, Mrs Pye. Jake, from the boats. About the petition.'

His name rang no bell in her mind. She invited him in, offered him coffee. He refused, shaking his head and visibly flinching – as if he feared it might be poisoned, she thought. Even when he sat down, he remained on the edge of the chair, his eyes, which were a very light blue, fixed on her warily.

She said, cheerfully, 'Tell me about your petition. I'm glad the wretched Waterways Board are doing something at last.

You must be pleased, too. It will be a relief to have proper services laid on, electricity and rubbish collection, all that sort of
thing.'

He nodded, and cleared his throat. 'We want to be on good
terms. We don't want no hassle. That's why we're calling on
everyone in the street.'

'I have no objection to the boats,' Fanny said. 'I know some
people do object, but I am sure they would feel differently about
properly regulated moorings.'

Jake said nothing. He was frowning. Almost as if he didn't
understand her, she thought. As if she were speaking some
strange foreign language.

She said, 'Your boat is opposite my house, isn't it? The
Adelaide May. I've seen you . . .' She hesitated before his sharp
look of renewed alarm and went on in a gentler voice, 'That is,
I've noticed you. Your boat, and you on the towpath. I often
look out of my windows at the back. It's such a pretty view.'

He gave a gusty sigh and said with sudden boldness, 'It would
be funny if you didn't recognise me, wouldn't it? Since we're
neighbours, like. And we get a nice view, too. I mean, of the
gardens and houses. I used to be moored down the Basin and
there was nothing to see except them tumbledown warehouses.'

She thought, well, that's his story, he was admiring the architecture, might as well let him think I accept that. What's the
alternative? Accuse him of keeping an eye on the house so he
could burgle it when it's empty? She said, smiling, 'And it's
more convenient for the shops and the buses.'

'All that,' he said. He was still watching her closely but
seemed no longer ill at ease. His gaze was appraising. Even
admiring. If it had not been so risible at her age, and his, she
thought she might have been flattered. He was an attractive

boy with a fine delicacy in the bones of his face and the curve of his mouth. His torso was concealed by a bulky jacket but he had nice hands and long, graceful legs. Fanny wondered what he would look like naked and he smiled suddenly, in a knowing way, as if he knew what she was thinking.

She thought, oh no you don't know, my lad, it wouldn't cross your mind for a minute.

She said, 'I suppose I should read it first. But I expect I will sign your petition.'

3

Stevie Trench, Ivy's husband, had a stroke on the second Friday in November. Fanny, who had been away for the weekend, did not hear the news until Monday morning when she telephoned Ivy.

'Oh, darling,' she cried, 'why didn't you let me know? I was only at Harry's, you have his number.'

'No point in spoiling your little break,' Ivy said. 'Poor old devil, he wouldn't wish it.'

The attribution of any kind of altruistic sentiment to Ivy's husband seemed ludicrous to Fanny. Ivy must be in deep shock to make it! Fanny said, 'I could have done something, Ivy. At least driven you to the hospital. It was a filthy weekend to be hanging about catching buses. Never mind. I'm here now . . .'

'And upset to find the house as you had left it, I expect,' Ivy said. 'I'm sorry I didn't get in on Friday. I meant to do a bit of clearing up for you after the builders, but we were all sixes and sevens here waiting for the ambulance and then I was stuck until ten at night hanging around until the doctor could see me. I can come later on and give you a lick and a promise.'

'I wouldn't hear of it,' Fanny said.

'No trouble, I'll have to look in at Bart's and see Stevie, I thought I'd go fairly soon, before lunch, and you're on my way home.'

'I'll pick you up from the hospital,' Fanny said. 'Drive you back to the flat, go shopping, whatever you want. Only you're not coming here to cope with this mess. It's not so bad, anyway, and Mr Jones says the worst bit is over now he's got the old timber out, just noise and dust from now on.'

'Oh, if you don't need me,' Ivy said in an insulted tone.

'Rubbish,' Fanny said. 'Wait and see how you feel.'

How Ivy felt was clear to see. She looked devastated; her rosy face pale, her mouth trembling. Her hands shook too much to fasten her seat belt. 'There,' Fanny said, tugging at it across her stout body. 'Straight home, I think, don't you?'

She held her friend's hand for a moment. Ivy attempted a smile. 'You think about it,' she said. 'But all the thinking in the world doesn't prepare you. He couldn't feel me holding his hand. Though he knew I was there, he could see me. His eyes looked so angry.'

She spluttered hysterical laughter. 'Sorry,' she said, 'did I spray you? Nothing to hope for, the doctor said. He could go any time. Tomorrow, next week, six months, no one knows. Not much to live for, I suppose, poor old man. But it's a shock when it comes.'

Ivy was quiet after that; a few low, moaning sighs which Fanny interpreted as protests against her style of driving rather than signs of distress. 'Training to be a rally driver, are we?' she grumbled when Fanny jerked on the brakes outside her tower block. But then she said, 'You know, Stevie would have liked a car. We did look into getting one with the money from the compensation after the accident, it could have been adapted so he could drive it, but we left it too long, it seemed such a big item, and there was the worry of where to keep it so it wouldn't be vandalised. Then, of course, he lost interest in cars and in just about everything, gave up altogether.'

She heaved herself to her feet. 'D'you want to come in? The lifts were working when I left.'

When the tower blocks had been built in the Sixties, they had won plaudits and prizes. The fact that the responsible architects preferred to live in the same kind of Georgian houses that had been flattened to make way for them was not thought to be ominous. Who would choose five floors and an outside lavatory in a run-down terrace or square when they could have a carefully planned apartment with a modern kitchen? A few of the tenants who moved into the blocks regretted the neighbourliness of the little streets but more remembered the dirt and the inconvenience, the lack of a bathroom.

Now they found themselves in a cold, concrete prison; a wasteland of car parks and windy walkways. The young trees hopefully planted in the few open spaces had died from lack of sun and water, and the struggling, yellow grass stank of cats. The reinforced concrete had weathered to a dirty grey, stained with damp, most of the outside lighting was broken; the lifts, the chilly stone stairways and empty landings were playgrounds for young thieves and muggers and fear of these dangerous children kept the old and the frail indoors at night.

Beleaguered but warm, Fanny thought. Entering Ivy's apartment was like walking into a furnace. 'Can't do much about it,' Ivy said. 'Though I was glad of the fug for Stevie's sake, he didn't complain all that much, bless him, but he was a martyr to the cold. Oh, my poor Stevie!'

She plumped herself down in her husband's special chair

(supplied by the social services, high from the floor, with a lifting mechanism in the seat) and began to sob noisily.

Fanny went into the kitchen to make tea. Whisky would be a better medicine, and in fact she had a quarter bottle in her handbag. She would not drink herself, since she was driving, but a slug in her tea would do Ivy good. For her own taste, neat whisky would do better, but Ivy would consider tea the correct tipple in the circumstances. She was amused at the way Ivy appeared to have elevated Stevie Trench to the ranks of the angels after vilifying him all these years but she wasn't surprised; emotional turmoil had strange effects sometimes. She did wonder, however, how Ivy would react if the old man were restored to her. People did make amazing recoveries, hospitals were not all that keen to have their precious beds occupied by untreatable geriatrics, it was not unthinkable that he might be discharged, dumped home without warning.

Perhaps *she* should warn Ivy. It might stop her moaning, Fanny thought, with a sudden lift of the spirits that she recognised as spite. Though why should she feel spiteful towards Ivy?

She stood at the window from which an astonishing breadth of sky was visible; the delicate spires of Wren churches, even the tall towers of the City looked tiny beneath the huge sweep of space which altered from second to second. In the time it took for the kettle to boil, grey, billowing clouds, suddenly appearing on the eastern horizon and sailing stormily towards the calm blue of the centre, overtaking it, swallowing it whole like some great, flying whale, were already threatening the paler clouds, edged with gold and red, in the west. And, while she watched the sky change, a heron flapped slowly beneath her, thin legs trailing.

She made the tea, carried it to the living room, set it down on the table by Stevie's chair. She said, 'Something to be said for living on top of a tower block. So much wonderful weather, clouds fairly belting along. And I saw a heron.'

'Oh, you often do, there is a heronry on Wanstead Flats, they go backwards and forwards to Regent's Park,' Ivy felt for the handkerchief tucked into the waistband of her skirt and blew her nose like a trumpet player cleaning the spit from his instrument. 'You wouldn't call the weather wonderful if you lived here. They don't think, do they? Lovely view – but you open a window and the wind rips it out of its frame. Unless it's dead calm, you have to choose between the heat and a hurricane. Stevie liked the birds, though.'

Fanny said, 'What will you do if they send him back, Ivy?'

'They won't do that,' Ivy said, giving her nose a final, vigorous polish. 'The doctor said he's beyond me now. Lifting and feeding as well as the other business.'

'A nurse could always come in to give him an enema and a bed bath. I believe the community care is not bad in this area. Delia says so, anyway.'

'Since when have you started paying attention to Delia?'

'I suppose she could be right sometimes,' Fanny said slowly, trying to sound like a careful and honest woman, giving credit where credit was due and proper consideration to what she was saying. 'And Stevie might well be happier in his own home with familiar things round him. His own bed.' What else was it credible to suggest could make that sour cripple 'happy'? Photographs of his family? Hardly. According to Ivy's previous accounts it was years since he had been even approximately civil to any of them. 'His own bed,' Fanny emphasised. 'And the birds, as you say.'

126

'Why are you sticking up for him all of a sudden?' Ivy was looking both suspicious and fearful.

'Sticking up for him?' Fanny spoke in an incredulous voice, as if she were uncertain what these words meant. 'Sticking *up* for him? I don't know, Ivy, I thought I was trying to look at the situation from your point of view.'

'You know my point of view very well,' Ivy said crossly. 'I've had hell on earth from him these last years. Which doesn't mean I'm not sorry he's come to this at the end and find myself thinking of times when he was different.'

'I'm sorry,' Fanny said. 'But you sound like yourself again. I was afraid you were going to work yourself into such a state that you would offer yourself up as a sacrifice. Beg to be allowed to have him home, something like that.'

Fanny was pleased to discover that her attempt to stir Ivy up had sprung from such an acceptable motive. She was aware that her impulse had not been particularly admirable to begin with. On the other hand, since she had expressed it so easily, without thinking, a genuine concern must have been at the back of her mind all the time.

'You don't really think they'd send him home?' Ivy asked.

'God knows. Or, if He does, I know that I don't! All I'm sure of is that you have to know what you want, what you're prepared to take on, because if he does last, beyond the end of the week, say, they'll be looking for what's possible, what's expedient. Whatever the doctor may say to you, what it comes down to, when they've done all they can for him, is a question of finding somewhere they can send him that isn't an acute bed in a big teaching hospital. There are long waiting lists for old people's nursing homes. So if you seem willing they'll jump at you!'

'I couldn't do it,' Ivy wailed. 'Really I couldn't. I can't think it will come to it. You haven't seen him, Fanny! He can't move, he can't speak . . .'

She was trembling. Fanny took the bottle of whisky out of her handbag and poured a little into Ivy's cup. And, after a slight hesitation, she added rather more to her own milkless tea. Ivy said, 'I was ashamed of myself, I suppose. I was sitting there, by his bed, thinking. I can get out of this place now he's going to die, get out of the flats. I can go and live with Rosie, in Bow. She suggested it, Saturday night, she said, Mum, I've never said it before and perhaps it's too soon. But we've talked about it, Graham and I, and decided that when the time came, we'd like you to come to us. Of course I'd never consider it if they didn't have room, but they've got that house that belonged to his parents and there's a flat, one big room and a kitchen and bathroom on the ground floor that they used to rent out until it came vacant this summer when the people went off to Australia. It's stood empty since and I've wondered why, but you don't like to interfere, do you? And it turns out they'd seen this coming, seen Stevie fail and go down, and been thinking of me.'

Ivy's tea-coloured eyes were wet. 'It's so good of them, Fanny. It chokes me up, really.'

Fanny's heart ached for her. She said, 'Is that what you would really like, Ivy? To live with your children?'

'I shan't be with them, exactly.'

'Well, no. But in the same house . . .'

'I don't have much choice, do I? I don't mean I want one, just that I haven't. Either here or there, and there looks a lot better to me.' Ivy looked at Fanny with a sudden, sly hint of malice. 'Don't worry. I'd still come to you. There's a bus. Takes a bit of time but it's almost door to door and no changing.'

'I wasn't thinking of myself, I was thinking of you,' Fanny said, hurt. 'I can see it would be lovely for you to be near Rosie. But there could be other ways. You could get another flat through the council. An exchange. Or a little house. You could be independent.'

She waited. She felt a delicious, quivering excitement at the prospect of Ivy's astonished pleasure. She had told Harry she would wait, but the propitious moment had come and it would be foolish to let it slip by. Emrys Jones hoped to finish the roof extension by February; the house could be on the market by March. Time for Ivy to make her plans comfortably. To recover from the shock of bereavement. It wasn't callous to take Stevie's death into account since Ivy was already preparing to look to her future without him.

'Oh, I wouldn't want to live alone,' Ivy said. 'Funny you should mention it, though. It's one of the things Graham suggested. He's had his eye on a couple of houses in the next street, just been waiting for the prices to come down a bit. They need doing up, but that's easy for him, being in the building trade, and property's still the best investment, especially with me being a dependent relative giving him tax relief on the mortgage. And he could get the house back if he wanted to sell, I wouldn't stand in his way, but neither of us mentioned that side of it, naturally. He said, he and Rosie would rather I was in the flat, nice for them and for the kids to have Granny so near, but it was up to me. If I wanted my own front door, I just had to say. I said no, of course.'

'But it sounds a marvellous idea.' Fanny spoke with more enthusiasm than she felt. It seemed mortifying to admit, even to herself, that she felt cheated. Though was it unreasonable, if you had intended to give someone an unexpected and generous present, to resent being pipped at the post. Perhaps what seemed to be wrong about the way she was feeling was that she feared it included an element of class-conscious pique. Lady Bountiful, affronted to find that the peasantry could buy their own houses. She said, 'Why say no, Ivy? An investment for them, your own home for you. Is it that you don't want to feel in their debt?'

'They would have offered before, I think. Only it was in Graham's mind that he didn't want Stevie living round the next corner so that Rosie would feel she ought to be popping in all the time, helping me out with her father. Graham's protective of Rosie. He's a bit like your Daniel used to be in that way. But I might have said yes if they'd suggested it then. Now it's different. I don't want to live alone. I've seen you try that, turning inwards with no one else to give heed to. I know Becky's not much to write home about but you're more your own self now she's there. Though you're the sort needs a man really.'

Fanny laughed. 'I didn't know I was so feeble.'

'That's not what I meant,' Ivy said. 'Of course you can *manage*. But you know what you are.'

She sounded fretful. Gazing through the window at the vast expanse of sky, she seemed too weary to elaborate further and Fanny, though mildly intrigued, did not press her.

She said, 'I think you should rest, Ivy. Take your clothes off, relax properly, on the bed. I'll stay with you if you'd like me to. Answer the telephone. Take you to see Stevie later. Whatever you want. Anything.'

Ivy shook her head. 'There's nothing, dear, really. It would only be a worry, you hanging about with me too tired to be company. And Rosie will come this afternoon and take me to see poor Stevie again. Not that there's much point, but you never know, do you?'

Fanny felt a sudden, strange desperation. There must be something she could do, surely? She could see that Ivy was perplexed, sensing her need, though not understanding, of course, the true cause of it. Fanny smiled at this thought and said, 'Well, all right, then. As long as you know I'm just at the other end of the telephone.'

Ivy was frowning. Casting around for a suitable errand? 'I suppose I could do with something to read. I mean, if you've got the time, and you're passing the library, you could change my books for me. You know the sort of thing I like, dear.'

It was comic really, Fanny thought. To get one's come-uppance so neatly. She should have told Ivy about her intention before; at least she would have had that little pleasure. But was giving so selfish? Had that really been all she wanted, thanks and praise? Had she wanted to bind Ivy to her? Or worse. Perhaps she had never meant to buy Ivy a house in the end. Perhaps it had just been an idea to be played with? To torment her children? No, that was not true. When it first came to her it had simply seemed the right thing, the just thing to do.

Now she felt forlorn; bereft and rejected. And furious. She growled angrily, through clenched teeth, accelerated through a yellow light as it turned red, and swerved across the oncoming traffic on the main road to park her car in a small street at the side of the public library.

Ivy's taste was for detective stories and thrillers that were not too bloodily violent; Emma Lathen rather than Micky Spillane. Fanny collected a Julian Symons and a Ruth Rendell, both of which she knew she would enjoy herself, and a collection of

Famous Murder Trials. She hesitated over *The Princess Casamassima* before deciding to take it; even if Ivy found it a little long-winded the marvellously convincing plot about terrorists should appeal to her. As long as she didn't think that by producing a novel that was obviously 'literary' as opposed to a 'good read', Fanny was trying to make a snide comment, put her down in some mysterious way.

'Rubbish', Fanny said. Her voice sounded loud to herself but when she looked round, abashed, no one else appeared to have heard it. There was only one other woman in sight, semi-crippled, with swollen legs and feet in pink and white running shoes, shuffling along on a walking frame and peering at the shelves, and a few elderly men snoozing comfortably at the tables at the end of the stacks. Perhaps Fanny had disturbed one of them; a man wearing a stained and ancient overcoat with a greasy fur collar and a black cloth beret on his long, curling, grey hair, woke up briefly, with a startled snort.

When Fanny had been young, living in an East London suburb, the sacred hush of the public library (reverently guarded by a tiny female dragon in pebble glasses) had been for the benefit of students in the reference section. If this library had a reference section Fanny had not found it, and in general it seemed a poor place to her, overstocked with badly bound paperbacks and pamphlets extolling the social services provided by the local council, and short of what she thought of as 'proper' books in hard covers, as well as any indication, such as a subject index, that the occasional visitor might be after something other than a threadbare copy of a Henry James novel or a warm place to rest for a while. Delia would say that the library was there to serve the community, as if that was an answer. And Harry – no doubt speaking in the indulgent tone he had begun to use to her lately – would tell her that old people were always complaining that things had got worse. Well, of course, you would have to be fairly old to make that particular complaint, Fanny thought; old enough, anyway, to remember when things had been better.

Thinking of making this response to Harry at the next opportunity restored her good temper. She picked up *The Franchise Affair* because she knew Ivy had enjoyed it when it had been on television, and decided to abandon *Famous Murder Trials* which was a library book of the kind Fanny remembered from her girlhood, printed on good, thick paper and so stoutly bound that it would be wearisome for Ivy to hold if she were tired. An old-fashioned library user, Fanny wondered where the book belonged. She had found it in CRIME FICTION but assumed it had simply been discarded there by someone else who had found it too heavy in the hand. Even if there was no subject index there must be some order in this library; hadn't she seen a shelf marked LAW somewhere?

Turning round the end of the stack she came upon Jake so suddenly that she almost tripped over him. He was crouching down on his haunches, his head on one side, peering at titles. She said, 'Oh, I do beg your pardon,' and clutched wildly at the nearest shelf, dropping two of the books she was holding.

He jumped up, held her elbow briefly, to steady her, then stooped to pick up the books. 'I'm so sorry,' she said, feeling suddenly clumsy and old – since everyone else in the library had seemed practically moribund, she had felt comparatively young until now – and more mortified than she would have been if she had stumbled over a stranger. Just vanity, of course, she told herself, pushing back her hair and smiling deliberately, lifting the slack muscles round her mouth to make herself younger.

She thought he hadn't recognised her to begin with. When he stood up, holding her books, he looked at her properly for the first time and blushed furiously, the colour throbbing beneath his pale skin, his blue eyes very bright. He said, 'Oh, it's you,' and looked nervously around as if he were seeking a way to escape.

Harry was lunching with Ella Carberry. He had had a drink with her in the BBC club bar the week before, when she had come to pick Felix up to go to the theatre; Felix had been late, caught up in a meeting, and Harry had seen her waiting at the door of the bar, signed her in and bought her a drink. He had told her a funny work story; he couldn't remember afterwards what it was, only that she had laughed at it rather louder and longer than he thought it warranted. And then a couple of days later she had rung him at the office and asked him to lunch. It wasn't a straight invitation. That could have been side-stepped or, at least, postponed for a long enough interval for him to find out from Felix in a roundabout way what it might be about. But the way she put it – How did he feel about having lunch with her? – made it hardly the sort of question Harry felt he could easily or decently be very negative or offputting about.

It also meant that he was put in the position of having to invite her, rather than ungallantly waiting for her to invite him, and of booking, and paying for, a meal in a more expensive restaurant than she would have been likely to choose herself. Harry could not be sure this would be true in Ella's case, of course, since she had never taken him anywhere, but it was his experience that on the whole women were meaner than men in that sort of matter, and it was natural for him to argue from the general to the particular.

He could not even take her to the little Polish restaurant round the corner, just three minutes from the BBC bar, where he could have entertained her more cheaply than in Soho. Too many of his colleagues went there, Felix among them, and although Harry had nothing to hide, he wasn't sure about Ella.

Of course, he had thought – when it was too late and they were already sitting in the upstairs room of L'Escargot in Greek Street – he could have suggested they went to the Polish place and seen how she reacted. If nothing else, he might have found out whether Felix knew she was meeting him and been spared the discomfort of feeling shifty all this last week, whenever he and Felix were on their own for a minute. He hadn't told Poppy either, for reasons that were less clear in his mind. It would have been easy if he had told her immediately, or at least at the first opportunity, but they had met at a friend's house for dinner that evening with no time to talk together beforehand, and afterwards Poppy had said she was tired and had slept all the way home in the car. After that there was no point at which it did not seem faintly awkward to mention it, calling for unlikely circumlocutions, falsely casual statements. *Oh, by the way, I forgot to tell you.*

Best really to tell her after the event, he had decided, when he would know what Ella wanted to talk about. As long as it wasn't private, or something that Poppy would prefer not to know. Poppy had a normally healthy appetite for gossip but she did not care, for example, to hear about adulterous affairs among their friends. Oh, she acknowledged the facts of life, accepted that married people might fall in love but they should keep it to themselves, get over it alone, not break their promises. This was such a firm imperative for her that Harry had sometimes wondered if she were unconsciously yearning after an affair herself – there had been a time, early on in their marriage, when he had watched her flirting at parties and brooded jealously – but now he knew that there was nothing equivocal or Freudian about Poppy. She was simply being true to her upbringing and she had been brought up in what seemed to him, and would seem to most people nowadays, he thought, a quite extraordinary way.

Poppy had been the late and only child of school teachers who had lived their working lives on the same council estate as the children they taught and whose education and future they cared about deeply. By the time Harry met them they were retired but their old pupils still came to visit, brought their growing families to see them, and it did not occur to them to move away because 'their children' might still need them. They managed, on a small income, to live generously and cheerfully; they were always ready to listen, to give advice if it was asked for, but they never offered it, unasked, or judged unkindly. They were loving and helpful to their many friends and they always took great trouble with the young.

They were not religious; their moral discipline seemed innate, a natural grace, a gift bestowed by some good fairy in their cradles. To their minds, it was a form of good manners, Poppy had said once, endeavouring to explain to Harry, putting it in terms that he might understand.

It had seemed to him that his parents-in-law pretended things were simpler than they were. They had never had to face the sort of complications he met every day. Not necessarily in his own life but in the lives of his friends and acquaintances, in the lives of the men and women he and Felix were responsible for in their department. 'Your mother and father were lucky to have secure jobs and a happy marriage,' he had answered Poppy sternly, knowing it was not the answer, that they had made their lives secure and happy because they had chosen to abide by the kind of rules that most people found too hard to keep.

Harry had missed them when they died, Poppy's mother of a sudden viral pneumonia and her father several months later of what was clearly grief, but while they were alive he had envied them, and resented them a little. They had made it seem so easy to be good and occasionally, lying awake at night and listening to Poppy's soft and regular breathing, he thought that *she* had been lucky too, brought up by two people who had made life so simple for her that she assumed it must be simple for everyone. Not that he wanted her to lie awake, unhappy and tormented. He was delighted that she always slept so sweetly.

Now, looking across the table at Ella, smoking a cigar and drinking the double gin and tonic she had demanded the moment she walked in, Harry felt an agreeable surge of indignation. A bit smug of Poppy, wasn't it, to expect to be spared the harsher realities? What if Ella did drink too much? Or have a lover? Half a dozen lovers. No doubt Felix led her a wretched life. But Poppy did not care to hear about that sort of thing! About the way ordinary folk managed to cope with their miserable existences! Poppy had such tender sensibilities. Fine for her, fine and dandy, but what did it mean in practice? That people like poor Ella had to cope with all the grubby bits alone? What about her sensibilities? Or his, for that matter?

Harry thought, what hypocritical nonsense! He grinned, to himself, and at Ella. He said, 'Shall we order, get that out of the way? Then we can settle down and be comfortable.'

He had already looked at the menu. He assumed Ella had been given one without prices. Still, she and Felix probably ate out a lot, more than he and Poppy did, anyway, so she would know which were the dishes that no ordinary wage slave could be expected to pay for without taking out a bank loan. He was not really hungry himself. He had suggested discussing the food because it seemed the only opening gambit he could think of. He couldn't remember the names of her children; Poppy usually briefed him on that sort of thing. And he could hardly ask if Felix was well since he had only just left him.

Ella finished her double gin. 'Oh, God, I needed that. But I won't have another unless you are going to join me. Miserable, getting sloshed on one's own.'

'Sorry,' Harry said. 'It's having to work in the afternoon.' Though true, this sounded priggish. He went on, enthusiastically, 'I was really waiting for the wine. I can order as soon as we've decided what to eat.'

'You decide for us both,' Ella said. 'Something light. I'm not really hungry. Nothing to start with.'

Perversely, Harry felt disappointed. He had begun to suspect that a browse. through the menu might sharpen his appetite. And, after all, he could put the bill on Diner's Club instead of writing a cheque. Although if he did that, he would have to tell Poppy that he had been lunching with Ella when he went home this evening. Couldn't put it off any longer. Poppy dealt with their finances, paid the bills, paid the mortgage, filed the bank statements. It was part of being a serious wife which was the role she had cheerfully adopted within weeks of finding out that she was pregnant with twins. No point in their exhausting themselves as a couple trying to run two careers and two babies, she had argued. Harry's job paid better than hers and for the most part he enjoyed it more. Poppy had gone into teaching to please her mother and father – well, not to please them exactly, more because she had assumed she would come to feel, as they did, that next to composing great music or writing great literature or making great scientific advances it was the most worthwhile job in the world. Instead, she had simply discovered that she wasn't much good at it, or had thought she wasn't, anyway, which had more or less the same effect when it came to measuring enjoyment. It turned out that she didn't really care for children, or not in the way she had imagined she would when she had been a lonely little girl longing for a younger brother or sister. Her children, hers and Harry's, would be different, of course. Nothing like the monsters she had tried to teach English Literature to! Her own children would want to learn from her. And they would benefit from having one parent reliably at home to provide comfort, food, and a listening ear.

It was true, Harry thought, that his daughters were turning out well. They were composed, well-mannered, self-assured children. And it was undeniably pleasant to compare his comfortable domestic circumstances with those of his colleagues who arrived at work in crumpled shirts and odd socks, haggard with taking their full share of family responsibilities. On the other hand, ironed shirts and paired socks could be achieved by paying for domestic help and money would still be left over out of a professional income, even out of a teacher's pay, for things like an extra holiday or a small second car, which a BBC salary didn't quite run to. And there were times, driving home in the fog in the winter, or sitting through a particularly boring departmental meeting, when it seemed to him that Poppy had chosen the soft option: now the girls were old enough to get themselves backwards and forwards from school she was free as a bird for much of the day. There was housework, of course, cooking and shopping, but Harry drove her to the supermarket once a week and usually made the coffee after dinner and helped stack the dishwasher.

Certainly Poppy had an easier time than Isabel, or than Ella who had a bigger house to run and a small business to occupy her. The business was something to do with designing interiors; not houses, Harry thought, something more unexpected like showrooms, or could it be department store windows? Although it would have provided a conversational topic he could hardly ask her because presumably he had been told at some point or other and either had not listened to the answer or simply forgotten.

He said, 'What about the Dover sole? Potatoes. A green salad. Then see what we feel like after that?'

Dover sole was always expensive but since it was being left to him to decide it seemed vulgar to let himself be guided by cost. Besides he liked Dover sole himself very much indeed. When was the last time he'd had it? At the Roma, probably, lunching or dining with Fanny.

Ella said, 'How is your mother, Harry? I used to get fairly regular bulletins from Felix but now the excitement's died down, I don't hear so often. Has she got over it all? Being mugged, and the fire?'

Fanny's health and the progress of the building work at Sickert Terrace occupied them while Harry ordered the food and the wine – a 1986 and not particularly expensive Chablis. Ella appeared to be listening to him, nodding from time to time, but a certain fixity in her wide-eyed, liquid gaze suggested that her mind was not fully engaged. Or had switched points to another track, anyway.

When the sole arrived and their glasses were filled, she squashed her cigar in the ashtray, picked up her knife and fork, and said, a little aggressively, Harry thought, 'You're damn lucky, you know. Felix's old mother is becoming quite exceptionally tedious. That's partly what I wanted to talk about.'

The cigar was still smouldering. Harry moved the ashtray to the edge of the table. He would have liked to stub it out firmly but he fancied Ella might suspect a rebuke. He said, 'Fanny's marvellous now. But we've been through it a bit these last months, you know. There were times when things looked pretty gruesome. More gruesome for her than for us, of course. Losing bits of memory must be horribly frightening. For us it was just another responsibility.'

'Oh God, all *that*!' Ella said. She sounded dismissive. She speared a chunk of sole and regarded it thoughtfully. She added a slice of potato to the fork and raised it to her mouth. Then looked at Harry. 'At least you know what I'm talking about on that score. But it's only part of it, as I said. I mean, I can cope with her all right, if I have to, though why I bloody should when Felix wouldn't have my mama stay in the house overnight when she lost her marbles, I simply don't know. Mind you, he had some reason, the poor old thing was terrified of being incontinent and the Home said she was always wandering about looking for the loo and of course they had a proper night staff to cope with that sort of thing which we hadn't, but that's not quite the point is it? Or not altogether. Felix just didn't want to be lumbered. He doesn't want to be lumbered with his own mother, come to that. He just can't see any way round it if he's to get his mitts on the money.'

She put the fish and potato into her mouth and swallowed it without chewing and washed it down with several lusty gulps of Chablis. She pushed her glass towards Harry and he refilled it.

She said, 'We don't need it. Not income, anyway. I mean, you know what he gets, and I make rather more. It's capital Felix is after. He's been watching it wasting away in that huge, leasehold flat for a long time. Now she's really three sheets in the wind, it'll have to be sold and he can't bear the prospect of seeing a solid lump of cash waste away in nursing home fees. Well, you know they're enormous and going up all the time. We won't get as much for the place as we would have last summer when she turned down a simply vast offer from the Arabs upstairs and although there's a chance they're still interested, I'd guess they would expect to get it a hell of a lot cheaper now. It must be obvious to them that she can't go on living there on her own, they've found her several times wandering in the street and taken her home and rung Felix or me. They've been very good to her actually, the woman is especially nice, it was she who told us the really tiresome bit. Told me, rather, because I think she'd have been too embarrassed to explain it to Felix.'

While she was talking Ella had been pushing her sole round her plate and mashing potato into the wine and cream sauce. Now, although she paused, it was to drink, not to eat. She looked at Harry over her glass, and laughed sharply, as if she felt some embarrassment herself. 'It seems that Felix's mother has taken to propositioning just about every man she comes across. Not just verbally, either. She *touches* them. Makes a grab at their bottoms or penises. Or fondles their knees. She catches a bus to the park most days at just about the same time and it was the conductor who told the woman upstairs. They'd got on at the same stop, apparently, and he saw them together and managed to get across to this Arab lady, who doesn't speak all that much English, that he was having a bit of a problem with her friend who was one of his regulars. He didn't know what to do. What could he do, after all? Throw her off the bus? Call the police? I mean, she's well on in her seventies and weighs about as much as a leaf! I wonder how he did deal with it? How often had it happened? He didn't say, or if he did the lady upstairs didn't pass it on! Oh God. It would be funny if it wasn't so bloody awful.'

'Does she realise what she's doing?' Harry asked. He had almost finished his sole and was still feeling hungry. He wondered if Ella would be offended if he offered to finish what she was obviously going to leave on her plate. He also wondered why she was telling him this unhappy tale. He had no experience of senile behaviour, no advice to offer. He guessed that Felix probably felt more distraught about it than Ella. He knew how he would feel in Felix's place. The thought made him shudder.

Ella said, 'Oh, she's always been keen on men. Though not on Felix's father, so Felix suspects. Since she's been widowed she's had quite a number of gentlemen friends. Went off on holiday cruises designed for the old folk and usually brought one male old folk back with her. That sort of thing. Nice blokes on the whole, though none of them *took*, so to speak. A couple died, the others just drifted away. Or got older. Then I suppose she got older too, and the men got harder to get and she – well, I don't know how it started exactly. What happened was that she suddenly always seemed to be boasting about how attractive some man or other had found her, or had told her she was, and that just seemed a bit sad. But then it got worse because she began to imagine they were actually *after* her, either crossed in love, or wanting to rape her. Anyone. The milkman, the window cleaner, her hairdresser, her chiropodist. And you can't just ignore what she says altogether. Old women do get raped after all.'

She made an expansive gesture with her wine glass but there was not enough left in it to spill. Harry filled it again and poured the last drops into his own glass. He caught the waiter's eye and ordered coffee and double brandies. He said, 'What does her doctor say?'

'That it's nothing unusual though it's more often old men who get randy. Just that she needs looking after. He could put her on tranquillisers but he's not keen to do that. Or not yet.' She pushed her plate away with a sigh. 'I'm sorry I couldn't manage it all. I'm not that keen on finny fish, actually, they don't really agree with me. I'm better on shellfish. Funny, that. It's usually the other way round, isn't it?'

'If I'd known, I'd have ordered lobster,' Harry said. He was both relieved that he hadn't known, lobster being roughly twice the price of the sole, and angry with her for not telling him. He said, insincerely, 'I wish there was something I could do beside saying I'm sorry.'

'Talk to Felix,' she said, speaking with a sudden brisk competence that reminded him of Isabel. Cutting the cackle.

'About his *mother*?'

Ella grinned at him, not very pleasantly. One of her large front teeth was very obviously crowned; the image that sprang to Harry's mind was of a sparkling new marble tombstone in a very old churchyard. She said, 'Why look so horrified? Though as a matter of fact that's not it. Felix has won that round, and, to be honest I wasn't altogether unwilling to lose it. She's got cataracts, and funny little ways with the gentlemen, but the old girl is still *human*, not vegetable. She likes to get out and about. I couldn't bear to shove her in one of those waiting rooms for

144

death as we did with my mother. What we've locked our horns over is where we're to live *with* her! It's the old story. Felix wants to move to the country. Well, we both did, at one point.'

'There was that oast house in Kent.' Harry was pleased with himself for remembering.

'That fell through. Now what he's found is a converted stable block in Surrey. Very nice too, I thought to begin with. I could work from home some of the time and there'd be enough money left over from selling this house for a small flat in town. But not, repeat not, if Mother comes too. I can see it might suit Felix okay, wifey and batty nymphomaniac granny tucked away out of sight and of mind but not me! He says we could get a woman to live in, his theory being that some country-loving old biddy would be so thrilled to be offered a loose box to live in that she would put up with a minuscule salary. My God, we'd need to be lucky! Guess who'd be stuck in the sticks with Felix's Mummy? Not Felix!'

Harry said, 'And it wouldn't be so difficult to get help in Clapham. Felix must see that. It looks like a straight swap to me. You take the main burden of looking after his mother, you decide where to live!'

'Just tell that to Felix,' Ella said. 'Oh my God, Harry, you must know what he's like. He has to *win*. Not just the war, but every single battle. His mind sets like *concrete*.'

She lit one of her small cigars, coughed over it, and then stubbed it out. She pulled a face. She said, 'Dirty habit.'

Harry thought she looked older than when he'd last seen her. That was only about ten days ago, in the BBC bar; she could hardly have aged very much in that time. But her face seemed thinner to him, all the same, and the skin under her eyes looked fragile and sore.

Harry said, apologetically, 'What do you think I could say to Felix? I mean, I'm willing to try. Though there's a chance I might make things worse. Does he know you're having lunch with me, for example?'

She said wearily, 'No, he doesn't. Not that it matters. I don't know what I thought you might be able to say or do, anyway. I suppose I hoped you might think of something. You work with him, I know he trusts your judgement, he's often said so. He quotes you sometimes.' She smiled. 'Though that's usually about politics, and not because he thinks you might be right to vote Labour, but because of your aunt. He's impressed by titles, though he'd hate you to know it.'

Harry said, 'I suppose I could say, if the subject came up, that it might be a bit silly at this stage in his career to bury himself in the country.'

Though it wasn't himself Felix was planning to bury, of course. The converted stable in Surrey for weekends, perhaps, but a discreet pad in London for the working week was what he was after. He was probably already planning the rota. Already pencilling in young Caroline, Harry thought, remembering Felix coming into his office a few days ago and stopping by the desk of this pretty and pleasant girl, to bestow upon her his special, bright look of awakening interest, making her simper uneasily, though she wasn't the sort of girl to simper in the ordinary way, much too sensible. Harry wished he had the courage to warn her. But if he did she would be unlikely to thank him.

He said, 'You could try that tack too, couldn't you?' feeling sorry for Ella, smiling at her, wondering if he should put out his hand and touch hers, just a friendly pat, to show sympathy. But she was swallowing her brandy, picking up her bag, opening it to put her cigars away, taking out a frayed and crumpled tissue to dab at her nose. She snapped the bag shut and beamed at him, shedding years.

She said, 'Darling Harry, you are an angel to put up with me. Thank you for lunch, and above all for listening to me maundering on, that's more help than anything. The way Felix argues always muddles me up. I always end feeling I must be in the wrong about everything and yet I know that I'm not. Telling you helped me get things straight. You thought Felix was being bloody unfair, didn't you?'

Harry made a deprecatory sound in the back of his throat, half laugh, half groan. He knew what she meant about Felix's way of conducting an argument because he had been bewildered by it himself – was still bewildered sometimes, though less than he used to be before he had realised how it was done. Felix's trick was to start from a false premise and build upon it a delicate and convoluted edifice in which each step apart from the first was obviously and entirely rational. This verbal sleight of hand was performed so quickly and gracefully, Felix's smiling dark eyes expressing nothing but good will towards his opponents, his *victims*, that they were trapped in a web of confusion, forced to concede defeat. What could the false premise be in this case? Perhaps that the decision to move to the country was, as politicians said, paramount, although Harry suspected that it could be subtler, and nastier: Felix might be a dirtier fighter as a husband than as a head of department.

Ella said, 'It's okay, pet, no need to commit yourself. Harry is a *judicious* chap, is what Felix says. I look after his mother, I choose where to live, that's what you said, isn't it? I hope a judge might take the same view. A good wife, living in the matrimonial home and taking care of her husband's elderly mother is entitled to stay put if she wants to. So no chance of Felix selling the house over my head if it came to what estate agents call a divorce situation.'

She leaned across the table for Harry's hand which anxiety had momentarily clenched round his brandy glass, and stroked the back of it gently. 'Don't worry, I'm just checking the soundness of my fall-back position! Not actually planning to go off and leave the old bugger.'

'Thank God for that,' Harry said heartily, so relieved that he squeezed her fingers enthusiastically and looked intently into her face. Her eyes softened and filled and he felt something more was required. 'Felix doesn't know how lucky he is.'

'Oh, come *on*,' she said fondly. 'Don't start pretending. You've never fancied me.'

It seemed churlish to agree with her. He said, 'How do you know? I *like* you very much, as it happens. But it wasn't what I was thinking about. It was the way you, well, take things on.'

'Like Felix?'

'Heavens no! Of course not.'

She laughed outright. 'Oh, *Harry*!'

He said, quickly, 'Oh Lord, you know what I mean. Your family, your job, and now Felix's mother! I really admire you for that.'

'Poppy would do just the same, I'm quite sure,' Ella said, withdrawing her hand and frowning a little. 'Though with luck, she won't have to.'

Fanny was accustomed to shy young men. She had learned not to show too much direct personal interest in them to begin with, but to talk away soothingly, like an aunt, perhaps, or a much older sister with her own affairs to consider, and then

148

draw them in gently with a question that could be easily answered or a relaxed moment of silence they might feel able to fill. She had always found the embassy gardens especially useful. Fanny had never gardened herself and could never remember the names of the plants but that was useful, too: most of the young men she had walked round after afternoon tea or before drinks on a summer evening had known more than she did and even those who knew nothing had been amused and encouraged to find that their hostess was as ignorant as they were and not ashamed to admit it.

A neglected inner city library did not provide quite the same atmosphere but Fanny did her best. She spoke in a soft, breathy tone, out of respect for libraries in general rather than for this particular one, and also because she thought that this shy young man – who was not, after all, a fledgling diplomat who would automatically be aware that English ladies were supposed to be knowledgeable about gardens – might not be so nervous of her if she were to sound mildly potty.

She explained that she was getting books for a friend whose husband had been taken to hospital. Her friend liked crime stories, so that wasn't too difficult in a way, but she didn't care for the sort of violence that American books were so full of nowadays. Fanny liked the same kind of crime novels, but she had lived abroad for so long, and although she had been back in England for quite a while now, almost five years – goodness, could it really have been as long as that? How time flies – she hadn't really had time to catch up on all the new books and new authors. Because even though they had had English books sent out to them it wasn't the same as browsing through the shelves of a library. Not that this library was all that wonderful. She had been trying to find the shelf that this book belonged on so she could put it back in its right place. It looked quite a nice book, if you could call *Famous Murder Trials* 'nice', but she thought that her friend, who was feeling so tired, worn out with the daily journey to hospital, might find it too heavy to hold.

By this time Fanny began to feel she might be overdoing it. 'A nice book' indeed! But Jake was listening to her with a politely attentive expression, a little uncertain, perhaps, not quite sure what response was expected, but not puzzled. She smiled at him. 'I'm sorry,' she said, 'old women do run on, don't they? And I interrupted you when you were looking for a book. Perhaps I can help? I must have looked along most of the shelves. What are you looking for?'

He didn't answer and she wondered if she had been too direct. Not inconsequential enough. 'Never mind, even if I'd seen what you wanted, I don't suppose I'd remember,' she said.

'It was just a law book,' he said. 'A book about the law.'

His eyes were such a pure, pale, glassy blue, Fanny wondered if he were wearing coloured contact lenses. She was wearing bifocals herself, with reading lenses in the bottom half and plain glass in the top. She pushed them up the bridge of her nose and tilted her head back to get a good look at him, at the clear, brilliant eyes, the satiny skin with no sign of a beard breaking through, the sweet, glossy curve of the mouth. Very pretty, very young, she thought, removing her ugly and ageing spectacles and tucking them into her pocket.

She said, 'What aspect of law? What is it you want to know?' Something about the position of the boaters on the canal, probably. She couldn't remember whether the planning committee had given their verdict yet. Dora Partridge had tried to tell her something about it the other day, catching Fanny on the doorstep, but Fanny had been on her way to the National Film Theatre and in too much of a hurry to pay proper attention. She thought now that it may have been something about the planning meeting being cancelled. Or adjourned. What layman's book on the law would be useful? Something on vagrancy? Until official moorings were established the boats were illegally parked. Water gypsies.

Jake said, 'Just on the law. Something sort of general.'

'It's a large topic,' Fanny said, smiling.

For about half a minute he stood, looking down at her, watching her cautiously. Then he jerked his chin and said, speaking in a quick, determined way, 'It's just, there's this friend of mine in a bit of trouble. Something he did that he didn't mean to do that went wrong. He's scared he'll get done for it, though it was a good while ago now, but another friend said there's a time limit. I mean, they can't do you if it was too long a while back.'

'It's called the Statute of Limitations, I think,' Fanny said. 'I'm not sure how many years it is before your friend would be safe from prosecution. Or if there is a different period for different kinds of offences. But you're right, there should be a book you could look it up in.'

Not, perhaps, in this library. Unless the local Council, who were so strongly opposed to the Metropolitan Police that they had refused to allow constables into the primary schools to instruct the children on road safety, had put out a pamphlet to advise the neighbourhood criminals. What might it be called? YOUR RIGHTS IN AND OUT OF PRISON. And why shouldn't there be such a pamphlet, Fanny thought. If Isabel and Max were correct in their view of this area of London, thieves and other criminals made up a fair proportion of the population. And since, excluding their unsociable occupation, a good many of them would be ordinary citizens with ordinary needs, schools, hospitals, libraries, who even – though this might be less certain – paid taxes, why should they not have their special needs taken care of? If they were gay, or single parents, or an ethnic minority, those needs would be recognised by what Delia would call the community. She must remember to put this point of view to her sister next time she saw her, Fanny thought, hoping she would remember it long enough to write a reminder in the back of her diary. A coded reminder, in case Delia should decide to go snooping.

Jake said, 'What's so funny, eh?'

'Nothing,' Fanny said. 'Or just a silly thought.'

'You were grinning away.' He was smiling himself. 'I think I'll pack it in for today. Give me them books, I'll give you a hand to the counter.'

He waited companionably beside her while the books were stamped, shaking his head when the librarian turned to him enquiringly. 'Got enough to read with the Want Ads in the paper,' he confided to Fanny, still carrying her books, pushing open the heavy glass door to the street and standing aside for her.

'Looking for a job?' she asked, thinking that even given the latest horrendous unemployment statistics he shouldn't find it too difficult; he seemed intelligent, he spoke well enough, he was a pleasure to look at.

'Why not? Might as well give it a try,' he said, sounding cocky, but it was probably a defence, Fanny thought. She was grateful that all her grandchildren were some years away from this particular hurdle. Though neither Harry nor Isabel seemed to worry about their future. Perhaps they thought unemployment, like mental illness or cancer, was something that only happened to other people.

It had been sunny earlier, a lovely, crisp day with a playful breeze rattling the last fall of leaves in the gutters, but in the short time Fanny had been in the library the aspect had changed from bright to sullen; the sky had clouded over and a bitter wind was whirling up rubbish and grit from the street. Fanny turned up her coat collar. 'What sort of thing are you looking for?'

He shrugged his shoulders. She interpreted this as a warning not to be nosy. She said, amiably, vaguely, 'Oh, I know it's a difficult business. Goodness, isn't it *cold*?'

She shivered elaborately. Jake watched her silently, hefting her books from one arm to the other. He said, 'Shall I run you home?' His eyes lit up with amusement. 'Not out of my way as you know, so no problem.'

He turned before she could answer and was at the kerb in two strides, wrenching at the rear door of an old and battered red Peugeot hatchback that was brazenly parked on a double yellow line. He off-loaded Ivy's books – treating them with respect, Fanny noted with pleasure – slammed the door shut, leapt to the passenger door, opened it, and then stood to attention, clicking his heels and smiling expectantly.

She laughed at this pantomime. She was about to explain that she had her own car parked round the corner. Instead other words came; words that seemed to tumble out before she was conscious of the thought that had formed them. Like a medium, she was to think afterwards, or someone under hypnosis, although immediately she had spoken, several seconds before Jake reacted, she knew that she alone was entirely responsible for what she had said, and that it could in no way be explained or rescinded.

She said, 'I thought you had a Vauxhall.'

Isabel answered the telephone sounding so breathlessly eager that Fanny felt almost apologetic for not being the lover her daughter was clearly expecting. Even when she announced herself, Isabel's responding voice sang with a joyful note: she was clearly too happy just at this moment to be cast down by a small disappointment.

'Mummy darling, how *are* you? How are things going? I've been meaning to get up and see how the builders are getting on – and see you, too, of course! – but there's been so much to do, nothing that *sounds* much, just that things pile up, and Gaga has not been too well.'

In spite of the turmoil she was in, Fanny felt a prick of irritation at the name with which Isabel had endowed her mother-in-law. Obviously, it had been the children's name for her when they were tiny, and Isabel had found it a convenience to adopt it, but in Fanny's view Adam and Jennifer and George were of an age now to address their grandmother in a more dignified fashion.

'What's wrong with Dolores?' Fanny asked, thinking that Dolores wasn't much of a name for anyone either, and Isabel confirmed this by laughing immoderately, almost choking over the telephone.

'Oh, don't call her that, she absolutely hates it. If you think Gaga is really too awful, why don't you use her second name? Margaret. But even *Max* calls her Gaga now, and I don't think she minds. What's wrong is some sort of gut thing. She's been to see the consultant and she's got to go into hospital tomorrow for some quite beastly tests that are going to take all day and I've promised to go with her and stay with her, she says she can manage and I'm not to bother, but I know she's terribly nervous and I think if I'm there she'll feel easier. At least she'll have someone to complain to.' She stopped short, and made a stifled sound, half giggle, half sigh.

'Then you'll be performing a vital function,' Fanny said drily, unable to resist making this point, but expecting Isabel to fall on her reproachfully and extol her mother-in-law's saintly capacity for silent endurance.

But Isabel only said, in a conspiratorial tone, 'Mummy, darling, you mustn't *encourage* me. What did you want? I mean it's lovely to have a chat, but was there anything special?'

She was aching to put the receiver down. Fanny said, 'I was just wondering if you might be free sometime tomorrow, that's all. But since you're not, it doesn't matter.'

'Sure?'

'Yes, dear. I'll ring to see how she is – how Margaret is – in the evening.'

Fanny felt winded. She sat down and leaned back in her chair. Maybe it was just as well Isabel couldn't come tomorrow; what had she imagined she could say to the girl, after all? I'm frightened I may have put myself in great danger? That was overstating it, surely? Some danger, then. But she wasn't even sure of that, was she?

She wondered if it was too early for a drink. Four o'clock. Obviously a good time to telephone Isabel, and for her to expect a call. The children rarely returned from school before five. And Dolores-Gaga-Margaret napped in the afternoon until four fifteen when she rose and prepared a pot of weak China tea in her room, of which she then drank just *two* cups with lemon and a *few* grains of sugar while she watched the children's programmes on BBC television. Fanny knew this because Max's mother assumed that the details of her daily regime were bound to be of widespread general interest, and had acquainted Fanny with them on several occasions.

Isabel had sounded so wonderfully happy. Fanny was glad for her, but afraid too; all happiness was precarious but this kind was especially fragile. And Fanny wondered if Isabel had the emotional stamina. Or the restraint. As a child she had never been able to keep a secret for long. *Do you know what that parcel is, Mummy? It's your birthday present, don't tell Harry I told you.* Red cheeks puffed out, and fat little shoulders hunched up with excitement. Bursting to tell.

But Max would take it very badly. As Daniel would have done had she ever told him there was another man. It would have been impossible to explain her need to him, how it seemed the only way she could feel in control of her life, the only way she could make something happen. There were days when she had felt she danced on puppet strings – Delia's pawn, Daniel's foot soldier, she thought fancifully. Conducting a love affair on the other hand, she had been a general, planning the campaign, exploring the possibilities, mapping the territory it was safe to move in, predicting the ambush.

'Rubbish,' she said aloud, with a snort. 'You are just an ordinary woman who got fed up with playing second fiddle.'

She got up to make tea, changed her mind when she came to the top of the basement stairs and went back into her study to open the corner cupboard and take out the bottle of whisky. The house was empty today. Emrys Jones and the two sons who were on this job with him were away for the best part of the week; they had gone to Wales for a family wedding. Except for the damp sound of the heavy duty polythene sheeting flapping on the top floor and the occasional creak of old boards expanding, contracting, there was a silence that Fanny felt to be suddenly threatening.

The pulse in her throat was thudding quite painfully. It was darkening outside. She moved her chair away from the telephone, turning it so that she could look out of the window but placing it well inside the room so that until she put the light on, she would not be visible. There were lights in the street opposite, on the other side of the towpath, in the windows, but none in the canal boats as yet. Fewer of them were occupied now winter was coming on. But Jake and his girl were still living in the *Adelaide May*.

He had stared at her. Then his colour had risen, crimson blood surging up his white throat to set his face on fire. His mouth had twisted as if he were about to scream with pain. He had snarled, 'What the fuck are you playing at?'

She had not been able to answer. She stood, like a fool, mouth agape, drying with terror, although there were people about, walking past, one or two hesitating, looking towards her and Jake.

He had banged the passenger door, flung round the front of the car, hurled himself into the driver's seat and driven off, grating the gear, gunning the engine.

And all Fanny could think, watching him go, was that he had Ivy's books in the back of the Peugeot.

Fanny sipped her whisky – pouring it in the dark she had unintentionally made it much stronger than usual – and tried to think calmly. He had yelled at her. True. But there could be another explanation than the one she was dreading. She had watched him in his boat, making love to his girl. She had intruded upon him in the library and forced conversation upon him. A young man of such singular beauty must be accustomed to receiving attention from women of all types and ages. Maybe it had amused him to have this grandmotherly lady show interest in him. But then she had said something crazy, and scared him.

An innocent, then. So why was she frightened? What did she know, actually *know*, as distinct from fearfully guessing, inventing?

Harry had once had an old Vauxhall; his first car, bought with the money he had earned working in a brewery one summer vacation. He had been eighteen or nineteen, roughly the same age she thought Jake might be. In her mind, therefore, a Vauxhall had been a young man's car. Which was why, when the policewoman had told her, early on, in the hospital, that Mrs Hobbes had been certain the other car was a Vauxhall, she had accepted it as a fact that was known, undisputed. But she had only accepted it – and remembered it – because she had always associated young men with Vauxhalls, meaning by young men her son Harry, not the other man involved in the accident. She had told Isabel he was young, and Isabel had found this significant. How significant was it? Andrew Hobbes had been young. And because he was young, Fanny had simply assumed that the men who had beaten him up were young too.

Fanny whispered, under her breath, 'They didn't just beat him up. They beat him to death.'

Suddenly the light was on, dazzling her. Becky was saying, behind her, 'Why are you sitting in the dark, Auntie Fanny?'

Fanny shrank from the black, naked window in front of her,

seeing herself mirrored in it, dangerously exposed to the night. Then a bulky shape interposed itself, a shape that to Fanny's dazzled eyes momentarily appeared as a creature from space, or out of some Nordic fairy-tale, a troll, or a goblin, before it turned its benign gaze upon her and smilingly revealed itself to be human. One of God's nastier jokes all the same, Fanny thought sadly: a heavy body, so wide and so solid that its short legs and arms seemed vestigial, a broad, squashed face, with almost no forehead, in which a small and beautifully fashioned nose and pretty, pink bud of a mouth could be seen as an extra refinement of cruelty, taunting their owner with their incongruous perfection whenever she looked in the mirror. Out of this rosebud mouth came an exceptionally sweet and musical voice with a gentle tinkle about it that made Fanny think of a harpsichord. It said, 'Auntie was having a bit of a zizz, I think, Becky.'

'I wasn't asleep,' Fanny insisted robustly. 'I was just sitting here, with my whisky, too lazy to get up and close the curtains and put the light on.'

'It's been dark quite a long time,' Becky said, speaking lightly and teasingly and sounding much more confident than Fanny had ever heard her. She went to the window to draw the curtains; then she switched on the lamps and turned off the harsh central light. She smiled at Fanny, looking unusually bright, almost sparkling. She said, 'That's better, isn't it? This is my friend Angela, Auntie Fanny.'

'Pleased to meet you,' the lovely voice said. 'Becky has told me so much about you. I hope you don't mind my calling you Auntie?'

'Well,' Fanny said faintly. 'Yes, yes, of course you may. If you want to.'

Becky laughed her high, nervy laugh and Fanny assumed she was embarrassed by her friend's odd request. She said, much more warmly, 'I'll be very pleased, Angela.' She began to get up from her chair but she was feeling unaccountably tired, her legs heavy. She abandoned the effort and settled for smiling sociably. 'Do sit down, Angela. Would you like a drink? Becky dear, would you?'

'A drop of gin would hit the spot, I think,' Angela said, perching on the frailest chair in the room, an elegant Victorian spoonback which was the survivor of a pair that Fanny had found in the most expensive antique shop in the Precinct. Harry had sat on the other and broken its back. Angela must be heavier than most men, Fanny suspected. If she had been a man it would have been easy to ask her to move but as it was it would seem too painfully pointed. Perhaps if she continued sitting as she was now, weight slightly forward, balancing her barrel of a body above her widely spread knees, the chair might support her. The damage would be done if she got up in a hurry.

Becky was standing on a stool to reach the corner cupboard. 'Can you manage, poppet?' Angela said, and looked at Fanny, drooping one lard-pale eyelid in an old-fashioned music hall wink. 'She's such a teensy little wisp of a thing, you want to wrap her in cotton wool, don't you?'

The words didn't matter, Fanny thought, only the music. She asked 'Do you sing, Angela?' and listened with amazed delight to the wonderful laugh; a full, rich burble of sound that was more like a harp than a harpsichord.

'Bless you no, people are always asking that, Mum and Dad used to try and get me to join the choir, they're very churchy people, but the plain old truth is, I sang too loud for the others.

However hard I tried, this big voice belted out. Anyway, who'd want to look at my fat ugly mug with its mouth open, I ask you?'

'Oh, Ange, don't,' Becky said. 'She's always running herself down, Auntie Fanny. She thinks she's too heavy, but I tell her it's just that everyone is built differently. By the way, there was a bag of books on the doorstep. I brought them in, they're library books I think, not new ones, but you better look some-time and make sure they belong to you. It was a Sainsbury's bag and you don't go to Sainsbury's all that much, do you?'

She poured Angela a glass of gin and Angostura bitters, which was not a drink Fanny would have expected Becky to be familiar with, nor one she had ever heard anyone younger than about sixty-five asking for. Angela hadn't told Becky how she liked her gin, so presumably Becky knew that this was her preferred tipple. Which suggested that Becky and Angela were well acquainted. Fanny said, 'I think the books do belong to me, Becky. I left them in a friend's car and I expect he has kindly returned them. Does Angela work with you?' She smiled at Angela. 'I'm sure Becky has told me and I've just forgotten.'

She was relieved about the books, she decided, even if the thought that he had come to the door and she had not heard him dismayed her. Her hearing was as good as it had ever been. He cannot have rung the bell. And since it was well known that anything left on the doorstep of a house in this neigh-bourhood mysteriously disappeared within minutes, swooped upon by some invisible, amateur garbage collector, Jake must have waited with his Sainsbury's bag until he saw Becky and Angela turn into the street: Angela must have been a surprise to him, but Becky's stick-like silhouette in the lamplight would be unmistakable.

Becky said eagerly, 'It would be marvellous if she did! For me, that is, but I'm afraid she'd be bored. Ange likes meeting people, she'd go mad in an office. In fact, she works at the coffee bar where I have lunch, she's almost always there when I go, and to start with I was just glad because she made the best sandwiches, better than the other girls there, but then we got to talk a bit and discovered that we agreed on, oh, simply everything! Then we found out that we stopped work at the same time and so we started to meet at the wine bar at the corner, and sometimes when you've been out, Auntie Fanny, and not expecting me back to supper, we've been to the cinema.'

Fanny had never heard her talk at such length before. And although nothing could make Becky look pretty, there was a gleam to her skin that made her look healthier.

'I see she doesn't go without her dinner, Auntie,' Angela said. 'A girl as thin as her can't afford to. Sometimes we get really scrummy cream cakes left over at the end of the day and I slip a couple in a bag for her. So you don't have to worry about her, nor do her Mum and Dad. I'll always see she eats properly.'

'I don't think anyone needs to worry about Becky's appetite,' Fanny said. In fact, how much her skinny niece could put away had astonished her. Though perhaps it wasn't such a huge amount by Angela's standards.

'The thing is, Auntie Fanny,' Becky said quickly, 'you did say I should look for somewhere, for when I have to leave here. I told Ange and she says lots of people come in the coffee bar and she'll keep her ears open for me. I don't need a very big room, after all. As Ange says, I don't take up all that much space.'

'No more space than a dicky bird,' Angela chimed in tenderly. And to Fanny, with a hint of reproach, 'The poor little thing's been so worried.'

Becky was looking exceptionally fragile, Fanny thought irritably. She said, 'Really Becky, you couldn't have thought I would just throw you out without warning!'

Angela answered for her. 'Oh, she knows you wouldn't do that, you've been so kind to her, Auntie. But she says she doesn't want to have to go home to her Mum and Dad. And when Mr Jones has finished the house you'll be selling it, won't you?'

'Oh, I don't think so,' Fanny said. 'There's no reason why I should now.'

Sitting by the window in the bar of the House of Lords, Delia laughed so much Fanny feared she would burst a blood vessel. Earlier, she had been in a belligerent mood; she had sprained her right wrist falling over a broken paving stone in Whitehall and had been breathing fire and brimstone in the direction of Westminster Council. Fanny's news about Ivy had restored her good temper completely.

'Lord above,' she moaned, wiping her eyes with the back of her bandaged hand. 'Yes, as a matter of fact I did know what you meant to do because Harry told me. I think he half thought I might talk some sense into you but I told him that really it was none of my business if you wanted to give some of what was, after all, your own money to Ivy. As a matter of fact I was rather impressed that you should think of it, Fanny. I mean you've never been all that much interested in that kind of thing.'

'What kind of thing?'

Delia looked at her suspiciously. 'I never know if you really are being stupid, Fanny, or only pretending. Anyway, I do think it's damn funny. Harry will be mightily relieved, so will Isabel, I imagine.'

'They were both perfectly agreeable when I suggested it,' Fanny protested.

'Now you are being stupid.' Delia spoke with some satisfaction. 'Honestly, Fan, if you believe that you can believe anything.' She glanced at the monitor in the corner to see who was speaking in the debate at the moment and said, '*That* old windbag's bound to drone on over the limit, easy to see why they booted him up from the Commons, so there's time for another drinkie if you can manage it. I'd better not or I'll be forgetting my lines. Of course your children wouldn't say what they really thought, they're both much too well mannered. Take after Daniel. But although neither of them is on the bread line exactly, they're not all that flush . . .' She caught Fanny's eye and added quickly, 'You know what I mean. Not by middle-class standards. In fact, Buffy says, if you're going to buy a smaller house and make a bit on the move, it would be sensible to hand each of them a lump sum now rather than later. As long as you live seven years you'll save on the tax. That may sound a bit premature, Buffy says, compared to him you're still young, but anyone can fall under a bus.' She sighed suddenly. 'This is Buffy's advice not mine. I don't approve of inherited wealth as you know.'

She looked ruffled. Fanny said, soothingly, 'Yes dear, I do know. And I'm grateful to Buffy for worrying about my financial affairs. But there's no need at the moment. I've decided not to move after all.'

Delia was struggling with her heavy leather bag, a combination purse and briefcase with a stiff brass clasp. 'Open it for me will you, duckie? It hurts to use my right hand and I was never much good with my left. Dear God this wrist is a nuisance. Can't do up my bra or put on my tights, can't wash my own hair, and Buffy's not much damn good at assisting. I suppose Becky wouldn't like to come home for a week or two? No, I don't suppose she would. Have you met Angela? Becky brought her down on Sunday. I was amazed that she dared. I mean, you know how Buffy can be with anyone the least bit out of the ordinary. But instead, he was spellbound. You know what he is about music. He says it would be criminal not to have that voice trained.'

'A drop of whisky would hit the spot, I think,' Fanny said.

Delia frowned, as if troubled by a distant echo. Then her brow cleared. She said, 'I thought you drank sherry, Fan. Never mind, not important, I'll catch the chap's eye in a minute. What d'you mean, you're not going to sell the house? Why on earth not? I understood it was all decided. Harry said he thought somewhere in Surrey would suit you. I suppose that would be easiest for Isabel, though Kent would be better for Harry.'

'I wasn't thinking of their convenience,' Fanny said.

She wondered what she had been thinking of. She was attached to the house, that was true, and she was enjoying the renovation of the top floor. Emrys was a good man to have around; they had pleasant interludes together sitting in her kitchen and discussing details of the work over cups of tea or beer and sandwiches. There was an agreeable element of sexual flattery implicit in their relationship, a chemical response between them that spiced their conversations, but more important to Fanny at the moment was the fact that she felt safe while Emrys was there. He would be in the house a good while yet, with his plumber and carpenter son, and when they had finished Archie would be coming to paint. But even Archie, who could be easily diverted and detained, would be gone in the end and she would be alone for most of the day, waiting for

Becky to come home in the evening. Not that she was really afraid, she told herself now. What was there to be afraid of? That *boy*? When she only had to lift up the telephone?

Or tell Delia now. That was why she had come, wasn't it, why she was sitting here, looking out at the grey Thames crawling by? For help from the big sister who had despatched the witch in the cupboard when she was little. For her advice, anyway.

Fanny said, 'I won't be driven away.'

She felt this very deeply. It was more than what Delia would call her 'mulishness'. She had thought several times of leaving the house; not selling it, or not immediately, just shutting it up and travelling for a while, perhaps visiting some of the friends she had treated so cavalierly since Daniel died, either not answering their tactfully enquiring letters, or writing back with a polite brevity that could be construed as a rebuff. But she had felt that to run away could be dangerous, loosening further the frail and cobwebby net that, in her worst moments, seemed to be all that held her mind together. To strengthen it she had to stay. To stay, and wait, and find out.

'What do you mean, Fan?' Delia asked, quite kindly. 'Who on earth is driving you away?'

Fanny looked at the whisky that had appeared before her on the polished table, and around her at other people in the bar. She saw one or two faces that were familiar from the newspapers or from television, but except for a Labour peer, a once fierce left winger, now notable for his increasingly ducal appearance and manner, she could give a name to none of them, and this common enough failure made her feel foolish and out of place. She should not have come. Delia could not help her unless she could explain what was wrong and she found herself unable to do this. Her memory was so uncertain and flimsy, her fear so incoherent and shapeless. Even if she could give it form and utterance what could Delia do? She could ring the police. But even if they could be persuaded to take Fanny seriously, what could *they* do? She could only offer a hunch, an instinct, nothing firm, no reliable evidence. Presumably they would interview Jake, perhaps even bully him – Fanny shrank from using a stronger word though she had recently read accounts of police behaviour that had shocked her – but unless he 'confessed', they would have to let him go in the end. He would blame her, and rightly, if he were innocent. And if he were guilty?

Fanny felt herself growing cold. She said, weakly, 'Oh, I don't know, Delia. People and events, I suppose. The children, and the fire. And Daniel and I were happy there.'

'Yes, yes, I know.' Delia sounded impatient. 'But that's in the past, duckie. You have to look to the future. I know you've always been fit, well we both have, but at our age you start walking a tightrope. One false step. You get mugged, I fall over that damn paving stone, and, bingo, you're in the geriatric ward with Alzheimer's and I can't pull up my knickers without a helping hand from my one-legged old husband.' She shook with merriment and looked up at the monitor. 'Look I've got to go, Fan. That's Tessa on now and she's a competent lass, sticks to the time limit. Next time we'll have proper lunch, I'm sorry about today, but I really couldn't skive off at the last moment. Honestly, though, you must be sensible, duckie. That's a silly house for one person, all those floors. And now you're going to have this, what d'you call it, studio flat on the top floor. What's that for? You're not going to start taking in lodgers, are you? I tell you what I'll do. Next weekend Buffy's got one of his old business mates coming, he doesn't need me around, and I can't stick this particular old mate anyway, hidebound Tory with no more brains than an ant and a good deal less feeling for social cohesion. Why don't you drive me round and we'll look at houses, Surrey, Kent, wherever you fancy. I'll spend Friday night with you, we'll have a nice cosy evening, you might help me have a good bath, wash my hair, that sort of thing. Then we'll get started first thing Saturday morning. November's a good month to buy, always a bit of a slump in prices and likely to slide a bit further this year, Buffy says. Okay?'

Delia was standing up now, awkwardly tugging at her waistband with her left hand, feeling beneath it for the elastic top of her tights, re-arranging her firm, fleshy bulges. Fanny felt affection and annoyance in about equal measure. She said, 'But I really can't leave my house, Delia. There's not just myself to consider. As you know, I do have a lodger.'

She laughed suddenly. An idea had come to her, a solution for her, someone permanent in the house to give her security, and the perfect riposte to her sister. 'As you say, the house is too big for one person. I thought I might give the top floor to Rebecca.'

Harry and Isabel would have something to say about that, she thought on the bus going home. Although Delia might not care to admit it, Buffy was rich enough to buy a house for each of his daughters. For one of them, anyway, and the older two, one a physician working with the World Health Organisation, the other comfortably married to a solicitor in Edinburgh, did not need his assistance. Would he offer to stump up for Becky? It seemed unlikely to Fanny. Even if he was prepared to put good money down, handing it over to his sister-in-law would offend Buffy's sense of business propriety. She could hardly accept payment, anyway. She had made the offer. She had had her reward in the look of sheer stupefaction on Delia's face. And it would bind Becky to her.

She wondered if she were getting like Great-Aunt Frances who had died the year she was born. According to Fanny's mother, this old maiden aunt had kept a Black Book in which she wrote down her bequests to her nephews and nieces, making adjustments when they pleased or displeased her, or as the fancy took her. Nothing better to do with her time, Fanny's mother, who was a hardworking puritan, would say somewhat tartly (although she told the story to amuse, she could never resist pointing the moral), but Fanny had thought even then that there must be more to it than a need to pass the time. Aunt Frances, apparently, had nothing much to give, a little jewellery, a nice porcelain tea set, three or four decent pieces of furniture. Her property, all the same, and to give or withhold it, was privilege and power.

There had been some of her water-colours in the attic, Fanny remembered. Her mother must have been fond of Aunt Frances. She had named her daughter after her; she had kept her faded paintings of willow trees and rivers and meadows. When their mother had died, Delia had turned up her nose at them; Fanny had taken them and stuffed them away in the attic and they had burned in the fire along with the photographs, the Christmas decorations, the bundles of old newspapers, the letters and postcards that someone, at some time, had thought worth preserving. Most of it, Fanny had realised, taking mental stock afterwards, had belonged to her mother or father and been kept by her out of family piety;

Daniel's parents, who had led a virtually nomadic existence, had left almost nothing of that sort behind them.

She and Daniel had been fairly nomadic, too, Fanny thought, getting off the bus and stopping at the stall on the corner to buy an evening paper. Moving every few years. Maybe that was one of the reasons why she was reluctant to move again now.

She bought the newspaper, folded it, and pushed it inside her bag. She might glance at the news later or she might not; she bought the *Evening Standard* for its film critic, Alexander Walker. He and Dilys Powell were the only ones she trusted. Who shared her tastes, anyway.

She crossed the main road well before the walking green man turned to red, still surprised (so much of her life spent in less orderly cities) that she could rely on the traffic to stop for pedestrians. She passed the carpet man at the entrance to the Precinct who rented a small lock-up shop and on dry days displayed his rugs on the cobbles outside. She noticed that he had a handsome Kelim and wondered if Harry and Poppy would like it for the wood floor of their entrance hall. She might ask Poppy when she next spoke to her. Although Poppy kept that floor so highly polished that to put a rug on it might be dangerous. And perhaps she and Harry preferred to leave the wood bare. Past the pub, turning the corner into the short street that led to the bridge over the canal, she tried to focus her attention on the children in the playground of the primary school on the left, but as she entered the danger zone, her pulse quickened and the blood rose in her face. It was as if her body led a quite independent existence; all the way home while she had been concentrating her mind on family matters, on houses and property, on film critics and carpets and slippery floors, her treacherous physical self had paid no account, simply lain low and bided its time to ambush and shame her.

Fanny was furious with it. With herself. She stopped on the bridge and looked down the shining reach of the canal to the dark mouth of the tunnel at the far end. She raised her hand to her forehead, to test the heat of her skin, and to shade her eyes from the afternoon sun that was slanting low over the water. She had told Delia that she would not be driven away and she wouldn't! She had done nothing wrong. If she wanted to stand and look at the canal and the boats on her way home from the bus stop she would do so whenever she felt like it.

Who was to stop her?

She thought – why doesn't Jake leave? It would be so easy for him. He has nothing to keep him here, no job, no child attending a particular school. He could sail his narrow boat somewhere else on the canal, stop anywhere between here and Birmingham. Well, not anywhere, there was a general shortage of licensed moorings but they must be easier to find, away from the centre of London. And surely he must realise that if he were no longer here, living at the bottom of her garden, in her daily sight, she might begin to forget him.

Though you could argue that to leave could look like an admission of guilt. While he stayed, faced her down boldly, he was an obviously innocent man. As of course he might be! Or did he feel safer, knowing she was within reach? That he could keep an eye on her, watch the windows light up at the back of her house, monitor her coming and going. Was he afraid of her? Did he feel drawn to her, as people sometimes feel drawn to an enemy, to someone who threatens them? When he had come to the house the other evening, had he hoped she would sense he was there, and open the door to him?

It bothered her that she had not thanked him for returning the books. She had thought of writing a note but it had seemed inadequate and perhaps cowardly. As if she were afraid to confront him. Now, coming to a sudden decision, she left the bridge and walked briskly down the concrete steps to the tow-path, and along to the *Adelaide May.*

A bicycle was padlocked to the railings beside it, but no one seemed about. The curtains were drawn in the main part of the boat, the living and sleeping area, but open above the sink in the galley kitchen. A jam jar of late roses, leaves streaked with mildew and petals browning a bit at the edges, stood on the sill next to a blue glass jar that held a small, grubby dish mop, a couple of wooden spoons, a pair of serrated scissors, and several sharp looking kitchen knives. There was a plastic bottle of Fairy Liquid on its side in the steel sink, and against the opposite wall, an electric hob with saucepans on a shelf above it and some rather pretty red and white pottery mugs hanging from a wooden tree at the side.

A cat began crying somewhere above Fanny's head; she looked up and saw it weaving its way through the pots of geraniums on the roof. It jumped from the roof to the deck, and from the deck to the shore, where it rubbed itself against Fanny's legs, purring loudly. It was a pretty little cat, part Siamese, Fanny thought. But she was no judge of cats. She said, 'Hallo Puss,' feeling it was churlish not to make some response to the increasingly voluble affection it appeared to be offering her. She wondered if it were hungry, and if it belonged to the *Adelaide May.*

Suddenly the cat arched its bony spine, hissed, and leapt for the boat, claws scraping frantically. Behind her, Fanny heard someone whistle. She was quite sure that it must be Jake. For perhaps half a minute she stood quite still, holding her breath. How ridiculously embarrassing to be caught peering into his kitchen!

The big dog barked as she turned and came skidding towards her out of the bushes at the side of the towpath with a rush of dead leaves and a scatter of feet. It leapt up at the side of the boat but could not reach the little cat that spat and feinted with its paw. The dog's owner whistled again. He was hurrying now, but not very urgently.

He was older than Jake – though still young to Fanny. He wore jeans and trainers and a black leather jacket. He said, 'He won't hurt you. Just got a thing about cats. Never catches one, though. Buster, *here*.'

The dog crouched, hunching its heavy shoulders, tail down but hindquarters squirming, and crept to its owner's feet, plaintive eyes rolling. 'There you are,' the man said. 'Soft old fool really.'

'You'd have to know that,' Fanny said. She was not afraid of dogs herself but she could see that this solid and workmanlike specimen might be threatening to people who were.

'That's the whole point,' Buster's owner said. 'You get someone comes to the door you don't fancy, you just whistle the dog up, and they're off down the street. I tell the wife, don't you answer the door without Buster. So I go off to work and I don't have to worry.'

Fanny said, smiling, 'There are more murders every day in Istanbul than in two months in London.' She couldn't imagine where she had got this statistic, nor why she had brought it out now; although it might mean something to her it could mean very little to Buster's owner. She bent to pat the dog's head as a form of apology and said, 'If your wife's anxious about answering the door, why don't you have one of those spyholes?'

'Nothing like a dog,' the man asserted with a touch of aggression. 'I'm in the business, so I ought to know. You fit all these things, burglar alarms, spyholes, panic buttons – just peanuts beside a good loud dog with a bad reputation. It may not deter your professional, though he won't make a point of picking a place with a Doberman or a Rottweiler, but it'll put off your average casual. I wouldn't live in one of them houses over there without a dog, not if I was paid to.'

Together they looked at the back elevation of Sickert Terrace; its windows, its balconies.

He said, 'Of course, when there's all those floors, a sensible villain will want to know habits. Whether people go up to bed early, or stay stuck downstairs with the telly. Even if they've got alarms, the bloody fools don't put them on half the time, almost never at night, when they're in the house. I tell them it's no good having the thing if you don't use it, but it's a waste of breath, they never listen. They think, they've paid out the money, that's done. So you see what I mean about dogs? You don't have to switch a dog on.'

Fanny wondered what made him so angry. All right, he disliked his job. Did he wish he had taken up dog breeding instead? Or had he simply grown scornful of people who were either so rich or so nervous that they needed a security system to defend their persons and property? Though he was obviously nervous himself, on his wife's account, anyway. Unless it was the only way he could justify Buster. A dog like that must cost a lot to feed. And it would have to be taken out regularly if only to empty its bowels, which from the look of the towpath and the neighbouring park, seemed to be the main object of most dog owners in London.

Fanny assured Buster's owner that she did indeed understand; she didn't have a dog herself but she could see how useful one might be. She coaxed a reluctant smile out of him as they parted, a small social triumph that made her regret having grown so increasingly solitary. As she let herself into the house she thought that now, for example, she would have liked to talk to someone she knew on an ordinary, everyday basis, someone with whom she was intimate enough to bring up the subject, not to *do* anything, just to clear her own mind. She could say something like, 'I seem to have got myself into a silly situation. I've half persuaded myself that I may have recognised one of the men who was involved in that accident. Well, more than an accident as it turned out, since the man died. What I mean is, it wasn't intentional. The difficulty is, once you've got an idea of that sort in your head, given it a voice and a shape and a name, it's hard to get rid of it. It grows like a fungus. I suppose if I was given absolute proof that my young man was in the north of Scotland that particular night I might manage it. Or the other way round. If I could suddenly remember the whole thing and know certainly, for myself, that he had been part of it. There seems to be nothing in between that would do the trick, does there? Which means that the longer I go on, without anything definite happening, no alternative offering itself, the more firmly hooked I become on what may be pure fantasy. And there is nothing I can do about it, as far as I can see. Even if I were totally convinced the other way, sure that it wasn't fantasy but a true memory that my mind, for some reason, didn't want to acknowledge, what Delia would call hysterical amnesia – even then, what could I do?'

She was standing in the hall, swinging her keys in her hand and looking at herself in the mirror that hung above a marble side table that she and Daniel had bought in Ravenna. She had been watching her lips moving silently. Now she saw herself smile. She thought that she could have said these things to any one of half a dozen acquaintances if she had been seeing them regularly. She couldn't say them to Delia; she had decided that already. Nor to her children, who would press her for certainties. The best sort of confidante would be someone like Alice Partridge; a woman of her own generation who would sympathise with her confusion and understand her inaction. But she had rebuffed Alice's friendly advances. And, anyway, she wasn't next door at the moment. She had gone to stay with a cousin who had bought a two-bedroom apartment in a retirement village near Andover. 'We thought it might be a good idea for Mother to take a look at it,' Dora Partridge had said, pushing up the sash window of her drawing room on the first floor, catching Fanny, trimming her geraniums on the adjacent balcony. 'Of course she doesn't need sheltered accommodation at the moment, but as Tom and I told her, it's always best to look ahead and plan your own future while you're still able to do it yourself, don't you think? That way you get what you want and not what other people decide is best for you.'

Perhaps she hadn't been as bald and blatant as that, Fanny conceded. Even Dora Partridge would wrap up that kind of message a little more tactfully. And it was inconceivable that either Harry or Isabel had put her up to it. To imagine such a thing for an instant would be absurd. Paranoid!

The small chandelier above her head jangled faintly. Fanny looked up; although she knew that someone must be walking across the drawing room floor, she was not alarmed, merely curious. She thought, perhaps it is Jake, and felt the pulse leap in her throat with a fearful excitement. This was the moment. She would have it out with him!

But it was Ivy. She appeared at the top of the stairs and Fanny, seeing her face, ran up to her and put her arms round her. 'Rosie doesn't know yet,' Ivy murmured against Fanny's shoulder. 'I was on my own with him. I thought, bad news can wait, so I got a taxi and came, and of course you weren't here.'

She gave a sob, like a child, and allowed Fanny to treat her like one. Settling her on the sofa with a cushion behind her, Fanny remembered how Ivy had comforted her after Daniel's death; always there when she needed her, unfailingly, unobtrusively kind. Then, feeling her friend's stout body, shaking with helpless tears, she was struck by her own, immediate loss. Here, in her arms, was the one person in the world she could have spoken to about Jake. Ivy would have understood the nature of the fix she was in, the almost farcical combination of embarrassment and danger. Out of the question now, for a while anyway, Fanny thought, and then, with an absurd lurch of laughter, poor old Stevie, awkward in death as in life, what an inconsiderate moment to choose.

4

Fanny was visiting (for the fourth time) the Museum of the Moving Image on the South Bank. Sitting in the model of one of the Russian Agit-trains that spread the Soviet message at the time of the Revolution, watching a clip from *The Battleship Potemkin*, she thought she recognised the silhouetted head two rows in front of her. It was the remarkable ears that made it familiar; large ears that stood out at the side of the head and seemed to be made of some thinner and finer matter than usual so that light would shine easily through them; a setting sun, for example, or, as in this case, the flickering white light from the screen.

At school he had been called Dumbo by his peers, and to begin with some of the bigger boys had singled him out as their particular prey and would pull him round the playground by these ludicrous protuberances, or hold lighted matches behind them to demonstrate their transparency, but by the time he was a Top Infant he had grown agile and angry enough to make bullying him a perilous enterprise; he bit and scratched and kicked so determinedly. When he moved up to the Boys – the sexes were segregated at eight in this primary school – he had become exceptionally sturdy and strong for his age, a match even for an eleven year old, and his particular enemies, who were by then twelve or thirteen, had moved to their secondary schools, out of the immediate area. Delia, who had been in his class in the Infants, had done her bossy best to protect him, shouting, and clinging to the arms and legs of his tormentors, and on occasions when his yells of terror and pain had been especially piercing, running to fetch one of the teachers. Perhaps he had been grateful, or perhaps it was simply that Delia had assumed a proprietary role, but for some years after that he had been her acknowledged boyfriend; calling for her to play in the park or, dressed up in his best grey flannel suit and spotted bow tie, to go with him to Sunday School in the Anglican church round the corner.

Fanny remembered this much with perfect ease, having had a blow by blow account of the bullying of Dumbo from Delia who was naturally eager to warn her baby sister about the dreadful things she must expect to happen once she was out of the nursery class, and Fanny's fearful imagination had made it more vivid and terrible than if she had actually been an observer. She couldn't, however, remember when the friendship had faded, though she thought it might have been some time before Delia was fourteen. That was the year the war had begun, but clearer in Fanny's memory than the war, was Delia's birthday party at which games had been played involving a great deal of kissing and giggling that Fanny had been too young to be allowed to take part in but had nevertheless watched with interest.

Dumbo had not been at that party. But she was sure he had been around in later years, towards the end of the war when Delia had been at university and the house had always been full of her friends in the vacations. Fanny, at this time, had done so badly in her Matric that her headmistress had advised her parents to let her leave school and go to a secretarial college. Although this was what Fanny wanted to do, longing to be out in the world and earning enough money to buy pretty clothes and go to the cinema whenever she wanted, she knew that it was a deep disappointment to her ambitious mother who had set her heart on both her girls rising up the educational ladder. From then on, until she met Daniel, Fanny rarely invited anyone home, feeling humbly and perhaps a little resentfully, that none of the girls at her college could match up to Delia's clever friends who talked with tremendous excitement about books and politics – the book talk pleased her mother, the politics her father. She thought that Dumbo had sometimes been one of the friends at this time, though he was not at university with Delia, nor singled out by her for any special favour. Fanny had a vague memory of him being in uniform, of an Army beret. Or had it been a naval officer's cap?

She tried to envisage him in her mind but remained undecided about his head gear; the only picture she could conjure up became misty above his winged ears.

And she couldn't remember his name.

Not that it mattered, she thought. It was unlikely that the man in front of her was Delia's Dumbo. Even if he was, he wouldn't remember her younger sister.

But it was Dumbo, and he did remember her. The last clip finished, the lights came on, and he stood up, and turned, and looked down at her, with casual interest at first, as he might have glanced at any other enthusiast for the early Soviet cinema, and then with astonishment.

'Frances,' he said. 'It is Frances, isn't it? Frances Hamilton?'

'Fanny, now,' she said. 'Fanny Pye. I'm sorry I can't – oh yes I can! Tim!'

'Tom. Tom Snow. Though your mother used to call me Thomas. I never knew why.'

'Delia told her to.' It was surprising, she thought, how swiftly the mental computer could function sometimes, flicking through endless images and coming up with the relevant one in a split second: Delia at ten or eleven, four square in her school uniform, maroon blazer and red and black velour hat with painful elastic under the chin, standing in the doorway of the narrow kitchen and saying to their mother who was doing something on the marble slab – Making a cake? Cutting sandwiches? – 'I do wish you'd call him Thomas. Tom sounds so common.'

Fanny threw back her head and laughed at this memory as she had not laughed for a long time. 'Oh,' she said, when she could speak, 'I'm so sorry. I think I used to call you Tom, didn't I? Though why should you remember?'

She had been Delia's boring sister. A tedious, smaller child, to be trailed home from school. Then, later, a dull girl only fit for the typist's pool. Though Daniel had not thought her dull. But then he had been even older than Dumbo.

He smiled. Fanny remembered the friendly smile, though not the wonderfully crumpled face. She reminded herself that it would not have been so crumpled forty years ago. And then thought how unfair it was that men should so often become better looking as they grew older. Those rubbery contours and crevices added a quirky distinction to what might have been an ordinary face otherwise. Though not ordinary with those ears, perhaps.

He said, 'Of course I remember. You were the beauty.'

'Good Heavens,' Fanny said, genuinely astonished.

'Sharp tongued, too. We were all terrified of you.'

'How could you be? You were years older!'

He laughed and took her elbow to lead her out of the train. She had remembered him as being tall, but that memory must date further back than her secretarial college years, probably right back to the time when he used to knock on the door to escort ten-year-old Delia to Sunday School. Fanny was wearing two-inch heels which made them now much the same height. She could look into his smiling eyes, which were a deep brown-flecked blue, without tilting her head back uncomfortably.

He let go her elbow, went ahead of her down the steps of the train, and put out his hand to her. She jumped the last step, to demonstrate that she didn't really need that kind of assistance, but rested her hand on his all the same.

They walked on together quite naturally. He said, 'You being such a kid made you all the more formidable. You seemed to know exactly what you were up to. None of us felt that we did. We'd sit around, drinking coffee and boasting how clever we were to cheer ourselves up, and you'd come back from whatever you were doing in London and look at us layabouts scathingly.'

'I may have tried to give that impression. But I think I was too shy of you all to be effectively scathing. You were at university getting yourself a proper education which I was too stupid to do.'

'I was in the Army. Doing my National Service. So I was out of things, too. And I didn't have your advantages, either. Maybe you didn't look down on us, consciously. You just were superior. Cool and beautiful.'

His tone was detached. He wasn't trying to flatter her. He was making a statement that seemed to him to be true.

Fanny said, 'I wonder which film star I was trying to copy.'

He answered instantly and seriously. 'Veronica Lake. You wore your hair just like Veronica. Straight, and hanging down over one eye like a curtain. Or waterfall.'

'A bang, I think it was called. You know, I'd forgotten Veronica Lake. But you're quite right, I remember now. Though I suppose I would rather have looked like Hedy Lamarr.'

'Not your type. She was too sultry.' He looked her up and down thoughtfully. 'And fatter than you in the hips, I would say.'

He was teasing her now. She said, 'Do you remember *Ecstasy*? I never got to see it until after the war by which time it seemed fairly tame. But I remember Delia coming home and raving about that daring sequence. Hedy naked, but of course only seen from behind and from a fair distance.'

Fanny thought it was a long time since she had spoken of a film actress by her Christian name. There had been a time when the film stars had been her ideal acquaintances, her close friends, as well as mentors to be admired and carefully emulated. She had never told Daniel about this private side of her life; the evening before they were married, she threw out all her film magazines and signed photographs and copies of the letters she had written to Hedy, or Veronica, or Gary, and made her mother promise never to mention them to anyone, ever.

Now she wondered why she had worried. Had she thought Daniel would despise her? She said, 'When I was between about fifteen and twenty I lived through the cinema. Only I called them the pictures then. I did all the things girls are supposed to do. I helped my mother, got a job – and didn't do badly at it either – but my real life was acted out much more grandly. You remember those uplifting endings with orchestras playing and heroines looking noble? Either renouncing something or other or dying beautifully. I used to practise that kind of expression in train windows. I suppose it's silly to say that my imaginary life was my real life, but it was certainly more fun than being a typist.'

'I hope the rest of your real life has been more interesting.'

Dumbo was looking amused. But that could be mere politeness. She said, 'That's enough about me. What Delia will want to know is what you've been up to.'

They had come to the splendidly baroque picture palace, all gold and cherubs and crimson carpeting. Next to the Russian Agit-train, this was Fanny's favourite exhibit. 'It's very well done,' Tom Snow said. 'What I miss is the smell. I've never met it anywhere since. Musty and heady at the same time. The smell of dreams, I suppose you can't recreate that. You'd have to go back and be fifteen again.'

They looked at each other. He was a solid, stocky, competent-looking man with curly black and grey hair, a face like a map, and elephant ears that looked less outrageously out of proportion than they had done when he had been a boy. His head had grown to accommodate them, Fanny supposed. He was wearing a Marks and Spencer reversible raincoat which Fanny recognised because Daniel had bought one just like it the month before he died. She had sent it, with all his good, hard-wearing clothes, to the Salvation Army.

She wondered what she looked like to Tom. To Thomas. To Dumbo. Talking to him, walking beside him, she had felt light as a girl. She thought, if only she could avoid looking into a mirror, it might be possible to safeguard this pleasant illusion.

He said, 'You know, I'm surprised you remembered me.' She nearly said, 'Who could forget you?' She stopped herself in time. 'I remember all Delia's friends. All the boys, anyway. Girls always remember their older sister's boyfriends. Have you kept up with Delia?'

'We used to send each other Unicef Christmas cards. I can't remember when we stopped but it must have been years ago. I just fell out of that particular habit. And I imagine she culled her lists occasionally. But it's an odd thing. I was planning to write to her.' He laughed and wheeled round, seizing Fanny's elbow again in such a firm grasp that she felt she had been taken prisoner. 'That's too long a story. Have you got time for a drink? I'd offer you lunch, only I have to get to Bow Street by two o'clock.'

He marched her to the National Film Theatre cafeteria. Deciding where to sit, and fetching cups of coffee was a natural break, Fanny thought. It had been a pleasant meeting but now the first flush of surprised recognition was over they would become strangers with nothing to say to each other.

She expected him to ask about Delia. But he said nothing. He sat, relaxed and comfortably silent, smiling at her across the table.

When she said, 'What did you do after the Army?' he raised an eyebrow, as if doubting that she really wished to know. Fanny thought he was both sure of himself and quite modest; an agreeable combination of virtues.

He had taken a degree in History and English Literature at the Army's expense and returned to the Education Corps attached to the British Army on the Rhine. 'There were so many youngsters bored out of their minds with their National Service once the war was over,' he said. 'I thought it might be a good idea to give them something to think about. Besides, I married a German girl, and I didn't want to take her away from her family while we could give them a helping hand, food and so on. Well, you know what it was like for them in the Fifties.'

Fanny nodded. She had known, she had been told. But she and Daniel had been living in Bonn, not Berlin, and her memories were not of bombing and devastation, of hungry people living in cellars, but of her own life as a young married woman, happy with her husband and children. They had gone to Bonn sometime around 1955; Harry had been a stout toddler, Isabel a damp, milky baby. She had taken them out, wrapped up against the deep cold, her boots crunching on the firm snow, and Harry had seen the Christmas tree angels in the shop window and was desperate for them, tugging at her gloved fingers, looking up at her, his round face scarlet with longing.

She had been so important to him then. It made her ache to remember.

Tom had children, too. Two daughters, one a nurse in Australia, the other living in England, in Faversham in Kent, with a husband and three girls of her own. The German wife was dead, had died years ago, in the late Sixties, of cancer. Tom had left the Education Corps and come home to England to take a post in a secondary school where the hours would make it easier for him to look after his adolescent daughters. He had found a job in Faversham, bought a house there, and continued to teach until the older girl had finished her nursing training and decided to emigrate, and the younger had got her degree and was engaged to be married to the man she had lived with her last year in college. Tom had taken early retirement from teaching, paid off the mortgage on the house and made it over to his married daughter when her first child was born.

When he got to this point Tom frowned suspiciously at his coffee, as if he suspected it suddenly of being an unhealthy or even poisonous beverage, and pulled a squashed packet of Marlborough cigarettes out of his pocket. He said, 'Do you want one? No, I suppose not. Not very fashionable, I know. May I?'

Fanny smiled, and watched him take a box of matches out of his pocket and light the cigarette and inhale the first lungful with a distant envy; it must have been nearly twenty years since she gave up smoking but she still missed the pleasure of that first puff. Watching Tom, she saw that when he wasn't actually smoking, he held his cigarette as she had seen working men do, between his thumb and forefinger with the lighted end turned discreetly away, tucked into his palm.

He saw her looking at him. He said, 'I never used to smoke. Not in the Army, nor when I was teaching. But the job I've been doing these last few years seemed to ask for it. Perhaps I'll give it up now.'

Until a month ago, when the local council had announced they could no longer afford the money to fund it, Tom had been the warden of a hostel on the East India Dock Road, between the London docks and the city. The hostel had once been a seamen's mission but for the last twenty years it had been a refuge for homeless men. 'God knows,' Tom said, when Fanny asked him why he had taken it on. 'They're mostly old men, old tramps, mental patients, burnt out schizophrenics. I think I had the idea that I'd done my bit at one end of society, perhaps I ought to have a go at the other. Oh, that's not true.' He stubbed out his cigarette rather forcefully. 'What really happened, was that I knew the man who'd been running the place, he was a friend of my sister's. He was ill and had been told to give up, but they couldn't find anyone to take his place. And I went along and looked at the flat at the top, rent-free for the warden, and talked to some of the men who were in for that night, his wayfarers, that's what my warden friend called them, and I thought the word suited them. There was one particularly spectacular old man, silver locks and a saintly expression . . . I'm not boring you, Fanny?'

'Of course you're not boring me. I did ask, didn't I?'

'All the same.' He gave her a doubtful look, but seemed reassured. 'That was when I smoked my first cigarette. He took two out of his pocket and I had to take one, it was all he could offer and it's important to be able to give, even when you're down on your uppers. Anyway, this old man had something romantic about him that made me think of George Borrow. What was that book called? D'you know the one I mean?'

'*Wild Wales?*'

'Something like that. Never mind. The point is, the romance tipped the balance for me. The nub of the thing was that I needed a place to go because I wanted to hand over the house to Hilde. My daughter. Her husband seemed to have taken up unemployment as a full-time profession – a position from which he has not wavered since, by the way – and I wanted her to have some security. So it was chance and luck as it so often is. And I haven't regretted it. I reckoned it was worth doing. Especially once they got busy emptying the old Victorian asylums and turning the poor lost souls, who'd lived there for ever, out into what's called the community! God, how I hate that word!'

His ears had gone a rich ruby colour. He thumped his large fist on the table. 'Just as I hate this bloody Government! That's why I was going to write to Delia. Just in case she could help. Not my hostel, my old men, too late for that, but if she took it up, made an issue of it, she might save some others. Oh – I'm sorry to visit all this on you. Not the sort of thing that interests you, is it? Or so I remember.'

Fanny found herself, suddenly, equally angry. 'That's spiteful, Dumbo. Taking it out on me! You're as bad as Delia. Putting me down, telling me what interests me and what doesn't. Why on earth should you think I don't care what goes on? Just because I've not stood for Parliament or helped run a doss house? Look, I'll tell you what I think. There are always sick people, and poor people, and homeless, and there's nothing much anyone can do except the best they can, step by step, individually. I know it would be fine if there were enough money to keep your hostel going, and enough money for good schools and good hospitals so that everyone can have a heart and lung transplant, or a new liver or kidney, just for the asking. But there never has been enough money to do everything that everyone wanted done has there? Perhaps because we are all too greedy, or because there are too many of us – not to feed, but to keep occupied, busy. I don't know what the answer is. Only that people like you and Delia are always blaming someone else, or *something* else, like the Government, because there isn't an answer. Who are the Government, anyway? Just ordinary people who are as stupid and ignorant as the rest of us.'

She was shaking with fury and humiliation. She leaned across the table and hissed into his astonished face, 'I don't know why you didn't marry Delia. You could have had a wonderful life being indignant together.'

He gave a kind of startled hiccup. He said, 'Oh, Frances. I mean Fanny. Honestly, I wasn't getting at you, it simply occurred to me, what a bore I was being. Did we always make you so mad? Not just me and Delia, the whole crowd of us.'

He was trying so hard not to laugh, it made her want to laugh, just to see him. She said, 'I'm sorry. I was too young, I suppose. Or you all thought I was. It was the election in 1945, wasn't it? You were all so caught up in it, I suppose I was jealous. It wasn't only being left out, it was knowing I didn't feel what you felt. Well, perhaps I felt some of it. But not passionately. And then, when I married into the diplomatic service, as you might say, you had to be discreet about what your politics were. You were supposed to be representing the whole country, not just a part of it. Daniel – I mean my husband . . .'

'Fanny,' he said. 'I know who your husband was. I came to your wedding.'

He was looking at her intently. She couldn't tell what he was thinking. She wondered if he had been married himself by then.

She said, 'I don't remember much about it. Only the photographs that were taken. I wonder if people remembered more, or remembered differently, before cameras were invented.'

He didn't appear to have heard her. He was looking at his watch. He muttered something, then said, more clearly, 'Must go. I've got to bail someone out, I said I'd be there at two. Bow Street. I can make it if I run. Mind you, I'll almost certainly have to hang around but you can never be certain. Sorry, Fanny. When can I see you? Except for today, I've got all the time in the world at the moment. Lunch tomorrow?'

'I've got to go to a funeral,' Fanny said.

The blood came up in his face. He said hastily, 'Okay. Well okay, then. Really, I have got to rush. It's been great seeing you. Regards to Delia. Sorry about the funeral.'

He was gone. It was only as he turned at the door, to lift his hand in farewell, that Fanny understood the reason for this awkwardly hurried departure. She didn't doubt that he was off to stand bail for one of his wayfarers; standing bail was presumably a residual occupational hazard. But he had assumed that she had made the classic excuse to dismiss him. She stood up, gathering her handbag, her raincoat, thinking as she did so that she was making an undignified spectacle of herself, shouting at the poor man like a fishwife, and then chasing after him. But she couldn't bear him to think she would be so vulgar as to invent a funeral to avoid having to see him again. Not that she did want to see him, particularly. If he wanted to see her, he could look her up in the book.

He had said he would have to run. She guessed that he had a fair turn of speed, and wished that she had worn flatter heels. She found a taxi setting down a passenger at the stairs for the National Film Theatre and hailed it. Crossing Waterloo Bridge, she imagined herself snarling throatily, 'Follow that short guy.' A long-legged Dietrich figure, wearing a mannish hat and smoking a cigarette in an ivory holder.

The lights were turning green for the traffic, red for pedestrians. As her taxi accelerated past him he looked up and saw her. She thought she might shout, 'See you after the funeral,' but she couldn't quite bring herself; it seemed to mock Ivy's grief. Instead she waved and smiled, and then, through the back window, saw him looking after her. But without her distance glasses she couldn't see his expression.

'Thomas Snow. Great Scott, of course I remember him,' Delia trumpeted down the telephone. 'Takes me back a bit, though. Did he really remember you? I mean, it must be *forty years*! I suppose he would be unmistakable.'

'He seems to have grown to his ears. Or they fit him better now. Have I changed so much, Delia?' This sounded plaintive. Fanny said, quickly, 'He recognised me immediately.'

'He probably spent more time looking at you than I did,'

Delia said. 'God, you are vain, Fanny. If you must know, you're still very good looking but you've got a bit beaky this last ten years or so. How was *he*, that's more to the point?'

'Out of work. He's writing to you about that, anyway. Not about his job in fact, but a general principle. He's been running a men's refuge in the East End that's just been closed down. He's in a bitter rage with the Government.'

'I thought he was teaching. That is, he was teaching last time I heard from him. In the Education Corps before that. But the last time I actually saw him was years ago, let me think, Becky wasn't much more than a baby, mid-Sixties, it could be. He came to dinner in that funny flat we had in Westminster – do you remember that marvellous stained-glass loo at the top of the stairs? Anyway, he came with his wife who was stunningly pretty, but you know what Buffy is about Germans. I suppose he had cause, poor fellow, though he was lucky to spend his war in a German prison camp and not a Japanese one. All the same, though it was a sticky evening, it was more Thomas's fault than Buffy's. Thomas was always one for getting down to the nitty gritty and he was determined that Buffy should understand the German point of view, unfairness of Versailles and so on. I don't know what he thought he was doing, I mean any fool could see that's the wrong tree to bark up, just by looking at Buffy! Still, I don't need to tell you that, do I? You know how he could be with Daniel!'

'Buffy believes that barbarity begins at the Watford Gap as well as the Channel, and that all people who don't speak Standard English are barbarians,' Fanny said. 'Daniel was less insular by instinct as well as by profession. He would have found it hard to find a barbarian in Outer Mongolia. I think that was the only major disagreement between them.'

'Then I expect Daniel would have felt as Buffy does about this notion of handing over your top floor to Becky. He admits it's mighty generous of you and all that but he says it would cause frightful problems with Harry and Isabel and you shouldn't consider it for a moment. He's not even sure how it could be done legally. You can't make a completely separate flat out of it because the tenant would have to use the common stairway. Something might be done by dividing the freehold, Buffy thinks, but since it's a bad idea anyway, there's no point wasting money on advice from a property lawyer. You haven't mentioned it to Becky yet, have you?'

'No. But . . .'

'Then don't, duckie. Though it's had one good result. Buffy's decided that we ought to buy something for Becky. He was against it to start with, we hadn't done anything like that for the others, and so on, and so forth. And there was the question of *where*. No point in getting her a house or a flat and expecting her to make a life for herself; she'd have hidden indoors and peeked out of the windows occasionally. But she's stuck to this job and that's thanks to you, encouraging her to behave like a normal girl, and Buffy and I are both very grateful. But there's no reason on God's earth why you should be stuck with her for ever.'

'But I like having her, Delia! We get on very well together. We don't interfere with each other and I think she's quite happy.' Beginning to panic, Fanny grew humble. 'Truly, dear, I hadn't realised how lonely I was till she came. I would miss her quite dreadfully.'

'And you were so against the whole idea to start with! Oh, well!' Delia chuckled happily. 'Never mind. Water under the bridge now. Look, Becky won't leave you in the lurch, I'll see that she doesn't, so don't start to worry. But I ought to warn you, perhaps, I think it has already crossed her mind that she might fly the coop sooner or later. Maybe her funny friend Angela has something to do with it, suggesting that they might set up together some time or other. And though you mightn't expect it, Buffy's not too opposed to the notion. He says Angela is a fine girl, that's high praise, as you know. You wouldn't know it to hear him sometimes but he's been more worried about Becky than he lets on, and he says his mind is more at rest now. Look, I can't hang about any longer, Fan. Buffy's cooking this evening, one of his fancy dishes and he likes me to be at the table eight o'clock sharp, knife and fork at the ready.'

There had been noises off for several minutes; a crescendo of barks from the kitchen; the cow bell that was used to announce meals in that household, tinkling more and more frantically.

'Just one thing!' Fanny pleaded. 'I know Buffy can cook like an angel, but you mustn't let him become a dictator! Reverting to your friend Thomas. I often wondered, and never asked. You were so alike, the pair of you. Why didn't you marry each other?'

There was an empty silence. Fanny thought they must have been cut off. Then she heard Buffy's bellow and Delia's answer. 'All right, my lambie-pie, just a quick word with Fanny.' Then Delia, laughing very merrily, 'It wasn't me he was after, my duck. You knew that, I thought. You can't have forgotten.'

Oh, but she could, Fanny thought. It was extraordinary how some bits of the past remained clear as yesterday's daylight while others not only faded but disappeared totally. She could remember Dumbo in the front room at home, the 'best' room that her mother had more or less handed over to Delia and her friends for what they called the vacations and that Fanny, affecting not to understand the importance of nomenclature to her sister, had always referred to as holidays. Fanny had opened the door of this room and seen them all sitting there, six or seven young men and women, casually draped over the three piece suite or hugging their knees on the Axminster carpet. Dumbo, in his battle dress jacket, was standing in front of the fireplace. There was no fire, but his ears were aflame. Why was he standing? Because she had come into the room? Why should he stand up, when none of the others had bothered?

'Thomas has very good manners, I'll say that for him.'

That was her mother speaking, though where and on what occasion Fanny could not recall. Her mother's voice was a wisp, an echo in space.

Fanny tried to summon up her mother as she had been then, when her daughters had still been at home, one studying Politics and Economics at university, the other shorthand and typing at secretarial college. That mother had fastened her straight, light brown hair in a bun at the nape of her neck. Indoors, over her clothes, she always wore a flowered cotton apron that crossed over in front and tied at the back; if the front-door bell rang, she removed this garment in one swift, practised movement and then, as she walked up the hall, put both hands to the back of her head, tidying and tightening her bun.

How she would have looked to the caller when she opened the door, Fanny could not imagine. She could not summon up her mother's face as it had looked at that age; she could only remember her older, or younger. But then very few uncluttered images remained from that time of her life, Fanny thought; it was as if she had blanked out the years from late adolescence right up to Daniel's posting to Bonn when the children were small. There were plenty of photographs; of the wedding and the honeymoon on Lake Como, as there were of Harry and Isabel when they were babies. But it was almost as if these tangible records, these artificially trapped moments of time, had driven out other memories. Or perhaps only relegated them to some dusty mental attic where they would lie in an old tin trunk, forgotten for ever.

'Fanciful nonsense,' Fanny rebuked herself witheringly. She couldn't remember why she had begun to think of her mother. How had she *got* to her? From what starting point? Why?

She puzzled for a moment. Daniel? Delia? Dumbo? There was what she thought of at these moments as a white flash – a momentary illumination, or electrical discharge, that signalled she was on the right track; what she had temporarily lost sight of was just round the corner.

On this occasion, there was nothing more. Best to leave it alone, she told herself; she had often found that if she gave up pursuing the missing connection it would creep into her mind when she wasn't thinking about it. 'See if I care,' she grumbled aloud, dismissing her memory like a recalcitrant servant, and took herself down the stairs to the basement kitchen to prepare supper for herself and Rebecca.

She thought they might have a good bottle of wine. For no particular reason she felt somehow celebratory. Daniel had kept all the better wines in what had once been a coal hole under the pavement at the front of the house and was now a dark, dampish cellar. Most of the labels had either been washed off in the seepage of rain from the street or become indecipherable; ferreting about with a torch, Fanny extracted one bottle from its rust-crumbling wine rack that had a vague outline of a building that could have been a church, or a château, still visible on the label. Daniel had always made a great to-do about getting the wine up and opening it at a specified interval before it was needed. What that interval ought to be varied with the vintage, Fanny thought Daniel had told her, but since his death she had simply opened a bottle whenever she felt like it.

As she came out of the cellar, bottle in hand, she heard the hollow thudding of feet on the pavement above her, turning from the street, up the step, to her door. Then the familiar *thump* as the door was opened – an accumulation of layers of paint over the years made a fairly hefty shove necessary. Fanny wondered if she should ask Archie Olds to burn off the old paint when he decorated the front of the house, and then remembered the last time he had used his blow lamp in the terrace.

She was slightly surprised not to hear Becky's normal announcing cry of 'I'm back, Auntie Fanny!' Walking along the passage from the front of the house to the back, to the big kitchen, which was also the dining room, she called 'Becky?'

Jake was at the bottom of the basement stairs. He was smiling broadly and sweetly, and swinging her keys round his index finger. He shook his head at her reprovingly. 'Guess where I found these, Mrs Pye?'

He was too close to her. There was so little room in the passage. She pushed past him, quite roughly, and went into the kitchen. She put the wine down on the table and made herself take several deep breaths before she turned round to face him.

He said, 'In your own front door, that's where. You were lucky it was me found them. You get some funny characters about after dark. Someone could have took your keys away and come in late at night when you were in bed.' His eyes danced like points of sunlight on water. 'Thinking yourself safe in the Land of Nod.'

She filled her lungs again. She said, 'Thank you very much, Jake. It was careless of me, and I'm much obliged to you. I only wish you had rung the door bell. Coming in as you did, you alarmed me. It sounds foolish, I know.'

He said, in a mock-injured tone, 'I thought I'd give you a nice surprise! Sorry, I'm sure!'

She did her best to smile, and held out her hand for the keys. He dangled them in front of her for perhaps half a minute before dropping them on her open palm. She told herself that he was not teasing her, only thinking of what he intended to say, and this may have been true because then he said, speaking slowly and carefully as if repeating a prepared speech, 'I came to say I was sorry I got mad and shouted at you. When I brought your books back, I thought I might ring your bell, but I lost my bottle . . .' He frowned as if he wondered if she would understand what he meant and translated for her. 'My nerve. I mean I lost my nerve. I thought you'd be mad at *me*.'

She said, with relief, 'That's all right. That's okay. I must admit I was taken aback! But you brought the books back. That was kind. I came along the towpath to see if you were at home so that I could say thank you.'

'Yeah, I heard you'd been snooping around.' He laughed – this was not meant to be offensive, just another clumsy attempt at a joke. Then, solemn again, his clear eyes searching her face, 'What made you think I had a Vauxhall?'

Her breathing was becoming erratic again. She wanted to sit down, but felt that it might put her at a disadvantage.

She said, 'It will probably sound absurd to you, but my son, Harry, used to have one.'

She advanced her theory about her involuntary association of young men with this make of old car, interpolating her explanation with little, breathy gasps of laughter – a foolish old woman, amused by her own folly. He listened carefully, watching her steadily. She had no idea whether he believed her or not.

'Well, there you are,' she said, finally. She did sit down now, resting one arm on the table. Then felt inhospitable. She said, 'Can I offer you something? Coffee? A drink?'

He shook his head in a perfunctory way. He said, almost contemptuously, 'I've no time for that. You know, I told you about my friend, my friend what's in trouble, and you said something about a statue might help him?'

'Statue? Oh. Oh yes, of course. Limitation. Statute of Limitations.' She was careful to put the lightest of stresses on the final consonant. 'Did you find out about it?'

'There's nothing in that library. I spent ages. Looking in all the law books. I asked the librarian but she didn't know nothing.'

'I should think you might need a specialised library.'

She felt she was being dismissive. Ungenerous. Perhaps there was a real friend, a real trouble! And perhaps she could persuade him to leave the house now if she made him a promise.

She said, 'I've really no idea where to look. But I can try to find out for you, if you like. What this – this *law* says. There are several people I know who might he able to tell me. Or suggest where to go. I'll let you know, shall I?'

'Okay,' he said. 'Okay, then. That's really nice of you.'

He sounded as if he were really grateful. Well, she had

offered to do something for him. Perhaps he found this reassuring.

She stood up feeling so relieved that she was almost light-headed. She thought – the ordeal is nearly over. Though why was it an ordeal? He hadn't threatened her. True, he had come into the house without ringing or knocking. But he had come to apologise. And he had given her keys back to her.

He said, 'I'll be off, then.'

'Yes.' He was standing in the doorway of the kitchen. She would have to go past him to lead the way up the stairs, but she could think of no other way of getting him to the front door. She could hardly stand behind him and drive him in front of her.

She said, 'I'll see you out, then.'

'Right.' She was on the bottom stair when he caught her by her wrist, detaining her gently. She turned to look down at him, and he said, very seriously, 'I said I was sorry, didn't I? I hope you aren't frightened. What I mean is, I know I frightened you then, but I hope you aren't still frightened now.'

She held her breath. She couldn't breathe. She stared at him, fascinated by his eyes, his perfect eyelids, smooth and waxen as petals. Her ears were singing.

She was aware that in some way he was threatening her, but she had no real idea what that way might be. He was still holding her wrist, but lightly now, just enclosing it with his long thumb, and stroking her skin with the warm tips of his fingers, and smiling. She looked down and saw these fingers move up her arm, stroking tenderly, creeping under the loose cuff of her shirt. Although she was afraid to raise her eyes to his face, she knew he was watching her closely. But she was no longer his prisoner. She could remove her arm if she chose. If she wanted to.

She said, faintly, 'My niece . . .'

Playing it back afterwards, she was sure she had not heard Becky come in. Or not consciously. But Jake must have heard the door. He had let her arm go a fraction of a second before she had spoken, stepping back and laughing softly. Either embarrassed or mocking. And the next instant she heard Becky calling.

'I'm home, Auntie Fanny.'

Fanny went to the funeral with Archie Olds; he had offered her a lift as soon as the date had been fixed, and she had accepted at once, and told Harry and Isabel so that they shouldn't worry about picking her up and taking her back, nor quarrel about which of them was to do it. Although they would come to the crematorium, they might not have time to go back to Rosie's house afterwards or they might not be able to stay very long if they did.

So Fanny argued. But she was not only thinking of their convenience. There was also a curious *gap* that was either generational or cultural; Fanny was sure that neither her son nor her daughter would really comprehend the gravity of this occasion to Ivy. They had both loved Ivy from childhood. But they would see their love for her as the only reason for their presence at her husband's funeral. Not, as Archie and Ivy would see it, as a mark of respect for the dead.

Fanny doubted that she could explain this to them, but she feared that if she had been forced to travel with either of them to Stevie Trench's funeral she would have had to try. She had woken up early this morning full of anger against both her children. Ready to quarrel. She had no idea why. She wondered about it while she tidied the house and bathed and dressed and drank a glass of whisky to fortify herself, but without finding an answer.

Unless it was Harry's remark when she had rung him to say she was going with Archie. He had said, 'Why not, if you want to, though why can't you take your own car?'

Why should that make her angry? Before Archie had made his offer she had intended to drive herself, hadn't she? And why should it make her angry with Isabel?

Maybe she had had a dream in which both of them had behaved badly to her, she decided at last. This had sometimes happened with Daniel. She would wake from a nightmare and berate him for some peccadillo or other of which, once she was fully awake, she would realise he was totally innocent. The offence was always trifling, but in her dream it had seemed monstrous to her. Daniel had been dismayed to begin with, recognising the intensity of her anger and feeling that he must be somehow to blame for it, and she had been ashamed of herself for accusing him falsely. She had reassured him by making a joke of it, a funny story to be related to friends, and trained herself, when she woke with a pained, thumping heart, to lie quiet, not to disturb him.

Nowadays she still woke sometimes with the anger, but she could never remember the dream. What could Izzy have done to set it off, anyway?

She arrived at the crematorium to find Isabel already there; when Fanny got out of the car she was in Ivy's arms and it was Ivy who was comforting her, not the other way round. Isabel turned a tear-stained face to her mother and gave her a sad smile. She was wearing her green woollen suit, and a yellow silk scarf at her throat. And she was carrying an untidy bunch of yellow chrysanthemums that she had presumably picked from her garden.

Why should she be surprised, Fanny thought. She had known all the time, in some hidden part of her mind, that Isabel would not think to wear mourning clothes. It was curious, when the girl had a wardrobe stuffed to the gunwales with gloomy black garments, that it didn't occur to her that a funeral might be the appropriate occasion to wear them. And the flowers? That was her own fault, Fanny admitted. She should have warned Isabel to get a proper wreath made and sent to the undertakers. Now Ivy would think that Isabel hadn't 'bothered'. Though she would forgive her, of course. Ivy had always been indulgent to Izzy.

Fanny kissed Ivy and pressed her hand. She kissed her daughter and said, 'You look very gay for a funeral!'

Harry, she was glad to see, arrived in a dark suit, with a black tie. He was late, but others were later; the men from the London Fire Service among them. Fanny could see that Ivy was on tenterhooks waiting for them, and her own stomach tightened in sympathy 'Are you all right, darling?' Harry asked her, drawing her hand through his arm and thinking, she realised, of Daniel's funeral, the last funeral they had attended together, and assuming that she must be grieving. But when she explained about the representatives from the fire service he understood the importance at once. 'Don't worry, I'm sure they'll come, Mother. After all, he was actually injured on duty! It's the sort of thing they're bound to remember.'

'Ivy says they sent a wreath,' Fanny whispered.

'Even so,' Harry said, though more doubtfully. Then his face cleared. 'All right. Uniforms turning in at the gate. Four or five of them.'

Quite a respectable turn out, Fanny decided as they filed into the chapel. Ivy's immediate family; her two sisters and their husbands, her daughter and son-in-law, her son and daughter-in-law and half a dozen grandchildren of indeterminate ages, neither babies nor adults. There were three middle-aged men in suits, all so like the dead Stevie that it was easy to guess that they were his unmarried brothers, and an assortment of neighbours; eighteen or twenty on a rough count, Fanny made it. And the uniformed firemen.

Stevie's brass helmet was on the coffin. The sight of it brought a lump into Fanny's throat. He had been a brave man, after all. Harry squeezed her fingers. Isabel, of course, was sobbing into a handkerchief. Had she even *met* Stevie? Fanny looked at Harry and raised an eyebrow. He shrugged his shoulders and squeezed her fingers again.

Fanny hoped someone would have the wit to rescue the helmet before the coffin vanished through the doors at the end of the ramp. This anxiety gripped her tightly throughout the brief ceremony. She was uncertain what happened afterwards, did the coffin go straight, and entire, to the flames? As the machinery began to shuffle it along the ramp, Graham, Rosie's husband, wriggled out of his pew and threw himself gallantly forward. Holding the helmet against his chest like a breast plate, he returned to his seat next to Ivy, put his arm round her shoulders and his mouth to her ear. Fanny thought she heard Ivy laugh.

Beside her, Isabel gave a small, choking moan. Then she blew her nose and looked at Fanny, shame-faced. 'Oh, I'm such a fool, I know. But I can't *take* funerals just at the moment.'

Was she reproaching Ivy for laughing? Surely even Isabel could not be so stupid and self-regarding! Fanny reminded herself that her present irritation with her was hardly rational. Or at least, had no solidly identifiable cause. She took her daughter's hand, and patted it, and said in a neutral voice, 'Almost over now, Izzy dear. Just a look at the flowers, then the baked meats.' She remembered a silly thing Daniel used to say when the children were small and upset about something. 'Keep your pecker up, Charlie.'

'Oh, Mummy,' Isabel said, sighing deeply as she made the connection. 'I'm so sorry, dearest. I know it's much worse for you.'

Fanny decided not to dispute this. As they went to look at the flowers that were laid out on the paving at the side of the chapel, she said cheerfully, 'I suppose this particular ritual is a substitute for standing round the graveside watching the clods of earth fall on the coffin.'

Isabel was still carrying her chrysanthemums. She laid them down tenderly, apparently unconcerned by their shaggy appearance. Appearing at Fanny's side, Archie said, 'Beautiful floral tributes.'

Isabel said, 'It's such a pity that so many will have to be wasted. If they're made into wreaths you can't even send them to hospitals or old people's homes.'

'Rather a gruesome thing to do with someone else's funeral flowers anyway,' Fanny said. 'If you were stuck in a Sunset Home, you might not be so thrilled to see a hearse drive up with bunches of leftovers.'

'Better than leaving them to wither on the ground, isn't it?'

'It's a symbol, Izzy,' Fanny said patiently.

Archie Olds cleared his throat. 'That's what our vicar said when my mother was buried. But I couldn't help thinking how much she loved her garden, and how much she hated cut flowers. She wouldn't have them in the house. So it seemed a right shame to put them on her grave.'

205

Fanny smiled at him automatically. She had only half heard him. She had been watching her daughter, who had lost colour suddenly. Almost as if she were going to faint. Or be sick. Perhaps funerals – and death, and graves – troubled her more than Fanny had been able to credit. She had always been an emotional girl, but that did not necessarily mean self-indulgence. Or she may simply have come out this morning without eating breakfast. Fanny said, to help her recover herself, 'Are you coming to Rosie's for lunch, Izzy dear?'

Isabel breathed deeply. Then nodded, and smiled. She looked a little less pale, but still shaky. She said, 'Sorry, Mummy. Sorry, Archie. Suddenly felt a bit funny. Better now.'

'Can I get you something?' Archie said. 'A glass of water?' He looked around him as if he expected one to materialise out of the air.

'No, no, I'm fine now,' Isabel said. 'Sorry to make a fuss. Sorry. I'll see you at Rosie's, okay?'

Her agitation and embarrassment were inexplicable to Fanny. She said, apologising for her daughter to Archie, 'It isn't like her. Well, you know that, Archie. You've known her almost as long as I have!'

'It takes some young women like that,' he said knowledge-ably. 'Though as the old folk used to say, I daresay she'll be worse before she's better.'

'Oh?' Fanny said. 'Oh. Yes, of course, Archie . . .'

She felt such a fool! She couldn't face Isabel yet. She kissed Ivy and Rosie, she chatted to Ivy's sisters, who were very talka-tive, and to Stevie's brothers, who were monosyllabic. She agreed several times that the flowers were exceptionally beau-tiful, particularly for this time of the year, and said to one of the firemen that she was sure Stevie would have been proud to know they had remembered him. She observed herself performing these social functions with amusement. At least there was *something* she had learned how to do well!

She managed to get a lift with Harry but one of Ivy's sisters, who had a bad leg, was allotted the passenger seat and Fanny sat in the back with her husband. The only conversation she had with Harry was how to get to Tredegar Square in Bow. The sister, whom Harry had expected to guide him there, did not know the way; she and her husband lived in south London and rarely crossed the river. 'We'd have liked to see more of Ivy,' the sister said. 'But you know Stevie. Though I suppose I shouldn't speak ill of the dead.'

'You should have followed one of the other cars, Harry,' Fanny said helpfully. She had never been good at map reading and the sister's husband was either not disposed to help, or had left his reading glasses behind; he sat peacefully silent, big red fists clenched on his knees, gazing out of the window. Harry watched his mother in the driving mirror; when he saw her turn the map upside down he sighed heavily, exactly as Daniel would have sighed in like circumstances. She said, 'Tredegar Square is a turning off the Mile End Road but I have to make sure which side, don't I? So that I can tell you whether to turn right or left. So I have to point the map in the right direction. That is, the direction in which I assume we are going.'

Beside her, the sister's husband heaved with soundless laughter. He said, without turning from the window, but presumably addressing Harry, 'Women! All the same. The world over.'

Fanny said, 'The spatial side of the female brain is less well developed than the male. On the other hand there are better links between the right and the left side in the female brain.

Which means that even if men make better map readers women are better at making complex decisions.'

'Like, whether there is any point in going there in the first place?' the sister's husband said placidly.

'Right,' Fanny said. 'No, sorry, I mean *left*. You've missed the turning Harry. Turn down the next one, that's Coborn Road, that's right, I mean, that's *correct*, then left again . . .'

'Right,' said Harry, teasing her, smiling in the mirror.

Turning into the square, Fanny looked for Isabel's red Renault. Failing to see it, she became anxious. The idiot girl, driving off in a state because she hadn't told her mother she was having a baby. Why hadn't she told her?

'There she is, Mother,' Harry said. He was still watching her in the mirror. 'Just parked the car over there.'

Isabel was locking the doors of the Renault. She saw her brother and Fanny, gave a quick, jerky wave and ran up the steps of a tall, handsome house. She hesitated at the top very briefly and then went – *bolted* was the word that sprang into Fanny's mind – through the open front door.

Harry helped Ivy's sister out of the passenger seat. 'Oh, my silly leg!' she said cheerfully. She limped up the stone steps on the arm of her husband.

Fanny said, 'Harry. Did you know Izzy was pregnant?'

He was doing something to the driver's seat. Adjusting it backwards. He had shifted it forward to make more room for the man in the back. He looked up, a little red in the face; either from discomfiture, or from physical effort. He said, 'Yes, as a matter of fact. So she's told you, has she?'

'No she hasn't. It was Archie who pointed it out. Why didn't she tell me?'

'Better ask her that. I should think it was a mixture of things.

To start with, she wanted to be quite sure everything was all right. Her doctor thought she should have some tests done. How old is she now? About thirty-five, isn't she? And then, she thought you'd be angry. You remember the fuss before George was born. You said *three* was too many.'

'That wasn't me,' Fanny said, stung. 'That was Daniel! You know perfectly well how anxious he was. About Max taking on more than he could reasonably cope with and Izzy loading too much on his shoulders. Daniel thought she didn't appreciate the extra cost of a third child, both in money and energy. She wanted one so she had to have one! A spoilt child! I didn't agree with him.'

'Izzy seems to think you didn't disagree, either.'

'I didn't quarrel with your father over it, if that's what you mean. He was entitled to tell his daughter what he felt, I suppose. Even though I felt quite differently. I thought Izzy was the sort of girl who ought to have lots of babies!'

'Oh well. I don't know!' Harry said. 'Honestly, Mother, you must fight that one out with her. To tell you the truth, I've absolutely no idea who said what and to whom. All I know is what Izzy told me. That she was nervous of telling you.'

'I can't imagine why!'

Harry grinned at her and said nothing.

'Oh, all right,' Fanny said huffily. 'My daughter is terrified of me! The comic thing is, I saw how well she was looking the other day, and I'd quite forgotten that she always looks like that when she's pregnant. Like a cat full of cream. She was wearing that pretty green suit. I suppose she wears it for important occasions like going to a funeral or seeing her gynaecologist. And I thought she must have found herself a lover!'

Harry shouted with laughter. Fanny said, 'You won't tell her.'

'No. Come on now. We'd best go and pay our respects. What a nice house!'

'It's a famous square.' Fanny remembered Ivy telling her this. 'Graham's grandfather bought the house in the war. It was a boarding house, I think Ivy said, and the old woman who owned it wanted to leave London during the Blitz and sold it for a song. A few hundred pounds anyway. I knew it was a big house, I didn't realise it was quite so *grand*.'

'Must be worth a bomb!' Harry said.

The funeral party had gathered in the big ground floor room that was only sketchily furnished but had good plaster cornices and a very fine marble fireplace with a decorative overmantel. This was to be Ivy's sitting room when she moved in with Rosie and Graham.

'They've persuaded me it's the best thing to do,' she confided to Fanny. 'Though I'm not sure what to do with my furniture. Rosie thinks it's mostly too small for the room. What she really means is that it's a bit of a job lot, a bit gimcrack, only she's too polite to say so. I thought I might look for some second-hand stuff. Antiques.' She gave a shy giggle. 'You know me, I'm not really one for pushing the boat out but Stevie left this insurance, none of us had any idea it would amount to so much, and Rosie and Graham say I might as well spend it.'

She and Fanny had retreated to a corner, each with a glass of sparkling Saumur. Graham and Rosie were presiding over a long, well-stocked buffet table. There was a festive buzz in the room, bearing out Fanny's belief that a wake was often livelier than a wedding. She didn't say this to Ivy. She said, 'It's such a splendid house, it deserves pretty furniture.'

'It's a big, awkward place really, not at all modern,' Ivy said. 'But Rosie would love you to see it. We thought we'd have the party here as it was easier on the ground floor with people coming and going, and this is the biggest room, but they've made it very cosy upstairs and Rosie's got some nice things.'

The house had five floors and was built on the same Georgian pattern as the houses in Sickert Terrace, with a drawing room on the first floor and bedrooms and attics above, but it was twice the size, better built, and had been more systematically renovated and maintained. 'It was the old man's hobby after the war when Graham's daddy took over the business,' Ivy said. 'He'd been trained as a carpenter and cabinet-maker and was glad to go back to it, work with his hands again after all the old paper work. Graham's like him, he'll fiddle for hours to get a bit of moulding just right. It was Graham fixed these box shutters, took him weeks to get them free but that sort of thing's what he likes, more important to him than making a fortune which is just as well, Rosie says, he's got no head for figures.'

The box shutters were beautiful, gliding easily up from their wooden casings, one to cover the top of the window, the other the bottom. 'They're quite rare,' Ivy said. 'Graham says there are some still in good condition in one of the houses he's got his eye on in Coborn Road, mind you, he says it'll be a job freeing them, they're all stuck up with the paint. You don't get them in the front rooms, it's all folding shutters, for show. I suppose people thought they looked smarter. But I like the boxes much better. They're just that bit different.'

They were standing now in what would be Ivy's bedroom, on the ground floor at the back, looking out over the small square of garden. It was straggly and leafless now, but Fanny saw it could be pretty in summer; there was a terrace and a stone bench, a bed of roses, and a little pond. Ivy would sit on the terrace, and Rosie would bring her a cup of tea, or Graham would bring her a drink, and if Ivy tired of their company she could retreat to her beautiful room, knowing her family were still within reach, living their busy and useful and pleasant lives all around her. Fanny felt a brief flick of envy and shook herself free of it. She put her arm around Ivy's shoulders and hugged her – a bit awkwardly, but she felt some sort of physical demonstration was needed. She said, 'I'm sure you'll be happy here. I think the whole house is quite lovely.'

Harry, who at his own request was being shown round the house by Graham, repeated his earlier opinion that it must be worth a bomb.

Graham shrugged his shoulders. 'Only if we wanted to sell it. Long as you're *living* in it a house is worth nothing. Though my old dad did raise money on it at one time for the business.'

Like his mother-in-law, a little while earlier, he had been demonstrating the box shutters to Harry. Now, as he slid them down into their casing, he frowned as his finger touched a slight roughness: a knot, or a splinter.

He was in his early forties, a tall, thick-set man, with receding hair and a flourishing sandy beard. Harry watched his strong, stubby fingers feeling the shutter casing, and wished he was good with his hands. At the same time he noticed the frown and wondered if he had offended Graham by remarking on the value of his house. Some people were prudish about money. Although a house was slightly different and most people, even those who would be disinclined to discuss their bank balance or overdraft, would be pleased to be told that their property had increased in value. But perhaps Graham felt that kind of subject was altogether out of place at a family funeral.

Graham said, 'My dad was in building all his life. He always said the economics of the trade were a deal simpler than making tools. Or hats. The raw material is land, you improve it with bricks and mortar. Or you can just buy and sell like Harry Hyams – when he bought that site next to the Medici galleries, he made a hundred thousand pounds within a week. Even if you're just an ordinary bloke with a house to sell you can make a huge profit because of the dotty tax laws in this country. Any other manufacturer is taxed on the difference between his costs and the selling price of the goods. Capital gain on your own property is tax free. Plain daft when you think of it. Tax the sale of houses tomorrow, as they do most other places in the world, and the price of houses would come down overnight. I mean, it stands to reason. People wouldn't be so greedy if the more profit they made, the more they'd have to hand over to the tax collector. Of course, you'd have to take into account any improvements that they'd made.'

He looked at Harry, smiling, and pulling at his beard. 'Don't worry, that's the end of my Ancient Mariner bit. Positively my only contribution to the economics of the country. I just get fed up with seeing people who can't afford two rooms and a kitchen.'

Harry said, 'Would it really make so much of a difference? I thought houses were expensive because they were in short supply.'

'Plenty standing empty all over London.' Graham was chewing the ends of his beard now. 'You must see them. They belong to public bodies, private bodies, it doesn't make a ha'p'orth of difference. The owners hang on, they want to turn them into offices. Or they want a better price. There's a couple of little houses round here I'd be happy to buy and make over, but I need to get them reasonably if I'm to do a decent job and make a profit. They're both empty, two old ladies living next door to each other, both died in the same week. The families are asking fancy prices even though there's a lot needs doing and when it's done you couldn't expect to sell for much more than they're asking now. They'll come down eventually, but the longer a house stays empty, the more work it takes to get it back into shape.'

'But they'll pay tax on those houses, won't they? The families, I mean. It's only your own house, your main residence, that's tax free.'

'They'll pay inheritance tax. Not the kind of house tax I'd like to see. Not so high that the kids would get nothing when Mum pops off, just high enough to see that the place is put back in the housing stock as quickly as possible, at a price people who needed a house could afford.'

'Bit unfair though, isn't it? I mean, there's been this tremendous change. Once it was only the really rich who could leave money to their children, enough money to make a difference anyway. Now anyone who's got a house can leave a decent capital sum.'

'That wouldn't matter if the children invested it, but they don't, do they? They've not got the habit. So they go on a spending spree, buy an expensive car or put a swimming pool into the garden. It distorts the economy.' Graham shook his head disapprovingly. 'Let me put it this way . . .'

'Off your soap box, Graham.' Putting her head round the door, Rosie winked at Harry. 'You been getting the lecture on how the plebs can't be trusted with money? Sorry about that. Your mother's been looking for you. She's in good form, isn't she? My mum was fretting over her a while back. But she seems fine now.'

'I hope so,' Harry said.

He sensed a faint rebuke. Ivy had been fretting over his mother. He and Isabel should have been fretting more. Though Rosie was too sunny and open a creature to imply such a thing. She'd have to be sunny to live with Graham, Harry thought grimly. What extraordinarily old-fashioned élitist opinions! He would have liked to argue with him, well, not argue, what he would really like would be to *put him down*. Or, more effective, turn Felix loose on him. It was really monstrous to suggest that it was okay for the upper classes to inherit fortunes but the moment the lower classes saw a chance of escaping from the grind of wage slavery they must be slapped down. 'Why shouldn't I have a swimming pool in my garden,' Harry wanted to roar. To think it was to this unreconstructed working-class Tory builder that his mother had proposed making a present of a hundred thousand pounds. That was what her ridiculous desire to buy Ivy a house would have meant in the end! When all the time Ivy's daughter and son-in-law were living in a house worth a damn sight more than his house, or Isabel's!

His mother was coming towards him across the big room. She was flushed and smiling and this filled him with anger. Surely, now she had seen Rosie's house, she should be *aware* of her folly! She should look shame-faced and repentant, not happy!

She said, 'Can you take me home, Harry? I don't think it's all that much out of your way.'

215

'I thought you were going with Archie.'

If she was surprised at his grudging tone it wasn't apparent. She was still smiling. She said, 'I haven't had a chance to talk to you, Harry.'

'Oh, all right. As long as you don't mind leaving now. Have you spoken to Isabel?'

'Not actually *spoken*. But she came to kiss me goodbye and said she would ring me. I said I was delighted about the baby, of course.'

'Good.' He looked deliberately at his watch. 'If you like, I can wait a bit longer. But I'm a bit tight for time. And if I'm to take you home.'

She said, very meekly, 'Yes, of course, dear.'

He watched her touring the room, making her farewells. Very much the gracious lady at this sort of function, he thought; a tiny bit patronising the way she was saying goodbye to everyone individually, conferring her attention, her handshake, as a singular honour. As if she were the Queen.

Unfair, he told himself sharply. It was how she'd been trained to behave. She had been married, after all, to one of the Queen's representatives. Fanny was the least patronising person he knew. It was *he* who was being patronising and snobbish, seeing himself and his mother as in some way superior to this nice, East End family. And yet he didn't feel superior, or not consciously.

What he consciously felt was resentful, he realised a bit later. They were in the car. Fanny said, with a contented sigh, 'I feel so happy about Ivy now. I hadn't realised the house was so large, I'd envisaged her stuck in a poky little granny flat. And how very nice Rosie is. I've known her a long time, of course. But it always strikes me afresh. Such a lovely girl.'

Unlike Isabel? Was that what she meant? Harry said, 'Can't say I thought much of Graham.'

'Didn't you?' Fanny spoke in a wondering voice as if Harry had given voice to a quite outlandish opinion. 'I thought he seemed an extremely nice man. I don't *know* him, of course. But then neither do you. And I've never heard Ivy say one word against him, and she's not uncritical. I gather he's a good husband and father, and a good son-in-law, too. It isn't just duty, either. He seemed genuinely fond of Ivy.'

This energetic defence of a man she couldn't really care two pins about depressed Harry. He said, 'Poppy and I did ask you to come and live with us when Father died. Or don't you remember?'

'It wouldn't have suited either of us, Harry dear.' She laughed gently. 'I wasn't making comparisons. No two people are alike. Nor are their circumstances. Ivy has had a much harder life than I have, for example. She is also several years older, and more dependent financially. And she can be useful to Rosie. She can be at home for the children so that Rosie can help Graham with the business. Poppy doesn't have a job she needs to be free for, and she is so competent, I can't think I would be able to help her in any other way.'

Harry said gloomily, 'There's not as much room in our house, as in Tredegar Square. I admit that.' He heard himself sounding disgustingly whiny and spoiled and said, 'You said you wanted to talk to me. It wasn't about Ivy and her family, I take it?'

She was quiet long enough for him to wonder if she had heard him. He glanced at her and saw she was staring straight ahead, her lips moving silently, as if she were rehearsing a prepared speech. At last she said, 'It's hard to know where to . . .

What I mean is, there's no obvious starting point. There is this young man who lives on one of the boats. You have seen him once, I think. I seem to have got myself into a stupidly confused state about him.'

She saw it was no good long before she had finished. To begin with, Harry was simply bewildered. Then sternly questioning. Had she recognised Jake or hadn't she? He realised that without a sudden lightning flash of total recall she had no means of being certain one way or the other. Her point about the Vauxhall could be looked into, presumably, but even if it did turn out that Jake had owned such a car, it could still be a coincidence. On the other hand, there were not all that many elderly Vauxhalls in the neighbourhood of Sickert Terrace. Harry had noticed this when he had been visiting Fanny. He didn't pay much attention to motor cars in the normal way but that first car of his was etched on his memory. Had a place in his heart. Did Fanny remember it had been christened Marlene? It might be worth asking the police if they had looked into this, but he guessed that it would be routine, and if they had found such a car in the area they would presumably have tracked down the owner. Would Fanny like him to speak to them for her?

'Please don't do that,' she said, shrinking.

She tried to explain why. It was so clear to her, she found it hard to understand why Harry should need to be told. 'If they question him, then he'll know that I told them.'

But Harry was frowning as if he thought this irrelevant. She said, unwillingly – the first time she had ever admitted such a thing to one of her children – 'I suppose I'm afraid of him.'

'Afraid? Oh, come *on*, love!' He dropped his hand from the

wheel and patted her knee. 'That's bees in the bonnet stuff! Not like you, either! What can he do to you?'

'Do me in, I suppose,' she said, making a joke of it, laughing. 'Unknown intruder murders old lady! Oh, I don't know, Harry dear. Perhaps I am just being silly. Too many frightening films on the telly late in the evening. But I do feel, well, *threatened.*'

'Give me an example,' he said, frowning again. She thought he had stifled a sigh. All this was inexpressibly tedious to him. He had already taken time off work to go to a funeral. Now his mother was presenting him with an insoluble problem.

Anxiously, Fanny shuffled occasions like cards in her mind. What would convince him? Something that did not involve her own feeble fantasies. She said, 'The other evening he walked into the house without ringing the bell.'

Harry was listening. He was taking this seriously, she saw with relief. He was nodding. He understood. He said, 'I can see it must have alarmed you, and it was bloody stupid of him to walk in like that. On the other hand, it was a neighbourly act, wasn't it? Not necessarily done with evil intent. He might just have walked off with your keys, after all. And you do *know* each other. He'd been in the house before, hadn't he? If it wasn't for this . . .'

He hesitated, searching, Fanny guessed, for a word to describe her obviously over-wrought emotional state that would not offend her. 'If you hadn't already got this *idea* in your head, that he might have been one of the men that night, would he have frightened you?'

She said, stubbornly, 'I don't know. After all, I do have this "idea" as you call it. All I can say is that I did find him frightening.'

They were turning into the Terrace. Harry parked the car opposite her house, turned off the engine. He said, 'In what way, exactly? Did he say anything? Do anything? Can you define it?'

She wished she hadn't begun this. She said, 'I suppose most of it is subjective. But, yes. There is something, some kind of sexual threat. I feel it. He knows it.'

'Oh my God, Mother.'

He gave a beseeching groan and began massaging his face with his hand, something he only did when he was in deep despair.

Fanny said crossly. 'You did ask! I was trying to answer. I don't mean he attempted to rape me. He simply touched me in a certain way. It is something to do with power I suppose.'

The anger she had felt earlier towards both her children was now focused entirely on Harry. She felt he had trapped her into an undignified admission. Though it was only undignified because it appeared to embarrass him. She unfastened her seat belt and opened the passenger door. She said, 'Look, forget all about it. Now I've told you, it doesn't seem so bad, somehow. Thank you for listening, though I'm sorry if you find it a burden.'

He was running his hands through his thick brown hair now, looking ruefully up at his mother. She bent to kiss him lightly on the forehead. He said, 'I'm coming in with you.'

She said, 'There's no need, Harry. The men are there today, Emrys and the boys. I'm not afraid to go into the house on my own, anyway.'

Harry got out of the car. He glanced up and down the street but the two parking meters were occupied. He shrugged his shoulders and left his car on the yellow line; a cavalier dismissal of the parking laws that signalled an exceptional degree of anxiety.

He followed her down to the kitchen without speaking a word, and went to stand at the back door and stare through the glass at the cold, winter garden. Emrys had already made tea for himself and his sons; the mugs were washed and draining in the rack, and he had put the pot and the tea-bags ready for Fanny, filled the kettle, set out the Royal Doulton cup and saucer that he knew she liked. Fanny smiled as she fetched down another cup for Harry; she thought she might tell him how much she was enjoying having a man about the house but decided that he would almost certainly find such an admission indelicate.

He had opened the door to the garden. She said, 'Do shut it, Harry, it's cold.'

But he had gone outside and was standing by the little wall at the end, by the holly bush that was bright with berries this year. Fanny followed him out, hugging her arms across her chest against the chill wind, thinking she might tell him that he and Poppy could have all the holly they wanted this Christmas. But when she reached him, he said, 'Which is his boat, Mother?'

'Opposite,' she said. 'Dead opposite the house. Over there.'

'Where, exactly?'

There was a plastic dustbin on the towpath that looked full of rubbish; an old broom, worn bristles uppermost, and a battered tin bath, leaned against it. The stretch of brown water before it was vacant.

Harry said, 'Has he just gone to the sanitary station? Where is the nearest one?'

Fanny shook her head. 'No,' she said, when she could speak. 'No, it's not that. He'd have taken his rubbish. There's a dump at St Pancras, I think. Where they empty the chemical loos or whatever. He wouldn't have left that mess behind him if he meant to come back.'

It was a message for her, she thought suddenly. He had guessed she might understand. He had wanted her to know that she had seen the last of the *Adelaide May*.

5

It seemed to Fanny that she was living two separate lives; one familiar and ordinary, the other, black and chaotic. Sometimes it seemed that these two lives were inside her, one her own, the other belonging to an intruder, a malevolent squatter who had moved in when she wasn't looking and refused to leave. At other times she felt that she moved, or was moved by some inscrutable agency, between two external and independent locations: a brightly lit, civilised room, and a dark forest, or desert, where she crouched or crept, blind with terror.

The panic would strike without warning. She was ready to leave the house. There was nothing at that moment to trouble her; or, at least, she had no conscious anxiety. Then her pulse leapt, her mouth dried, her legs would not carry her. She could not go out. She might vomit, or lose control of her bowels. She remembered a trick Daniel had taught her early on in their marriage when she had been jumpy before they went to some grand function or other, and cupped her hands in front of her mouth, or blew into a brown paper bag. The theory, Daniel had explained, was that you breathed in your own carbon dioxide and reduced the hyperventilation caused by your fear. She couldn't remember whether it had worked then, or not. It didn't work now.

She was registered with a local group practice. Her usual doctor was busy. The young man who saw her barely raised his eyes to her face. He commented that her condition was common among 'ladies your age', and prescribed tranquillisers. She took the pills for two days, waking up on the morning of the third so fuzzy in the head that she missed a step on the stairs to the kitchen. She was only bruised by her fall, but it warned her. She took the remaining tranquillisers back to the chemist and determined not to waste the Health Service's money or the doctor's time in the future.

After that, she told no one. There was no one to tell. Ivy had taken time off to move and 'sort herself out', as she put it. Delia, sympathetic to physical illness, would dismiss Fanny's affliction as a mere failure of will. Isabel was absorbed in her pregnancy which was clearly a source of such joy to her that Fanny was reluctant to spoil it. She had, anyway, felt herself at a distance from her daughter ever since Isabel had thought to apologise for keeping her baby a secret by saying that she 'hadn't told Gaga either'. And Harry had been behaving in what Fanny considered a most disagreeable and hurtful way, ringing her up regularly but only it seemed, as a duty. He would ask if she were 'all right' in a tone that made it quite clear that this was *all* he wanted to know, so that he could get back to his own interesting life without having to worry about her.

Above all, it seemed to Fanny that her condition was humiliating. She knew what caused it, so why could she not cure it? That was what psychotherapy was all about wasn't it? She understood that she was afraid both that Jake would come back and that he would not. As the weeks passed and December came and the streets and the shops grew gaudy with Christmas, his absence became a greater threat than his presence. She longed to wake in the morning and see the *Adelaide May* back in its accustomed mooring. Where she could keep him under her eye. As it was she began to fear that he would appear unexpectedly, suddenly; in an unfrequented, dark street, or in her own house at night; that she would hear a sound and come down to find him, at the bottom of the stairs, blandly and dangerously smiling.

The way to fight back, she thought, was to refuse to be taken by surprise; to expect him to appear everywhere, loping towards her with his loose, long-legged gait in the street, sitting several rows in front of her at the cinema, waiting outside the house whenever she opened the door. But although she fought hard, and imagined that once or twice she had managed to keep her composure this way, it gave her only a temporary respite. Either her determination was not powerful enough, or her madness – which was how she increasingly saw her involuntary physical terror – had a darker and deeper spring.

She left the house less and less. She went to the National Film Theatre twice, with Tom Snow. The first time they saw a Hungarian film of which she could recall nothing afterwards; feeling so sick, with such squirming discomfort in her intestines, that all she could think of was the distance between the seat that she sat in and the illuminated yellow sign of the Ladies. The second time she could not face the terrors of the dark auditorium at all and pleaded a headache; Tom took her to a pub where she drank whisky and calculated how long it would take her, *in extremis*, to reach the lavatory on the far side of the bar while he talked about his daughters, the nurse in Australia, and the married woman with the idle husband in Faversham.

Fanny was uncertain whether he noticed anything strange about her, whether he was an insensitive man or a tactful one. She decided in the end that he could be quite normally sensitive without being in the least aware of how she was feeling. She had developed over the years what Daniel used to call 'good social control'. She could hear herself laughing and talking quite naturally all the time she and Tom were together. And on the two occasions that she had seen Isabel – for lunch, in Covent Garden – Isabel had remarked on how 'wonderfully well' she was looking.

The expense of spirit that these excursions demanded began to seem exorbitant. They were expensive practically, too. She found she could not – literally could not, her legs would not obey her – travel by bus or by tube. Her legs would not even carry her up to the High Street to hail a black cab; she had to order a radio taxi. Enclosed, it seemed she felt safer. And she was able to go about locally, shopping, and to visit her dentist, though her dentist, being a brisk twenty minutes walk away, taxed her courage. She persuaded herself that if her legs became too weak and rubbery during these brief forays she could hold on to a railing, or lamp post, that as long as no one saw her who knew her, nothing really appalling could happen. Though if what she was really afraid of was shitting on the pavement, she told herself grimly, anonymity would hardly save her from some embarrassment.

She could not go into Marks and Spencer, or Sainsbury's, the two food stores near Sickert Terrace. She found a pleasantly anachronistic corner shop that sold groceries, a small butcher's shop in a back street, and a Welsh Dairy that had been in the same family since cattle had been walked from Wales to the green pastures of this part of North London. Very occasionally, driven by a longing for fresh fruit and vegetables, she would force herself to cross the High Street and brave the street market.

She decided that she must try to plan for the future, however much it alarmed her. She had had a letter from an old friend, once a colleague of Daniel's, now the British High Commissioner in Pakistan, renewing the invitation he sent her each time he wrote, which was every few months or so. March and April were the best months in Islamabad, but as she must know by now, she would be welcome at any time. Fanny had always been fond of this young man. (Although he must be in his mid-fifties by now, she thought of him as young, partly because he had always been junior to Daniel, and partly because he was a bachelor: unmarried men, so she thought she would tell him, had a longer shelf life than unmarried women.) She wrote back to thank him and to say that she would like to come in the New Year, the end of January or early February. The thought of having to sit out the long winter alone was intolerable to her. She had agreed to go to Delia and Buffy for Christmas, which would leave only four or five weeks to endure before she could escape from her prison. Of course, she could go to Pakistan earlier still, immediately if she wanted to, but she knew she was not fit enough at the moment to get to the airport, let alone board an aeroplane; she could only hope that she would be more capable later.

It was Delia's constant complaint that although she lived in the country, she found it impossible to buy good country produce in the local shops; it was all sent to London on the early morning train. Fanny had promised her that she would buy the Christmas nuts from her local market; walnuts, and almonds, and the Kentish cob nuts, which were Buffy's favourites because he claimed to have gathered them, growing wild in the hedgerows, when he was a boy.

The afternoon she went to buy the nuts, Fanny was feeling better than she had done since Stevie's funeral. Jake had not bothered her – this was the shorthand she used to encompass the whole, dark range of her terror – for three days. She had not been out of the house for three days, but she refused to see this as relevant. She put on her coat and her boots without the smallest warning tremor; left the house and walked to the High Street, deliberately taking the slightly longer way, through the Precinct, along the wide street where Andrew Hobbes had died. Where he had been murdered. Fanny tested her sensations, her pulse, her guts, her leg muscles, the steadiness of her breathing, and found them as normal as they had ever been. She loitered in the Precinct, looking into the windows of the antique shops for presents; for Delia, for Harry and Poppy, for Isabel and Max. The children were all at an age when they were delighted with cheques as long as they were large enough, but their parents would expect something that showed more personal effort. Now she seemed to have recovered she would enjoy searching and choosing. She would make a preliminary sortie today, on her way back from the market, and spend the whole of tomorrow browsing luxuriously.

She was quite unprepared for the force of the panic that struck her in the street market. One moment she was happily strolling, rejoicing in her new freedom to walk abroad, to be part of the Christmas crowd, to enjoy the coloured lights and the glitter, the next, she was pole-axed with terror.

Jake was behind her, she knew. A few yards behind her, in the narrow space between the two lines of stalls. If she turned he would disappear instantly. As easily and as completely as he could disappear if he knifed her, and fled. But she did not dare to turn. She stood, staring at a stall of oranges, with the wild idea of throwing herself on the owner's mercy, imploring him to save her from the assassin who was silently stalking her. But she could neither move, nor speak. She was shaking, dissolving; her ears were drumming. When something, or someone, touched her shoulder, she let out a groaning cry – so low, and so stifled, that although the orange seller glanced at her, it was only momentarily; he continued without a second's break to count fruit into the bag that two little girls were holding between them.

Tom Snow said, 'Did I make you jump, Fanny? I'm sorry.'

'Oh God,' she said. 'Oh, my God.'

He held her elbow. 'Steady now. I say, you are in a state. What's the matter?'

She shook her head. 'Come on,' he said, speaking quite roughly, pulling her hand through his arm, locking it against him – taking her into custody again, she thought, and began laughing hysterically. The orange seller was looking now. The two little girls ran away, giggling.

'Stop it Fanny, love,' Tom said. 'Pull yourself together. I'll take you home, but I don't want to walk through the streets arm in arm with a loonie.'

'Oh,' she said, spluttering, 'I'm so terribly sorry. Oh, Dumbo.'

'Don't call me Dumbo!'

This brusque injunction startled her out of hysteria like a slap in the face. She drew her breath shakily. 'I didn't know you minded. I'm sorry.'

His face crumpled into a smile 'I don't mind that much. Not from you. Though I don't like it all that much either. I just wanted to shut you up.'

'Okay,' she said. 'Better now. Thank you. What are you doing here?'

'Looking for you, Fan.' He laughed. 'Well, not quite true. Not altogether.'

He had taken the oldest of his three sisters to a clinic at St Bartholomew's Hospital, and walked up from there to the market. 'I thought I might get you some flowers and drop in on you,' he said, looking mildly embarrassed as if he thought she might find this an eccentric notion. 'I don't mean to make a convenience of you, though I admit I didn't want to hang around at the hospital. So if you'd rather I didn't, since you're not feeling well.' He looked worried. 'I'll buy you the flowers, of course, anyway.'

He said this quite seriously. Fanny was feeling so limp, it was easy to keep a straight face. She said, meekly and wearily, 'Thank you Tom. Unless you prefer to be called Thomas? I don't want the flowers but I'd love it if you would come home with me. If you have time. I can give you tea. Or a drink. Food. Anything. Are you hungry?'

'A cup of tea would be very welcome, if it's not too much trouble. I had lunch with my sister before we went to the hospital.'

'I hope it's nothing serious,' Fanny said, automatically. Although her first panic was almost gone, she longed to be home. She dreaded the second wave, the *fear* of the panic which she found in some ways more debilitating. She felt she should be able to control it intellectually: if what she was afraid of was being afraid, then that was entirely a matter of reason, nothing physical, and she should be able to argue herself out of it. While Tom told her about his oldest sister's chronic arthritis, and, by extension, the various, and variable, uncomfortable ailments from which the other two suffered, she both leaned on, and steered him.

She said jauntily, 'It doesn't sound a very healthy household you're living in, Thomas. You'd better be careful you don't catch something.'

'Oh, none of them have anything infectious. It's anno domini, anno domini with them, all the way.' He paused. 'I can't imagine why one says anno domini.'

He was wagging his head, looking solemn. Fanny decided that the second panic was receding fast. In fact, she was feeling better by the minute. She said, 'That can be catching, too. Daniel was older than I was and fairly obsessed with ill health. While that didn't make me ill, I think I may have drifted into an artificial old age out of sympathy. Or perhaps he encouraged it, so he could feel I was keeping him company. He was always telling me that I should take things more easily, have a nap in the afternoon, wear flatter shoes, and my distance glasses when I was driving.'

As she put her key in the door, she wondered why Tom hadn't married again. His wife must have died when he was still fairly young. The natural thing, surely, would have been to look round for another woman to help bring up the girls. Then he wouldn't be stuck, as he seemed to be now, with these three sickly sisters. She must ask Delia about them. Delia's memory was prodigious. She could ask Tom, of course, hut she suspected she might not get a real answer. Not an untruthful answer, he was almost certainly incapable of lying, just an unhelpful one.

The front door stuck, as usual. And as usual, she gave it a thump. Tom said, 'It needs a bit shaving off, I think. If you like, I could do it.' He examined it, running his hand up and down, looking at the hinges. Closing it, he said, 'Do you have any tools? If not, I could bring some from home.' And, as they went down the stairs to the kitchen, 'You know, I don't want to interfere, or be accused of making you old before your time as you say Daniel did, but if you need glasses for distance, you really should wear them when you are driving. It isn't just your own safety involved after all. A car is a lethal weapon, everyone should always remember it!'

She said, turning at the door of her study, smiling at him, 'How true, Tom. How very true. I'll try and remember it. Now. If you don't think it's too early, what I would really like is a whisky.'

'There were four sisters, actually,' Delia said. 'One of them used to work in the shop. The fish shop, the one up the hill just before you got to the station. That sister was the one that got away, she married an American soldier and went to the States as a GI bride. Never came back, sensible girl. None of the other three did a job as far as I know. Daddy owned a whole chain of fish shops and had genteel ambitions for his daughters. The dark secret was that their mother ran away with a blind piano tuner. I remember hearing our mother telling someone or other that the real sadness lay in the fact that the piano tuner was only in the house because poor Jack, that was Snow, the fishmonger, was so keen that his children should have a good musical education, and I couldn't quite understand her logic. I don't know how old I was, it was some while before the war, anyway. I suppose the other three girls must have done some sort of work during the war, yes of course they must, they would have been called up, wouldn't they? Unless they had something wrong with them. Hang on a minute, I think that was it. They were all three supposed to be delicate. TB or something

232

like that. Thomas was all right, and the GI bride, and I suppose old Jack Snow. I can't remember what the girls were called. One was Audrey, I think. Yes, that's right. Audrey and Shirley and Eileen. The one in the fish shop was Elizabeth; she had a moustache, I remember. That's about all, except Jack Snow danced attendance on his girls and I would think only son Thomas was expected to do the same. In fact that's almost certainly why he got married in Germany, away from home would be his only chance. And why he didn't marry again, poor old fellow. Well, you can see the scenario. Daddy passes on, leaving them all comfortably fixed financially, and in the old family home, but no useful male *servant*. Luckily young brother is near at hand, no female owner just at the moment, so the harpies latch on to him to make sure there will always be someone around to change the light bulbs and run down to the chemist for their prescriptions.'

Delia drew breath for a minute. Then she said, 'Why did I ring you up, Fan? It wasn't to give you Thomas Snow's family history. Oh, yes. Could you go to Fortnum's for me next week and pick up the game pies? I know they'd send them but you know what the post is like. I'd be eternally grateful.'

Fanny called up the nightmare of Piccadilly at Christmas. Then said, 'Yes. Yes of course I will. Delia.'

She could order a radio cab and ask it to wait. *Would* it wait? At this time of the year, outside Fortnum and Mason?

'Good,' Delia said. 'Bless you, duckie. One other thing. You know you asked Buffy about the Statute of Limitations? Well, he says there ain't no such thing in England for criminal offences. Only for civil claims, and then the length of time varies, and there are exceptions and complications. In criminal law, in general, no such animal. Some minor cases, most traffic offences for example, can't be brought to court unless the process of prosecution is begun within six months. There are a number of specialised offences, like election offences and carnal knowledge of girls under sixteen. Also Customs offences and income tax. But unless there is a special statutory provision, a prosecution can take place any time at all after the crime. Let me see – what else? Actually he's writing it all down for you, these are just bits that I gleaned. He said if you could let him know what crime you had in mind to commit – Ha ha! – he could be more helpful.'

'Manslaughter,' Fanny said.

'Really? What are you doing, Fanny, writing a novel? Oh, Lordie, I'm sorry, I quite forgot that poor man. I think if you want to know if the chap who did it can still be prosecuted, the answer is yes. Murder and manslaughter can only be murder and manslaughter if the victim dies within a year and a day of the act. But that's not really a limitation, just an arbitary rule to avoid endless arguments about what caused what. The murderer can always be charged with a related offence like grievous bodily harm with intent. Don't tell Buffy I told you all this, he's very happy pecking out a detailed report for you on his typewriter. I just thought you might need to know before he presents you with it at Christmas.'

'I didn't mean to put him to a lot of trouble,' Fanny said.

Fortnum's van would surely deliver in the London area. If she rang, would they deliver the game pies to her? She and Daniel had never had an account there. Did Delia? She could hardly ask; it would sound as if she were unwilling to pay for them.

Delia said, 'He loves finding things out. Gives him a chance to ring up old chums for a chat. Pretending he's just picking their brains. He feels a bit out of things sometimes. I say, Fan, you're not still worrying over that horrible business? Oh, I know you must be, how could one not, a dreadful thing to have lurking at the back of one's mind. And yet, Buffy says, since you'd be a useless witness now even if you could remember, there's really no point.'

'No,' Fanny said.

'So I hope you're not *seriously* worrying.'

'A shiver from time to time,' Fanny said. 'Goose walking over my grave. Several geese sometimes. I've got the nuts, some good walnuts and Buffy's cob nuts. I'll get the game pies. Anything else you want, let me know.' She pulled a hideous face at herself in the mirror above the marble side table. 'I've got nothing much to do at the moment so it's really no trouble.'

Harry saw his mother outside Fortnum and Mason, carrying a green and gold plastic bag and creeping along very close to the plate glass of the window as if she felt safer there. He thought she looked like a whispering ghost, pale-faced and muttering. He hesitated – he was due to meet Ella in Jules Bar in Jermyn Street and he was already a few minutes late – then braced his shoulders back and marched firmly towards her.

Although she appeared to be looking straight ahead, she didn't see him until he was immediately in front of her. She looked up, startled, then blushed like a girl. She said, 'Oh, *Harry* . . . What are you doing here?'

'Just a lunch date,' Harry said cagily. He thought he knew what his mother would make of it if he told her he was going to share a fish cake in Jules Bar with a woman he wasn't married to. There was only one interpretation she would be likely to think of. He laughed at her playfully and kissed her cheek.

'What are you doing, is the real question. Talking to yourself in the street.'

'Was I? Oh, dear.' She was looking around her, beyond him, as if seeking a way to escape. She said, fretfully, 'I need a taxi . . .'

'You, and the rest of London,' Harry said. 'Have you tried the doorman round the corner?'

'There's such an enormous queue.'

He thought she was looking wretched, almost as if she might cry. He said, concerned, 'I'll have a go, shall I? You look as if you ought to sit down. I suppose if we went inside Fortnum's they might . . .'

She shuddered. 'Too many people . . . It's all right, as long as I keep moving, I'll be all right . . .' She blinked at him, and smiled unconvincingly. 'You go off to lunch, Harry. I get these silly turns sometimes. It's the crowds, perhaps. Christmas tension. A sort of *electricity*.'

He wondered if she were really ill, as opposed to just tired from shopping. Was it the kind of emergency that expected him to abandon Ella and call an ambulance? He would have to go with her to hospital. Or would it be adequate just to put her into a taxi? If he could get one. Of course the decent thing would be to take her home himself. The taxi could wait while he nipped into Jules and made his apologies.

He said, 'I know. You could go and sit in the Friends' Room in the Royal Academy if you're feeling rotten. You are a Friend, aren't you?'

She shook her head. No point in asking what she meant precisely; whether she wasn't a Friend, or whether she didn't want to sit down. He looked at his watch, took her green and gold bag with one hand, caught hold of her arm with the other, and wheeled her round the corner to the side door. The queue of exhausted shoppers, mostly elderly, stretched down the street. Harry said, to the doorman, 'Is there any chance you could get a cab at once for my mother? I'm afraid she's not at all well.'

He expected Fanny to protest. When she acquiesced, nodding and drooping against him, he felt his first, real alarm. The doorman had only to look at her; at her beseeching, pale smile, and as the next taxi drew up, his gloved hand was on the door, opening it to let Fanny in. Then he stood back, still holding the door, waiting for Harry.

Harry leaned in. He put his mother's purchases on the seat beside her. He said, 'Do you want me to come with you? I will, of course, if you feel you can't manage.'

She gave the faintest of laughs. 'I shall be all right once I'm home. Thank you, Harry.'

She was sitting on the far side of the cab. He wondered, as he closed the door, if she had assumed he would be getting in with her.

He said, 'Mother?'

But she didn't hear him. She was speaking to the driver. As the taxi drove off, Harry turned to the doorman and began to feel in his pockets. The doorman jerked his head backwards dismissively. Rejecting a tip since the lady was ill? Or refusing to touch the tainted money of a man who had played such a cheap trick on him?

Two women at the head of the queue were looking at Harry as if they thought hanging was too good for him. He said, loudly, 'Thank you all very much. It really was necessary.'

The doorman ignored him, one of the women laughed, and he retreated hastily, angry with Fanny for turning him into a social outcast, and angry with himself because now she had gone home alone, he knew that he should have gone with her. It had been a shock to see her looking so grey and defeated, and talking to herself under her breath. He hadn't really taken it in. What had she meant about *electricity*? Had she gone crazy?

When he realised that he was muttering as he hurried along Jermyn Street, he snorted with laughter. Anyone can behave oddly when they believe themselves unobserved. And she lived alone, after all. Virtually alone, anyway; he couldn't imagine that she and Becky had much conversation. It was a pity she hadn't made more friends in the street. She kept herself aloof. She was a little too choosy. She claimed to like spending time on her own; that was fine, as long as it didn't give rise to foolishness, fantasies of rape, and the like. He should have asked her if that young man had come back with his boat.

Ella was already at the table. There was a bottle of champagne in a bucket beside her. 'My party,' she said, when she saw his eye rest on it. 'I've ordered the fish cake. If you haven't eaten Jules's fish cakes you haven't lived. But they are so enormous, it's best to order them one at a time.'

It seemed a curious meanness to him. Especially as he was hungry. He said, 'Whatever you say. Sorry I'm late.'

'Never apologise, never explain.' Ella poured a glass of champagne for him. He saw that the bottle was already half empty, and reminded himself, charitably, that he had kept her waiting. She lifted her brimming glass to him and said, 'Hail. And farewell.'

He raised an eyebrow enquiringly. And then saw tears in her eyes.

She said, 'I'm going into purdah after all. Exiled to a stable with a madwoman. Don't ask me why because I couldn't tell you. Felix talked me into it. Nothing more to be said. There are always winners and losers. Which do you belong to, Harry boy?'

He said, feeling his way, never quite sure how drink was going to take her, 'Losers are usually nicer people, I think.'

'How amazingly *English* of you.'

He shrugged his shoulders. He would have done better to go home with his mother and not merely for her sake. This was the fifth lunch with Ella, two at his instigation partly out of idle courtesy, going along with what she appeared to expect, and partly out of curiosity. He had no intention of being unfaithful to Poppy but he couldn't help wondering what Ella was after. Now he decided that what she had mostly wanted were fixed opportunities to moan about Felix. But meeting secretly, as if they were lovers, had produced what seemed to Harry a kind of false intimacy, or at least an assumption of intimacy on Ella's part that licensed her to be rude to him. Why should she accuse him of being *English* in that contemptuous way? She had asked him a meaningless question and he had given her a meaningless answer. Did she despise him because he had not made a pass at her? She might equally well ask herself why he should find her attractive, he thought nastily.

She rapped him quite hard on the knuckles with a fork. 'Harry, sweet Harry,' she said accusingly, 'I don't think you've heard one word that I've said.'

He shook his head, grinning apologetically, rasping his chin with his hand. Then thought, what the hell!

He said, 'Maybe not. The reason I was late was that I met my mother in Piccadilly. She was looking terrible and acting – well, to say she was acting oddly would be an understatement. I put her in a cab and sent her home by herself and now I wish that I hadn't. It isn't just this occasion. There have been a number of funny episodes recently. Each one could be explained on its own. It's when you put them together . . .'

He finished his champagne and pushed his empty glass across the table. He thought that if he had to buy another bottle it might well be worth it for Ella's advice. Cheaper than a geriatric psychiatrist, anyway.

This almost made him laugh. He cleared his throat instead. He said, 'You know about this sort of thing, Ella. What are the signs when an old person begins to go senile?'

'I forget things,' Fanny said. 'What did I come in here *for*?'

'To make coffee, I hope.' Tom Snow sat back on his heels, a plumber's wrench in his hand, flushed with crouching under the sink. He wiped the sweat off his forehead with the back of his hand. 'Hair pins,' he said. 'Who uses hair pins? You don't, Fanny. Everyone forgets things all their lives. It's only as they get older that they begin to worry about it.'

'Becky washed her hair in the kitchen the other day,' Fanny said. 'That great mass, no wonder hair pins get lost in it. I'm surprised you didn't find a nest of mice, too. Anyway, thank you, Tom. Though Emrys would have done it.'

She knew that sounded ungrateful but she didn't regret saying it. She had begun to feel that for Tom Snow she was the latest in a long string of good causes. And she knew that he would not take offence. An insult would have to be completely unveiled – naked as the day it was born, she thought – before he would see it.

He said now, 'If you keep asking him to do simple handyman jobs he'll be here till next Christmas. Besides costing a packet.' He peered under the sink. 'Have you ever thought of fixing a Wastemaster?'

'No.' Fanny remembered that she had come down to the kitchen to look for the Mont Blanc ball point pen that she had been using that morning to fill in the crossword while she was eating breakfast. Now she saw it beside the newspaper on the dresser where she had left it. She said, belatedly polite, 'Daniel said we would be always losing things if we had one of those. Pens. Rings. Fingers.'

She put the kettle on, wondering why Tom couldn't make instant coffee for himself if he wanted it, and immediately rebuked herself: She was glad he was around, wasn't she? Even if she didn't need him to unblock the drains, he was prepared to do other things for her that she found impossible to do for herself at the moment. He had gone to the Post Office for her, stood in line for stamps, when just to contemplate that particular purgatory made her feel breathless. There would be no food in the house if Tom had not bought it; she had felt so terrible when she had fetched the game pies for Delia that she had not been out since. She had even cancelled her last dentist's appointment. And Tom did not question her about what to most people would seem odd behaviour; seemed to think, indeed, that it was perfectly normal. When she had asked him to shop for her she had simply said that she had had a few fainting fits lately and he had accepted it. Perhaps three frail, ailing sisters had accustomed him to the idea that all women needed a man to run errands for them.

There was no doubt that it suited her at the moment to have him 'pop round', as he put it, every two or three days. And it was so clearly an escape for him, that she did not have to feel too heavily in his debt. He did not complain overtly about Audrey and Shirley and Eileen. He spoke respectfully of the many troubles that beset them. It seemed to Fanny that most of their symptoms changed daily but that each had one established affliction: Audrey was deaf, Shirley had arthritis and Eileen, what Tom delicately called a 'personality problem'. Mad, Fanny assumed, seeing the Snow sisters as a wailing Greek chorus, or perhaps Furies, shrieking together.

Poor Tom. She thought especially of his coming trials over Christmas. Shirley, the cook of the family, had taken up a vegetarian diet that claimed to cure arthritis, and could not be expected to deal with the turkey. Eileen and Audrey were determined church goers, attending different churches, some ten miles apart, and neither was able to drive. 'Not that it would make much difference if they could,' Tom said, settling down at the table to drink his Nescafé, 'there's a nasty knocking noise in the engine. I'll be lucky if the old bus gets me home tonight, let alone taxi-ing to and from all these religious occasions. Why can't they go to the same church, you ask? Well, I could tell you Fan, but it's too long a story and would take till next Christmas to develop full flavour. I should have put the car into the garage in good time, but I've been using it to get up to you, and it's been useful for shopping. Are you using your car over the holiday? If you're not, if it's just going to sit there in the garage as usual . . .'

'I'm afraid I'd decided to drive down to Sussex. I'm . . .'

'Okay, okay, fine. No harm in asking.' Tom threw up his hands, smiling his crumpled smile, forgiving her selfishness. 'I just thought you might be going by train, rather than joining the great motorway exodus. It was only the girls getting to church I was concerned about, anyway, and that's not your worry.'

Fanny said humbly, 'I am sorry, Tom. In the ordinary way I'd be happy to lend you the car. Trouble is, just at the moment,

I'm finding it uncomfortable to use public transport.' She endeavoured to laugh. 'These silly fits of mine! And besides, there are no trains the day after Christmas, and I might want to get back . . .'

There was no way of explaining the terror that seized her at the thought of being without the car near at hand, if not home and safety at least a temporarily protective shell for her craven self to crawl into. She began to shake; under the table, she clasped her hands in her lap, digging the nails into the palms, hoping the pain would distract her.

Tom said boisterously, 'Don't give it another thought, Fan. I wouldn't want to put you out for a minute. I know the trains get a bit crowded and I daresay you've got parcels to carry. I expect there will be taxis around, some people must work over Christmas. Though they'll be pricey, of course.'

He stood up, carried his cup and saucer to the sink. He crouched and inspected the joint, testing it with his finger for dampness. 'That'll do,' he said, getting up with a little groan and a wry grin. 'Wish my knees could be mended as easily. Is there anything else you want from Marks and Spencer, Fanny, before I go home?'

She thought angrily – why didn't he just say, 'Look at how much I've done for you'? She said, 'I don't mind your taking my car if you need it. As you say, there must be taxis. And it's silly of me to make such a fuss about going by train.'

'But I could drive you,' he said. 'I could take you on Christmas Eve, if you didn't mind going first thing in the morning. Just drive you to Sussex and drop you, I'd have to get straight back to see to things at home like stuffing the turkey, though naturally I'd like to say hallo to Delia. Then afterwards I'll fetch you whenever you want, just a telephone call and I'll

243

be there. Not in the middle of the night, perhaps. Though why not? None of the girls ever wakes, so you wouldn't disturb them. Is that okay Fanny?'

His blue eyes shone brightly; he was alert and excited as if this brilliant idea had only this moment occurred to him and Fanny was ashamed of herself for suspecting that he had had this plan all along.

If Tom finally guessed what an ordeal the journey was for her, he said nothing about it. And Fanny was grateful. She found she had suddenly tired of trying to put words together to describe how she felt and decided that it was better to hang on, endure, ignore, and wait for it to pass. She was quite convinced, now, that no one else in the world had ever felt as she did. She was also beginning to be afraid, not exactly unconsciously but somewhere just beyond the reach of her present powers of logical thinking, that a lunatic asylum was where she belonged, and that if she wished to stay free, she must keep her condition a secret. 'I'm fine,' was what she determined to say to every enquiry. And 'I'm fine,' – with a few synonymous variations – was what she did say. How much it cost her she didn't realise until the afternoon of the 26th of December when she stood at her bedroom window and saw her car turn in at the gate with Tom at the wheel. And wept uncontrollably.

Saying goodbye half an hour later, her face bathed and powdered to hide the traces of tears, she felt both guilt and relief. She kissed Delia and Buffy and Becky, and shook Angela's hand, and said what fun it had been to be with them all. She saw that Buffy raised an eyebrow but she was so anxious to be gone that she thought nothing of it. He gave her an envelope which he said contained the fruits of his research into the limitations on criminal prosecutions and hoped she wouldn't find it boring. She thanked him over-effusively – she could hear herself going on in what she thought of as her 'silly' voice. When she stopped, dismayed, she was feeling so heavy in her limbs that she was sure everyone must see how tree-like and rooted her legs had become. If Tom had not taken her by the arm with his prison-warder's grip she was convinced that she could not have moved, on her own, to the car.

'How'd you get on?' he asked when they were out of the gate.

She said, 'Fine,' and felt, rather than saw, his quizzical look. 'Buffy is a marvellous host,' she amended. 'He can't cope with his leg yet, the shock of it, I think, more than the physical thing. Though it hasn't stopped him smoking.'

Fanny thought of Buffy, a smouldering cigar in his mouth, playing the piano for Angela to sing carols. And his fascinated expression when she was talking.

She said, 'We went to midnight mass together. I didn't particularly want to but Delia thinks religion is vile hocus pocus, opium of the masses, and Becky and Angela wanted to watch television. And Buffy hung back as we went into church. He's not usually shy and he must know just about everyone, it isn't exactly a vast congregation. And when we came out, he waited then, too. He didn't want to be seen limping. I don't think it was vanity. More as if he were scared. It felt rather odd to me.'

Even though, or perhaps because, she had felt the same terror, hanging back in that church, shrinking away from the threat of those other people?

She said quickly, 'Otherwise everything was just *fine*. Buffy cooked the turkey, Delia made a huge saucepan of bread sauce with lots of onions stuck with cloves as our mother used to make it, and we all stuffed ourselves except Angela who eats no more than a bird. And afterwards Delia and Angela and Becky went for a walk and Buffy and I went to sleep. And then we played Scrabble and Angela won. Not because she is particularly literary but because she was so quick at working out what would get the best score. Now Buffy thinks she is a mathematical genius as well as a great opera singer. Potentially a great opera singer, that is. He really is stuck on her.'

'You seem fairly stuck on your brother-in-law. I'm surprised. I hadn't thought you cared for him all that much,' Tom said, rather sourly. 'Still, if it meant you had a better time than you'd expected I'm not complaining. I wish I'd been so lucky.'

'I found Buffy more sympathetic than usual, that's all. I'm sorry if you had a dreary time.'

'Oh, *dreary*. I could have coped with just *dreary*. I don't know that I can endure telling you even. It's just got to me, finally.' He struck his clenched fist on the steering wheel. 'There's a limit, you know. There's a *limit*.'

He began to cry – heaving, painful sobs, his mouth open. Luckily they had not yet reached the motorway and there was very little traffic on this minor road. Fanny persuaded him to stop in a farm gateway. He turned off the engine and sat for a while, his hands clenched on the steering wheel, his head on his hands. At last he said, 'Please don't laugh. Whatever you do, don't *laugh*. Audrey's all right, you see. If it were just Audrey, then it wouldn't be bad. She's a bit of a fool and she's deaf, but she's harmless. Perhaps even Audrey and *one* of the other two. But it's Eileen and Shirley who are the bad news. And I mean *bad*. They hate each other. Shirley had to look after Eileen when she was small. I think she was a bit odd even then, Eileen

I mean, and Shirley resented that. Oh, she resented it bitterly. Having to trail this half-wit around with her when she wanted to have friends and fun. Though Eileen isn't half-witted, not really, she's more malevolent. A bad spirit. She's got worse lately, more outbursts of temper. There was this stupid incident. Shirley can't – well, she can't cut her own toe-nails because of the arthritis and usually Audrey does it for her. But, oh I don't know what happened exactly, Audrey had gone to bed early, or was in the bath, or couldn't be bothered – when I say Audrey's all right, you must understand I just mean comparatively.'

He took out his handkerchief and blew his nose powerfully. He said, 'Sorry about the waterworks, Fanny. Can you bear it if I go on?'

Fanny put her hand over his. He put his arm round her and settled her against his shoulder, exactly, she thought, as if they were fifteen years old and in the back row at the pictures.

He sighed, and went on. 'This time, Eileen cut Shirley's toenails. I don't know precisely what they quarrelled about, I don't hang around on these particular domestic occasions. But it hardly matters. I heard Shirley shouting – oh, probably Eileen had jabbed her with the point of the scissors, I know scissors were mentioned, and that was when I went into the room because you can't trust Eileen, and though Shirley's big, she can't move very quickly. But Shirley was gone when I got there and Eileen was howling and clearing up – I think Shirley had kicked over the bowl of water. I thought she could be safely left, and I don't interfere if I can help it. I went back to whatever it was I was doing, and that was that. So I thought.'

He was quiet a minute. His fingers stroked Fanny's neck in a way she found pleasant. He said, 'Jump to Christmas lunch.

Turkey adequately cooked by yours truly, bread sauce out of a packet, Marks and Spencer potatoes and ready-cleaned Brussels sprouts. Mushroom quiche for Shirley. Quite a decent bottle of burgundy for Audrey and me, Coca-cola and Perrier water for Eileen and Shirley respectively. Not exactly a Bacchanalian orgy but the nearest the Snow household is ever likely to manage. I clear away with Audrey helping me, set fire to the pudding and carry it in. The next bit of ritual is one my old Dad devised to please Eileen. She puts the silver into the servings – charms, sixpenny bits, or whatever. This year she plays her part just as usual, takes the pudding to the sideboard, turns her back on us, then brings us our plates, one at a time, individually. So we all fall to. A ready made pudding but better than any of us would be likely to put together, as a family we're not exactly skilled in the culinary arts. Then, suddenly, Shirley begins coughing and spluttering bits of pudding all over the place, puce in the face, apoplectic, and Eileen starts laughing like a maniac, and pointing, and gasping – what she's done is put Shirley's toe-nail clippings into Shirley's portion of pudding. Not dangerous, even though bits of toe-nails could be sharp, I suppose; what's horrible is the venom behind it. Horrible to me, anyway. Do you think it's possible that for Eileen, from her point of view, it was just a grotesque kind of joke?'

'I can't answer that, I don't know your sisters,' Fanny said. 'It doesn't seem very funny to me.'

'You wouldn't notice anything too much out of the way if you met them,' Tom said. 'Eileen talks to herself a bit, and if Audrey didn't inspect her before she went out of the house she might look a bit thrown together. Apart from that I'd say that in public they'd seem fairly normal. Given the fact that a lot of people get a bit eccentric as they grow older. Though of course

I've got to remember the sort of old men I was working with were more eccentric than most. So maybe I'm not the best judge.'

Fanny felt claustrophobic suddenly. She rolled down her window and let in cool misty air and the sweet sound of early lambs bleating.

She said, 'What are you going to do?'

'God knows. When the hostel closed down, it seemed the obvious solution to move in with the girls. I could have rented a place but that takes an arm and a leg and I grudged the money. Hilde – I told you about my daughter and her useless husband, didn't I? Well, she needs all the help she can get. I thought – why shouldn't a man live with his old sisters? The house is big enough, plenty of room, four bedrooms and attics above. God! Buckingham Palace would be too small for the four of us. And I can't think they've always got on so badly. They'd be raving by now. I'll be raving if I stay there much longer.'

'You don't have to stay,' Fanny said. She hesitated – How would he take it? What was she offering anyway? – then said, 'At least, you needn't go back tonight if you don't want to.'

She felt his arm stiffen against her back. She choked back a laugh. She said, innocently, 'I love having visitors. The bed in the spare room is always made up. Since the fire, I've taken to sleeping on the ground floor, in my study.'

He was silent a minute. Then he cleared his throat, as if indicating a change of subject. He said, 'I'm sorry to be such a bore, I didn't mean to lumber you with the hideous details but you can see why it hasn't been exactly a burden to me to do a few jobs round your house. Somewhere else to go. Just about saved my reason.'

Fanny did laugh then, and after a pause for reflection he echoed her, rather awkwardly. He said, 'Not very gallant am I? Out of practice with the ladies, that's the truth of it. I've lived a thoroughly monastic life these last years. I should have said what a pleasure it's been getting to know you again, shouldn't I? And so it has, dear, no doubt about it.'

He squeezed her shoulder affectionately, and started the engine.

Fanny drove Tom to King's Cross in the morning and the car coughed and died on the way back. It had run out of petrol. She hadn't looked at the gauge until then. She had filled it on Christmas Eve, and assumed that Tom would top up if he was going to be doing the round of the neighbourhood churches all Christmas Day. She told herself not to be grudging; he had driven her to and from Sussex. But tramping up the Pentonville Road with a petrol can looking for a filling station that was open made her less charitable and by the time she returned to the car, half an hour later, to find a parking ticket on the windscreen, she could find no excuse for a man who borrowed a car over Christmas and returned it with the tank empty.

She wondered if it had been meanness or forgetfulness and decided, in spite of the unpleasant distraction of nail clippings in his Christmas pudding, on meanness. She had often given him lunch, a reasonably good lunch, too, but he had never contributed the usual widower's mite of a bottle of wine; even the flowers he had once said he was going to buy her had never materialised. Maybe he considered her delicious meals were no more than due payment for the jobs he had done for her, but in that case she would rather have *paid* him, she thought, not put herself to the trouble of cooking. For Heaven's sake – you did jobs for your friends as you cooked for your friends, without charging.

She put the car in the garage and walked back through empty streets. Although it was a Wednesday and in theory a working day, it seemed that most people had taken the week off. The Partridges had gone skiing for Christmas and Fanny's other neighbours were rarely there. It occurred to her as she settled down to read the post that had arrived after she had left on Christmas Eve, that she had been out and about for almost two hours without feeling in the least panicky. Perhaps a little healthy anger with Tom had been good for her.

She opened Buffy's envelope first. He had typed out more or less what Delia had already told her, and added a postscript in such minute writing that if she had not been conscience stricken by the amount of trouble he had obviously gone to, she might have put it aside without reading it.

He had written, 'If you think you could use him, the Happy Doctor I have been going to is first class and doesn't make you feel a fool.' There followed a name, an address, and a telephone number.

Fanny thought – dear Buffy! How extraordinary that he should have been the one person to recognise what was wrong with her. Though perhaps not. Set a thief to catch a thief. Or one madman to search out another?

She put the name in her address book. But she was feeling so well at this moment, so triumphantly in command of herself because she had walked through the streets without terror, that she could not imagine she would ever need Buffy's doctor.

She opened the letter from Pakistan next. As she had known it would be, it was warm and welcoming. Wonderful news that she was coming at last; she must come whenever she wanted and stay for as long as possible. He would telephone in the New Year. His unfeigned delight made her smile affectionately, happily. This was a cheerful, ebullient man she had known for a long time; not a lover, but a dear friend . . . And then, quite suddenly, she thought that she could not imagine why she had cut herself off so fiercely and finally from everyone she and Daniel had known together. She could only produce the absurd-seeming memory of a kind of humiliation; as if by her husband's death she had lost one of her limbs and had felt too awkward to appear in this amputated state before all those dear friends who had only known her as a whole woman. But that was a recent elaboration, she thought; all she could really remember for certain, was this strange, undefined shame.

The rest of the post was Christmas cards and she went through them quickly. Most people nowadays sent charity cards of varying sophistication; the first three Fanny opened were the same madonna and child. The fourth, and last, was – refreshingly, she thought – an old-fashioned card with a robin sitting on a tinselled log. She looked at the envelope but didn't recognise the handwriting. Nor could she decipher the post mark. She opened the card, which was from Jake.

He had written, using capitals like a child, HOPE ALL WELL. SEE YOU SOON.

The psychiatrist said, 'Is there anything in particular that seems to trigger off these attacks?'

'Just going out of the house, I think.'

Fanny put her head on one side and smiled brightly. There was no way she could tell this nice man the truth. What she thought might have caused her condition was probably irrelevant, anyway. And since he had seemed to recognise what was wrong with her instantly, as if it were something ordinary and everyday like a common cold, she must have told him all that he needed to know in order to cure her. To tell him about Jake would only confuse him. And introduce a problematical element: although she assumed a doctor's surgery was as privileged as a priest's confessional, she could not be certain.

She thought she had told him quite enough as it was. In the three quarters of an hour that had passed she had spoken at greater length about herself, her life and her circumstances, than she would have thought possible earlier, before she had entered this pleasant room with its softly-coloured Chinese carpet and comfortable armchairs. She had been fearing that he would expect her to lie on a couch, which struck her as not only undignified but likely to put her at a disadvantage, and she had determined to repeat the speech she had already used on her dentist when she had proposed replacing her old, upright chair with a modern one that tilted her patients helplessly flat while she worked on them.

Fanny rather regretted having no opportunity to use this good speech which she had been working on while she waited. She said, deliberately disingenuous, 'I thought psychiatrists always asked about one's childhood. So many things that go wrong seem to begin there.'

He looked over his very large spectacles. If he removed them, Fanny thought, he would look about sixteen. He said, 'Is there anything you want to tell me? I'm quite happy to listen. But usually, with someone your age, there's no point. If there was damage done, you have surmounted it. You don't need psychotherapy. In fact, I think it would be an insult to suggest it.'

When he took off his glasses and smiled he looked younger than sixteen, Fanny thought. She tried, without seeming to do so, to look at the photograph on his desk; as far as she could tell, without her distance glasses, it was of a pretty woman, too young to be his mother, and a large baby. The psychiatrist turned the photograph courteously towards her, and smiled. He said, 'There is no point, really, in going too deeply into causes. These attacks are often caused by a certain kind of chemical imbalance that pills will usually help. You may find these particular ones are no use at all. Or they could work quite amazingly. They may give you a dry mouth to begin with, which is unpleasant, but you can comfort yourself with the thought that if your mouth is dry, the pills are being effective.'

'I want to go to Pakistan at the end of the month,' Fanny said. 'I can't go in this state, with this – this malicious *other person* that seems to have moved in on me.' She laughed. 'Unless she's always been there, a sitting tenant like the old Irishman who was living in the attic of our house when we bought it.'

'Either way, we'll have to arrange for an eviction order, won't we?' Buffy's Happy Doctor said.

Harry, telephoning his mother between his afternoon meetings, found himself answered by an unfamiliar male voice. Assuming that this was another builder, a specialist carpenter or plumber, perhaps, he said, 'Tell her I called. No, never mind, I'll ring again. Did she say when she was likely to be back?'

'I should think about five,' the man said. 'Five or five thirty.'

'Ah,' said Harry. 'I suppose you don't know where she was going?'

There was a brief silence. The man said, 'Excuse me, you are Fanny's son Harry, I take it?'

Although Harry knew his mother was on first name terms with Emrys Jones and his sons, he was a little startled by this familiarity from a strange plumber. He said, with a laugh, 'Yes. Yes. I'm Harry.'

'That's all right then. Fanny had an appointment with a doctor. That was three thirty, I know. Wimpole Street, I *think*. Oh, sorry, I should say this is Thomas Snow speaking, old friend of your mother's. And of your Aunt Delia, of course. I've heard a lot about you but I don't suppose you know me from Adam.'

'No.' Harry wondered if he should apologise. Instead, he gave another pointless laugh. 'What doctor? I didn't know she was ill. I thought she had a local GP, anyway.'

'I don't know anything about that, you'll have to ask her.'

'Yes, well . . .' Harry said. 'Just tell her – no, don't tell her, Mr Snow, I'll ring later.'

'Okay, Harry,' Thomas Snow said.

'If you took the trouble to see a bit more of your mother,' Delia said, 'you would have met Thomas by now. He's a fairly constant visitor, I gather. Neither of us had seen him for years when Fanny ran into him in some museum or other. Why do I say that, I know which museum, the film museum on the South Bank. A good man, if a bit low-spirited some-times, just as well Fanny didn't marry him, she did much better for herself with your father. Though I don't suppose she had any idea that Thomas was keen on her, he didn't exactly put himself forward, he was a bit of a star gazer. A worshipper from afar.'

'We keep asking her to come and see us, Aunt Delia,' Harry said, injured. 'We asked her for Christmas, so did Isabel, but she was going to you. Did you know she was ill?'

'Buffy thought she was under the weather. But you know your mother, Harry. Tough as a boot. Has to be on her last legs before she'll visit a doctor.'

'Ah,' Harry said. 'Yes. Aunt Delia, what does this Thomas Snow *do*?'

Isabel said, 'He's rather a pet. I've only seen him once, just before Christmas, but he seems to be making himself very useful. He was clearing out the top of the kitchen cupboard the day I was there. There was some old china, just bits and pieces, Mummy was going to give them to Oxfam but Tom told her she should let me have first pick. He really is sweet.'

Harry thought that pregnancy must have softened his sister's brain.

He said, 'It sounds to me as if he's making himself very much at home.'

She thought about that for a second or two. 'I suppose it's nice for Mummy to have someone around. I mean Becky's not there as much as she used to be and she's moving out, anyway. She's looking for a flat to share with another girl, Mummy says. Uncle Buffy is putting down the deposit.'

'What's their relationship?'

'*I* don't know, Harry.' She sounded petulant.

Harry mouthed silently into the receiver, *Don't bother me now, I'm a mother-to-be.* Aloud, he said, 'You must have got some idea. Is he likely to move in, for example?'

'Move *in*?' Isabel sounded incredulous. 'How can I know? I only *saw* him for about an hour. What did you expect me to do? Ask if his intentions were honourable?'

'Don't be stupid, Izzy.'

'He must spend the odd night there. There were shaving

things and other men's stuff lying about in the bathroom. I didn't examine the bedrooms to see where he was sleeping, if that's what you're asking. You are really *crude*, Harry.'

'It's a reasonable supposition. You know what she's like.'

'I know what you've always *said*. But you don't have to worry about Dad being upset any longer. If she wants to be a merry old widow it's none of our business.'

'She's not well. She's been seeing a doctor – that's what this Thomas Snow has just told me, anyway. What for, I don't know. I've spoken to Delia and she doesn't know either. Merely implied that you and I hadn't been as dutiful as we might have been. But that's not the point. I think she's flipping her lid. Mother, that is, not Aunt Delia. I've been talking to a friend of mine who's had some experience. I think she may be losing her mind.'

Isabel laughed. 'Honestly, Harry!'

He sighed with exasperation. It was coming up to five thirty. The next meeting was scheduled for five forty-five and there were papers to go through beforehand. He said curtly, 'I'm not talking about men in white coats, Isabel. I just think she may not be in a fit state – there does come a point when children have to accept some responsibilities. I suppose I have to agree with you that it's none of our business if she takes a lover, though I'm not altogether clear in my own mind about that. But suppose this man, lover or not, intends to make use of her – none of us know a blind thing about him, Delia's not seen him since the year dot, apparently. Our mother is a fairly well off and susceptible elderly lady living on her own and probably lonely. You think about that for a bit, sister mine. Sorry, I know if I give you a chance you'll say I sound pompous, but I really have got to go now. If you've got time, give her a ring and try and find out why she's been to a doctor.'

Fanny said, 'How things do get around. Yes, I have been to see a doctor. A psychiatrist, actually.' She laughed, a little awkwardly. 'Now, don't say *Oh, Mummy*. I'm not off to the funny farm just yet. Although when I used that term to this pleasant young man he chided me rather. Psychiatric hospital is what they say now. I'm not mad, anyway. Although I must admit I had begun to wonder. I've been having some silly attacks which were really quite debilitating. But I'm reassured now. Not cured yet, of course, but I trust this nice psychiatrist chap absolutely and he says I will be quite all right by the time I go to Pakistan. What has helped more than anything is being told that the sort of thing I've been suffering from is really quite common, it can be caused by almost any kind of upset. He seemed to think your father dying, and my being beaten unconscious, and the house catching fire, was more than enough explanation in my case. So don't worry, darling. I've been a dreadful nuisance to you and poor Harry these last months and you've both been angelic.'

She sounded very far from mad, Isabel thought. Perhaps a little high, but if she had just been persuaded that what she was suffering from was not terminal, a certain amount of elation was understandable.

Isabel said, 'Why didn't you tell us you were feeling so awful? Harry guessed there was *something* wrong, he's been worried about you. There might have been something we could have done, after all.'

'What could you have done if I had told you I was losing my wits? Darling Izzy, it would have ruined your Christmas! No, that's a silly joke. I suspect the truth is that the fear of going mad is something people tend to keep to themselves. If I'd known Harry was worried, I'd have told him, of course. Now you can tell him for me – I don't really feel like going through it all over again. Even though I am feeling so pleased with myself. Tom and I are going out to supper to celebrate. The Roma is one place where I don't seem to get into a panic. Home from home, I imagine.'

Isabel thought it would give her great pleasure to tell Harry how wrong he had been. She said, 'I thought Tom seemed very nice, Mummy.'

'Yes. Oh yes, he's very nice, dear.'

Fanny spoke with an amused reservation that Isabel puzzled over after she had put down the telephone. Had her mother been warning her off? Since she must know that her children were likely to speculate about her relationship with Tom, was she making it clear that she did not intend to discuss it? Or had she simply been mocking her daughter for saying that Tom was 'nice'? Used colloquially, 'nice' was a perfectly good and very useful portmanteau word, Isabel considered. Kind, friendly, considerate, satisfactory, generally commendable.

Unless, of course, Fanny had simply meant that her friend, Thomas Snow, possessed all these agreeable qualities, but as far as she was concerned, that was all.

Tom Snow said, 'It's very modern, isn't it?'

'Emrys and I decided that there was no point in trying to reproduce a period attic, cobwebs and all,' Fanny said defensively. 'If it had been the main part of the house that was destroyed it would have been different. But these two rooms were small, and the front one was dark, and now there is light flooding in on both sides. I know you can't see the effect of that now, you must have a look in the morning.'

The electricity had been connected that day and this was the first time Fanny had seen the conversion at night. What Emrys called 'down lights', fixed in the ceiling, shone on new floorboards, smooth walls ready for painting, built-in furniture. Fanny was not sure that she liked the bed on its raised platform, so fixed and immovable, but she decided not to say so to Tom in case he agreed with her. She was cast down by his lack of enthusiasm for her fine new apartment, but as he had paid for their dinner at the Roma this evening, and had not been stingy with his tip, she was not disposed to have an argument with him.

She said, 'I'm pleased with it. Definitely. There's a good open feeling. And Emrys has fitted in the bathroom and kitchen so cleverly. Do you really not like it, Tom?'

'I only said it was modern! That wasn't a criticism. I was just surprised. This is the first time I've been up here without the builders banging and hammering in a cloud of dust. And it's the first thing that struck me. The rest of the house is pretty but cramped. But I've always liked the idea of a well-designed space which is what's been achieved here, I think. You could do all your living here without being cluttered.'

Fanny looked at him approvingly. 'Good for you, Tom. The popular opinion is that Georgian domestic architecture was the best ever. But you're absolutely right. Pretty but cramped is a perfect description.'

'I suppose the small rooms were easier to heat in those days,' he said, looking as if he didn't altogether understand why she was praising him. 'What are you going to do with it? This – what would you call it? Studio flat?'

'Just Fanny's Top Floor. I thought I'd take in a student. Or a young teacher might be more sensible. Older and more responsible than a student and more, well, what your old friend, Delia, would think of as socially useful. It's difficult to get anywhere to live on a teacher's salary.'

'Mmm. Yes. Good idea. On the other hand – no, I suppose not.'

'What?'

'Nothing, Fan. Forget it, anyway.'

'What are you talking about?'

She really had no idea as she spoke, although the next moment, when she had turned out the lights and was following him down the stairs, seeing his square, dependable shoulders and rough-haired, grizzled head outlined against the landing light, she knew what he was after.

They sat in her drawing room. He refused a drink, saying he had to drive home, and she waited for him to go.

He said, 'Emrys has almost finished, hasn't he? I thought you said March.'

'I think everything has gone unexpectedly smoothly. But it'll be a few weeks yet. The messy bit's finished, but it has to be painted.'

He sighed deeply.

She said, 'Are you tired, Tom? That was a good evening, a lovely treat.'

She wondered if she should suggest that he stayed, but decided against it. His earlier maidenly primness – as if he feared she might creep into his bed in the night hours and deflower him – had been succeeded by a cumbersome flirtatiousness she found equally tiresome. Arch looks and little, sad, meaningful sighs, just about tolerable in an adolescent were ludicrous in a man of Tom's age.

261

He said, 'I wouldn't ask, Fan. I wouldn't want to put you in an awkward position. But you know my circumstances.' He lifted one large, pink, useful hand as if bestowing a blessing. 'Enough said. I'll just leave it there.'

She was furious with him. Surely he must see that this was about the most awkward position he could devise for her? She said, 'It's not really suitable, is it Tom? As my children keep telling me, all those stairs. And we're neither of us getting younger.'

He smiled, his face crinkling up in the way that always disarmed her. He said, 'I must be a good six years older than you, and I haven't yet lost the use of my legs. As long as you don't tumble down them, stairs keep you fit, you might tell your children. That's just an excuse, isn't it? The truth is, you're a sweet, old-fashioned girl, really.'

He looked at her expectantly. When she did not respond he said, 'Would you feel happier if I married you, Fanny?'

Laughter bubbled up in her throat; she had to swallow hard to control it.

She said sedately, 'Thank you for thinking of it, Tom. But wouldn't that be rather a high price to pay for accommodation?'

His face turned red as a brick. He said, 'That's unkind, Fan. I expressed myself clumsily. I'm not the best wordsmith in the world. You must know that I would be over the moon if you said you would even consider it.'

Fanny thought she should be ashamed. She had meant to hurt him. She could not conceive of any circumstance in which she would agree to marry Tom Snow. She was also unwilling to dismiss him out of hand. She preferred not to examine this paradox closely.

She said, 'Dear Tom. I don't know what to say. That sounds

very Victorian of me, but getting married again, not just to you but to anyone, is something I simply have not thought about. I've been married. I don't mean that as a put down. Daniel and I were married and had two children and that part of my life is over. I don't mean I wouldn't think of getting married again, just that I can't see the point of it. Certainly not for the look of the thing, which is what you seemed to suggest to begin with.'

He clapped his hands on his knees and stood up. He said, looking down at her, 'So the two things are quite separate then. I could be the tenant of your top floor or your husband. Although the one doesn't necessarily exclude the other it doesn't automatically include it. Is that a fair statement? So what you must tell me when you've thought it over, is if I am to be either, or neither, or both.'

She nodded. She was fascinated by the fix she seemed to be in. If she turned him down as a husband, she would be bound, in all decency, to take him on as a tenant; a double rejection would be an unthinkable insult. What possible reason could there be for refusing him anyway? Did she want to refuse him? He would be a good tenant; clean, tidy, quiet and responsible, a handy man to have about the place. How could she say no to him? Since she had spoken of renting cheaply to a student, or teacher, she could hardly ask a higher, more economic rent from him in order to put him off. On the other hand, one would think he would offer it. It stole into her mind that he may have thought marriage would be the cheaper option.

He said, 'Then I'll wait to hear from you, Fanny.'

He left her in peace. She missed him. But she only missed him, she decided, as she would miss an old friend who was there when she wanted someone to talk to, someone to go to the cinema with her, someone to fix a new washer on a dripping tap. A cupboard husband, to be taken out of the closet for certain occasions and then hung back on his hook.

She thought, perhaps she was being hard on herself. She was not really so cold, so unemotional. The pills she was taking cushioned her feelings. The panics came, bad as ever, but she felt herself distanced from them, as if by a billow of clouds. In this numbed state, she was able to busy herself with preparations for her journey. She had her inoculations. She sorted out clothes for the heat, and bought several new dresses. She bought her air ticket, her travel insurance. She went through the additional accident insurances Daniel had been so keen on. One or two had been single payments; others needed renewing. She renewed them, glad to be doing something Daniel would have approved of and then, losing interest, stuffed them in the nearest box file with a wad of paid bills that she had thought she should keep, copying Daniel's way with receipts, but less tidily. She went to John Lewis and bought baby clothes for Isabel's child, thinking, as she did so, that Gaga, who was certain to be a good needlewoman, would despise these ready-made garments.

She spoke to Isabel and Harry on the telephone. She felt she had no contact with them. Nor even with Poppy, who came to lunch, and was bright and brisk with her. As if Poppy were a social worker, Fanny thought, and she was a client who was not only dim but delinquent. She drove to Bow to see Ivy who was sewing curtains; Fanny, who could not sew, put the hooks in the ruffle tapes while Ivy talked solidly, all afternoon, bubbling over with happiness in her new home, her new life. Fanny was glad for her, but sad for herself; she felt lost and alone, with no future.

Then, after twelve days, the miracle happened. She woke up and a veil had been lifted. The miserable wraith who had taken her over, set up house in her body, had packed up and vanished, leaving no trace behind. Fanny was herself again, in sole occupation. She sang as she made breakfast, and prepared to listen to the latest episode in Becky's house-hunting saga without dreading to hear that it had reached a successful conclusion.

She went to see Buffy's doctor in the late afternoon and said she wasn't sure whether to congratulate him or herself. He said he thought she could take most of the credit but just to hedge her bets, it might be as well to continue the medication. Happiness made her want to please everyone; she condescended to do what he asked her as she might have agreed to some curious ritual prescribed by a village wise woman, or a witch doctor.

She left his office and came out into a pleasant, damp evening; a fuzz of yellow light round the street lamps and a soft wind in her face. She walked for a while along the Marylebone Road, finding pleasure in movement, in the new and wonderful competence of her lungs and her limbs, in the way her whole body obeyed her.

The house was dark when she got home. It was too early to expect Becky, who had said something about going with Angela to look at a flat in Bayswater. Fanny went into her study and before she switched on the light she went to the window. It was a habit she had fallen into during her time of fear; she thought, amused at herself, that she would probably never again be able to live in a room without drawing the curtains at night.

Before she drew them now, she looked into the soft darkness

outside; at the lit houses on the far side of the canal, at the boats in between. And saw a light in the *Adelaide May*.

She telephoned Tom later that evening. She had her speech well prepared; the tone friendly but not in any way intimate. As he knew, the top floor was not yet quite ready, but if he liked, he could have the whole house to himself while she was in Pakistan and settle in at his leisure. She would be grateful, in fact. Becky had just told her that she had found somewhere in Ealing and was preparing to move as soon as the lawyers could fix it. It was always a good idea not to leave a house empty in winter, Fanny said, going on to speak about frosts and burst pipes, anxious that it should look to Tom as if she were in his debt, terribly afraid that he would have reconsidered. She had taken so long to reply to him; he had had ten days to reflect on her rudeness, her cavalier treatment, her plain lack of gratitude. A woman of her years should have been sufficiently flattered by a proposal of marriage to have made some response earlier. Even if she were to refuse him.

She didn't refuse him. She simply said nothing – and a little to her surprise, neither did he. She decided that he was so delighted at the prospect of escaping from the hell of living with his sisters that nothing else mattered. In a way, it was a relief to discover that he was not crossed in love; it made the prospect of a joint household a great deal more practical. He said he would come the next day, in the morning, to discuss details. He sounded friendly and relaxed. As she put the telephone down, Fanny wondered if he had simply forgotten that he had asked her to marry him.

She supposed she should tell her children. It was after ten, a little late to ring pregnant Isabel. Her reluctance to ring Harry puzzled her. It was something to do with the way Poppy had questioned her the other day, she decided. Was she taking the medicine the doctor had given her? Had she had her injections for Pakistan? Was she worrying about the journey? If there was any special attention she felt she might need, Harry would speak to the airline. (What had she meant? A wheelchair?) And when Fanny had said that travelling was one of the things she had learned how to do, and she supposed it was something you didn't forget, like riding a bicycle, she thought that Poppy had looked at her indulgently, as at a boastful child. Or an eccentric old woman?

Harry said, 'I wish you had discussed it first, Mother. He doesn't sound the most suitable tenant. An older man, you don't want to end up turning nursemaid. Besides, I thought you wanted a teacher. Some nice young woman – easier for you, I'd have thought, and more, well, socially useful. This Mr Snow – he's already got somewhere to live, hasn't he?'

There was music in the background, and chatter. Harry shouted something. Fanny didn't hear what he said, but the music stopped. She said, 'You're having a party, Harry, I'll ring tomorrow evening, it's not important.'

'Hang on,' he said. 'I'll go to another room.'

He put the receiver down. Fanny heard Poppy's voice; then a burst of soft laughter. She thought of the candle-lit table, young, flushed faces around it, and smiled. She was smiling when Harry picked up the extension.

She said, 'Tom is a very old friend, dear. I thought it would be much easier to have someone who wasn't a stranger. And he needs a home if anyone does! He lives with these dreadful old sisters . . .'

He said impatiently, 'How can they be *dreadful*, Mother?

According to you, he went to live with them voluntarily. Have you actually met them? It sounds to me as if he just thought you had a cushier billet on offer. Eye for the main chance, I'd say.'

She said, 'Don't be vulgar, Harry.'

But she wasn't angry. The picture of the happy evening she had just interrupted remained with her; she wanted to send her son back with a light heart to his wine and his friends and their laughter. She said, 'The sisters sound more mad than dreadful to me. Not in a dangerous way, more comic and sad.' She thought she knew the best way to explain this. 'There was this ridiculous thing that happened at Christmas . . .'

Harry listened in silence. He didn't speak when she had finished. She could feel his bleak disapproval like a black hole at the other end of the telephone.

She said, reluctantly, 'I suppose it isn't really funny. Though I must admit it gave me a wild thought about my own sister. You remember Delia sprained her right arm? Well, she was in all sorts of trouble. I thought, if I had cut Delia's toe nails and then lost my temper with her, I wouldn't have put them in a pudding, I'd have sent them to the House of Lords.'

Harry groaned.

Fanny said, 'Not in the best of taste, I admit. But it amused me in a mad sort of way. Wondering what would happen, what the security people would think. I mean, presumably they inspect the incoming mail.'

There was no way she could explain why she had laughed hysterically at this absurd scenario in the middle of the night. Not even to herself, let alone to Harry. She said, 'I suppose, living alone, you forget what sort of jokes are acceptable. Never mind. At least you can see why my poor Tom might welcome a more civilised household.'

He said quickly, '*Your* poor Tom? What d'you mean, Mother?'

'I told you, Harry. He is an old friend. I've known him since I was a small child.'

'Do you use the possessive pronoun about all your old friends?'

'Occasionally. About some of them.'

'You may have known him when you were young, but you haven't seen him since. You can't say you *know* a man when you haven't seen him all his adult life. Oh, come on, Mother. You aren't so innocent. Rip Van Winkle pops up out of the ground after a hundred years and you take him in – it might not be so easy to get him out, Mother. And he might turn nasty.' He paused. He said, with solemn emphasis, 'He might abuse you.'

Fanny said, 'Tom Snow is a decent and ordinary man. I don't think he will rape me, or steal all my money, or beat me. Nor do I think I am likely to end up in an acid bath. What was the name of that murderer, do you remember? Oh yes. Haigh.'

Fanny laughed – she had thought of a good way of ending this conversation. She said, 'Tom is such a proper old gentleman, though I imagine he would prefer me to say middle-aged, that he actually asked me to marry him.'

And then, since in spite of her laughter she was beginning to be angry with Harry, she put down the telephone.

Harry said, 'She's getting married.'

He enjoyed the effect of this remark on the company. Isabel sat upright and wide-eyed on the sofa, placing both hands protectively over her swelling stomach. Max, who had fallen into a doze, woke up with a snort and blinked blindly round him before he discovered his glasses had fallen on to his chest. Poppy, about to carry the remains of the Indian takeaway they had all dined upon into the kitchen, laughed and thumped the laden tray back on the table. She said, 'Is that really true, Harry?'

Having got everyone's attention, Harry felt weary. He sat beside his sister on the sofa and began rubbing his hand over his face. He said, 'She says that Tom Snow has asked her. Of course it may not be true, just one of the fantasies women have when they're slipping their cogs a bit. I think that's an established fact. Is there any more coffee?'

'I'll make some in a minute,' Poppy said. 'I want to hear this.'

'You won't like it,' Harry said.

He waited. Poppy didn't move. He shrugged his shoulders. 'Okay, then. One of the things that happens in senescence is that the inhibitions get weaker. People take their clothes off in public, that sort of thing. Sexy old men put their hands up their nurse's skirt. Some sexy old women do something similar. A friend of mine is having the most awful time with his mother. I don't think Fanny has got anywhere near that kind of debasement. But she may be fantasising. This Thomas Snow wants somewhere to live and he's pounced on *her*. Easy prey. He can probably understand her condition. He's got fairly dotty old sisters, apparently. But since Mother can only see her relationship with men as a sexual one, she imagines he's so desperate to get her into bed that he's even offering marriage.'

Max muttered, 'Jesus, Harry! For God's sake. I'll go and make the coffee if you don't mind. Unless Izzy wants to go home. Do you feel like going home, Izzy?'

'Not at all,' Isabel said. 'I think I'm beginning to wake up. It's not every evening one's brother goes raving mad. Or does he always go on like this, Poppy?'

Poppy shook her head. She was sitting on the arm of the sofa next to Isabel. She was holding her head very stiffly; the tendons stood out on her pretty neck. Isabel reached for her hand, drew it over her shoulder, and held it. She said, 'Harry has a *thing* about Mummy. He says she had a couple of love affairs while we were growing up – maybe more, but two that he swears he knew about, I don't remember how . . .'

'People talking,' Harry said, through his teeth. 'Aunt Delia and Uncle Buffy. Laughing about Fanny's "little Turk". Things like that.'

'There you are,' Isabel said. 'No real evidence. But it's always upset him. If it's true, he was the wrong age to find out, I suppose, you know what adolescent boys can be like about their mothers? And it's had its effect on him. He still isn't exactly reliable on this particular subject. Maybe Mummy is thinking of getting married again but that's not really what upsets Harry. What bugs him is the idea of his Mum taking up with some cheerful old lecher and having a good time.'

'That's not fair,' Poppy said. 'I don't think either of you should talk about your mother like this. Even if – I mean, *whatever* she's done. I think you should meet this friend of hers, and decide what you think about him. If he's a con man, a crook, which is what Harry is really suggesting, surely you should be able to tell? Although I don't know how you would stop Fanny marrying him, all the same. If she's in love with him. I know Harry says she's getting forgetful, and I thought the other day when we had lunch that she was a little distracted. Tangential. But she's not certifiably senile. You can't lock her up. I'm going to help Max with the coffee. We shall probably drink it in the kitchen.'

She closed the door firmly behind her. Harry muttered, 'Oh

God, Izzy. Maybe I am a bit obsessional. You were right to pull me up about that. But I honestly am terribly worried about her. I know she's not senile. Not yet, anyway, and pray God never will be. That doesn't mean we don't have to look out for her as best we can. Do our best to protect her.'

Isabel didn't answer for a minute. Then she said calmly, 'If he does move in, even if they don't get married, would he have a protected tenancy?'

'Don't know.' Harry looked warily at his sister. She sat, ankles crossed, hands folded over her burgeoning baby, the picture of tranquil maternity. He decided that he didn't want to know what she was thinking.

She said – and it seemed to him that her smooth, plump face grew pinched and sharp and calculating – 'It seems to me that the really important question is what would happen if Mummy died? Don't look at me like that, Harry. It's easy for you to pretend you're above such crass considerations, you've only got two children. If she dies, and after all any of us can die any time, and Mr Snow is living in the house, will we be able to get him out and sell it? That's what we're really talking about, isn't it?'

Fanny sat with a mug of instant coffee in her hand on a bunk in the *Adelaide May*. Jake lay on the bunk opposite, propped up on one elbow. The window curtains were drawn; an oil lamp shed a soft pool of light.

'It's very snug in here,' Fanny said.

She was finding polite conversation harder going than usual. When she had first arrived this dark afternoon, Jake had said, 'Oh, it's you.' He had reddened to the roots of his hair. She had stepped boldly into the boat and he had offered her coffee, and made it. He had not spoken since then, simply stared at her. Fascinated, she thought. Appalled. Afraid.

She said, 'I like the oil lamp. It gives such a pretty light. But you have electricity, don't you? You've got television.'

'Generator's bust,' he said, in a growling whisper. Speech seemed to release him from whatever spell held him. He heaved his long legs off the bunk and sat upright. He said, 'I wondered if we'd run into each other.' He attempted a laugh. 'I mean you can't sail away like I can.'

'That's the advantage of a boat.' Fanny smiled sociably, although she felt her throat tighten. She told herself that he was almost certainly more frightened than she was. She knew what she was doing, he didn't.

He said, 'You've got a bloke living with you.' Colour darkened his face again.

'Yes. An old friend. It's very convenient as a matter of fact. My niece, I think you've seen my niece, is moving into a flat and it's a big house for one person. Is your girlfriend still with you?'

'She's gone back up north for a check up. Manchester. Her brother's a gynaecologist up there.'

Fanny tucked this small item into her store of evidence about English social mobility, to be raided some time in the future to annoy Harry or Delia. She could say something like, 'I know you like to keep the working classes in their place, tidy and homogenous.' She said, 'When's the baby due?'

'End of the month.' He looked proud, and anxious. He said, 'She's got blood pressure. It's a bit of a worry.'

'It sounds as if she's in good hands,' Fanny said. 'But I know what it's like. A first baby.'

He said, suddenly hoarse, 'Why d'you come?'

Fanny felt giddy. His blue eyes accused her. They were alone in the boat. None of the other boats was occupied. She had not told Tom where she was going. That had been deliberate. The only way to conquer fear was to meet it head on, and alone. To deliver herself into its hands.

She laughed gently and put her coffee mug down. 'Two reasons,' she said, surprised that her voice sounded normal. 'I'm going away very soon. I wanted to say goodbye to you. And I wanted to tell you what I'd found out. You remember, for your friend who's in trouble?'

He nodded. His slender throat moved as he swallowed.

Fanny said, 'The answer is, if it's a civil matter, like not paying your rent, or your tax, there's a time limit after which they can't charge you. If it's criminal, burglary, manslaughter, something like that, they can always get you one way or another. That's about it, I think. I'm afraid it's not very helpful.'

She waited. The silence seemed interminable to her. At last he said, 'Who was it told you? Did you ask someone?'

'My brother-in-law,' Fanny said. 'I expect he rang up a lawyer friend and found out. I just said I was interested. Not any reason.'

She looked at her watch and stood up. 'I'd better be going, my son is coming to see me. I hope things work out all right for your friend.'

He stood up now. He was very close to her. 'He'll just have to live with it, won't he?'

Her heart had begun to beat very fast. She said, with some difficulty, 'That could be the worst thing. To have to live with oneself. With something wrong that one's done.'

She thought – what absolute rubbish, what *crap*. What stupid unthinking humbug!

She said, laughing at herself, not afraid any longer, 'That's nonsense of course. Prison would be infinitely worse.' She smiled into his bewildered and beautiful face and extended her hand. She said, 'I hope everything goes wonderfully well with your baby.'

She walked home, light and free. Harry and Tom were sitting in her study. Two heavy men, planted like trees. Beyond them, the window was black.

She pulled the curtains across it. She said, 'You've introduced yourselves, obviously. Why don't you sit in the drawing room. You look cramped in here. Do you want a drink, Harry?'

'I would have offered him one,' Tom said. 'But I didn't think it was my place to do so. We've managed to make each other's acquaintance without it.' He smiled his sweet smile. 'I think your son is feeling more at ease now he's met me. He was afraid I might be a bit of a ruffian. Up to some roguery. Making off with the family silver.'

'No, no, no,' Harry was waving his hands about in energetic denial. 'Nothing like that. Not at all.'

Tom said, nodding solemnly, 'I must tell you I'm really impressed, Fan. It takes courage for a young man to face down an older one. It's always a joy to meet a boy who really cares for his mother.'

Harry was the colour of beetroot. Fanny looked at him sympathetically and winked when she caught his eye.

He simpered uncomfortably. He said, 'Well, you know how it is, Izzy and I have been worried in case she . . . I mean, my mother has always had someone to look after her, she was very young when she married my father. I'm sorry if that sounds sexist but . . .'

'Not in the least, Harry,' Tom said. 'Women are superior to

275

men in most things, but it's helpful to have a man around all the same, even if it's only to do the dirty work. Isn't that right, Fan?'

'Oh, do stop playing the simple, bluff sailor man,' Fanny said, goaded. 'You too, Harry. I can look after myself perfectly well.'

She saw that in half an hour or so – she could not have been with Jake for much longer than that – they had entered into a masculine conspiracy against her. Even if they expressed it in ridiculous language it seemed to put her in an inferior, and foolish, position.

She looked at Tom with especial annoyance. She was accustomed to her son striking silly attitudes. She wasn't sure she could endure the same sort of behaviour from her old friend, Dumbo. *Taking her over* – that was not what she had intended.

She had wanted a bodyguard. Not a jailer.

She said, 'Harry dear, I have been on a tiresome errand and I would like a large whisky. Just ordinary Bells with a lot of ice and plain water. Fix yourself whatever you like. Tom likes a sweet sherry.'

'Tom is going to make himself scarce,' Tom said, grunting as he rose from his chair. 'A few things to sort out in the spare room. Would you like me to cook for us, Fanny? I got some nice looking scallops from that good fishmonger in the Essex Road. I thought, not a rich sauce, just lemon and parsley.'

Fanny took her shoes off, put them up on the stool, leaned back and closed her eyes. *If only she could have asked Daniel. Although whatever he said, she would have done what she thought the right thing. Or the best thing. The proper thing, given the circumstances.*

But she felt lost, all the same. When Harry came in she

opened her eyes and held out her hand for her glass. She said, 'I wish I had a cigarette.'

He said, reprovingly, 'You should have introduced us before. He's a nice man. Are you going to marry him?'

'No.'

'You could do worse.'

'Oh. Disappointed, are you?'

'It's none of my business.'

She said, smiling. 'No. But I think the arrangement will suit us both. I plan to do some travelling anyway, visit people I've not seen for ages. I've been stuck here too long. Daniel would have worried about the house if Ivy wasn't around to come in and out. Tom will take care of it. That seems a fair enough bargain to me. I get my freedom, he gets somewhere to live.' She hesitated, eyeing her son dubiously. Then said, in a rush, 'For the rest of his life.'

'Ah,' Harry said. 'Yes. Of course.'

Relieved, she sipped her whisky, and returned to the argument that had been running in her head all the while she was talking.

An eye for an eye, a tooth for a tooth, a life for a life. Retributive justice. What was the point, though? Dangerous people should be locked away to spare other people's lives, not their susceptibilities. Jake wasn't dangerous.

She wished she could ask Harry. She said, 'Would you say that I was an immoral woman?'

He looked startled. Open-mouthed. She wondered what he imagined she had been up to? Shop-lifting?

'Perhaps amoral is what I really mean. Not being ruled by the rules. Following the instincts of one's heart.' She laughed. 'Sentimental, but the best way I can think of to put it.'

He was staring at his glass of whisky, sloshing the ice about. 'I don't think you can judge other people.'

He sounded dull and tired, as if he feared this might become an intense conversation that he was not prepared for just at this moment. So Fanny talked instead of her Pakistan trip and the old friend she was staying with, the British High Commissioner whom Harry must surely remember. He used to be wonderful at family parties.

She reminded Harry of several of these occasions, all in different foreign cities, trying to entertain him, using all her acquired skills to draw him out of whatever gloom it was he was sunk in, and was glad to see him smile at last. He looked at his watch and said he must be off now, but he didn't seem over-eager. In the hall he lingered as if there was something he felt he ought to say before he left. Fanny opened the front door to speed him on his way and suddenly he grabbed at her clumsily and kissed her and said, 'As long as people aren't hurt, darling, that may be what matters, and I don't think Dad was ever hurt, so don't worry.'

Unable to make sense of this, Fanny decided that he was upset because she was going away; Harry had always been an emotional boy, thrown into anguish by arrivals and departures. At least, she thought, he would not now have to drive her to the airport, leaving five hours too early in order to make room for a number of unlikely but precisely envisaged emergencies. Thomas Snow, being a rational man, would allow just as much time to get there as he thought the journey would take.

In fact, she was early. Not for the scheduled but for the actual departure. The plane was delayed on the tarmac but this didn't trouble her. Once launched on a journey she had always been able to sleep. She slept now, waking herself up with a start, aware that she had her mouth open and fearing she had been snoring. She straightened herself, gave a self-conscious cough, and smiled an apology at the neatly-suited Indian seated beside her.

They were still on the ground. The pilot was making an announcement. She listened idly to his calm, pleasant voice that had a slight *burr* about it that reminded her of deep Devon lanes, a holiday years ago, her parents and Delia. She heard him say, 'I'll repeat that. I am told that the computer is throwing up a fault. The engineers have checked thoroughly and can find nothing wrong. My judgement is that the computer is on the blink and the plane is all right, and I am prepared to take it up now. But since there is this fault showing, there will be a twenty-minute delay so that anyone who wants to do so can leave the plane.'

Fanny expected a buzz of talk. Heads turned, eyebrows were raised, but no one in her vicinity actually spoke. The Indian beside her smiled at her and lifted his shoulders but seemed quite composed. Fanny craned her neck, and peered out of the window. No one was making a prudent escape. After the long and complicated ritual of actually getting into one's seat on this aeroplane – luggage, passports, visas, security checks – it would need more than a polite little speech to get one off, Fanny thought, it would need a bomb, at the least.

As she smiled, she reminded herself that this was the kind of remark Harry would find supremely unfunny. She wished she had been able to teach him that serious matters could also be comic; that laughter was the best means of survival. She wondered what the odds were. No way of knowing. Whether your plane arrived or fell out of the sky was all chance and luck.

She was unconcerned. She was confident that she would land

in Islamabad, and see her dear friend's polished bald head gleaming high above the rest of the crowd. When the children were little, his size had amazed and delighted them. He was a giant. He would pick them up, one in each hand, and whirl them round his head, terrified and ecstatic. Once, he had left a jacket behind him, hanging up in a guest room, and Harry and Isabel had taken every visitor to view this huge and wonderful garment; Harry had disappeared one evening and she had found him sitting cross-legged on the floor of this room, quite alone, staring at the giant's coat reverently, the tip of his damp, pink thumb in his mouth.

Remembering her children as small and dependent, she felt the exquisite pains of nostalgia. Would she have left this aeroplane after the pilot's announcement if they had still been dependent upon her? Probably not; once she was committed to a journey she had always been fatalistic. And she had left everything tidy behind her. 'Seeing to things,' was what Daniel had called it. She had seen to Jake. She had seen to old Dumbo. If this plane crashed, or blew up, he might be a slight nuisance to Harry and Isabel, a sitting tenant in the house she had left them. But they would have those enormous insurances, about a hundred and fifty thousand pounds, she thought she had made it . . .

This was a night flight. She made herself ready for sleep. She took off her shoes, fixed the cushion into the small of her back, and waited to tell the steward that she did not want to be woken. Then, as the plane banked and turned and she looked from her window at the glittering city, strung along the dark, thick, curling snake of the river, she remembered that she had stuffed the insurance documents into a file of old bills, looking like nothing of any importance, and that she had told no one about them.